A Touch of Nerves

D. C. Hampton

This book is a work of fiction. Characters, places and events are products of the author's imagination or are fictional recreations of actual events. The recreation of the events and actions surrounding the USS Vincennes and Iran Air Flight 655 incident, while based on reports of that incident, is the product of the author's imagination.

The United States is a signatory to the 1997 United Nations Chemical Weapons Treaty and has been systematically destroying its chemical weapons stockpiles. However, complete elimination did not occur by the treaty deadline of April 2012.

For the men and women who serve,
and the families who support them

Prologue

July 3, 1988
Aboard the USS Vincennes
Somewhere in the Persian Gulf

Operations Specialist 1st class Luis Acosta was seated at his console in the Combat Information Center aboard the *USS Vincennes,* a United States Navy Ticonderoga class guided missile cruiser. The *Vincennes* had been at sea for over two months, the last month on patrol in the Persian Gulf.

It was a hazy Sunday morning in the Strait of Hormuz, not that any of the men and women working in the Combat Center saw the haze, or the beautiful tan, blue and green waters of the Gulf itself. There were no windows and the room was darkened to make it easier to see the dozens of screens placed throughout the Combat Center. The large room was also sound-treated and air-conditioned to help them concentrate on their work. That work was to monitor and make sense out of the several thousand bits of information that arrived every second from the dozens of radar, sonar, radio and satellite receivers scattered about the ship.

The last few days had been hectic, with oil tankers moving through the narrow strait and in and out of the Gulf, the Iraq-Iran war playing out around them, and the increasingly aggressive harassment by the Iranian gunboats. Just a few months earlier, another Navy ship, the *Samuel B. Roberts,* had been seriously damaged when it struck a mine, a mine presumably laid by the Iranians.

Acosta had come on duty at 0600 and had been at his communications station for several hours. He was currently handling communications with Lieutenant Sheldon, who was piloting one of ship's Seahawk helicopters. Both of the ship's Seahawks had been on patrol when LT Sheldon radioed in, reporting he was taking fire from an Iranian gunboat. Acosta had been working with the helo pilot for several weeks and took his responsibility seriously. *Not bad work for a Hispanic kid from the Bronx who didn't finish high school until after he signed on with the Navy,* he thought to himself.

Captain Rogers and his second-in command, who was also the ship's tactical action officer, were both on duty and just a few feet away to Acosta's right. The Captain had been monitoring the sporadic running battles between the Seahawks and several gunboats. A dozen small Iranian gunboats had been identified and now both the *Vincennes* and the *USS Montgomery*, a destroyer escort, were moving rapidly toward them. Only about 10 nautical miles separated the *Vincennes* and the area where the action had begun, and several of the small boats were already on fire. But the Iranians were clever adversaries and the captain was wary of moving in too quickly. The Iranians put out mines almost every night, and although the Navy tracked the night movements of the small gunboats, you could never locate all the mines—as the *Roberts* had found out.

"Contact, Contact, Warning 1. Aerial contact, inbound, 42 miles," Acosta heard his buddy, Frank McCallahan, call out calmly next to him. McCallahan was a rated radar operations specialist. Acosta and McCallahan were on their second cruise together and had become good friends despite their very different backgrounds, he from the streets of the Bronx and McCallahan from a long line of Boston Irish. Some of the crew referred to them as Mutt and Jeff, especially when the six-foot, blond-haired Irishman, who weighed in at more than 220 pounds, stood next to Acosta, with his darker skin and black hair. Acosta was also about 6 inches shorter and 60 pounds lighter than his buddy, so the Mutt and Jeff label was OK with them.

Acosta had heard similar contact alerts dozens of times during the patrol. The Persian Gulf was a crowded and active area, with a lot of commercial traffic, and the Iranians weren't making it any easier with their harassing and probing. The Americans finally had enough and a few months earlier attacked several of the Iranian oil platforms, destroying a large part of the Iranian coastal navy in the process.

McCallahan worked with the air threat radar system, the heart of the Aegis missile defense system. The Aegis system could track more than 100 targets simultaneously and download the radar data in real time to the guided missiles and the automatic rapid-fire 5-inch cannons that made up the cruiser's offensive and defensive weaponry.

"Contact designated Track 4131," McCallahan continued in an even voice.

Acosta could hear McCallahan because he was sitting next to him, but everyone else heard him over the speakers scattered throughout the Combat Center. Chatter was kept to a minimum—Acosta's communications with the helo pilots were rarely put over the Center's speakers—but every new contact and contact update was announced to the room and it wasn't unusual for the room to be filled with calls coming in and going out.

To his right, the operations specialist saw Captain Rogers look up at one of the large screen monitors. The screen was filled with military and civilian air traffic, and Acosta had no idea which was Track 4131.

Rogers looked at the new contact. All Navy commands in the Persian Gulf Task Force had received several alerts in the past few weeks cautioning them to expect an increase in aggressive Iranian behavior. Iran was fighting for its life against Iraq, and although the United States had officially remained neutral, it was no secret that the Americans were providing information and material help to Saddam Hussein. According to the alert he had received last week, the Iranians had moved several F-14 Tomcats to Bandar Abbas International Airport, a provocative move. The airport was both a civilian airport and a military facility, used as an airbase by the Iranian Air Force.

"Sir, gunnery officer requests weapons release to engage gunboats."

The two American warships were tasked with keeping the Gulf clear for commercial shipping—nobody but the Iranians wanted to keep the oil tankers in port—and that's what Rogers intended to do. But the Ticonderoga class cruiser he commanded was a blue water ship, designed for naval battles at sea, not for the narrow and constricted waters of the Gulf. Rogers didn't like this mission, maneuvering through narrow straits and around small islands, in a narrow, almost landlocked seaway where pesky and very agile gunboats laid mines at night and attacked commercial tankers during the day.

"Permission to engage granted," the Captain replied. A few moments later Acosta heard the boom of the automatic, radar-guided 5-inch cannons, the sound only slightly muffled by the sound-treated walls of the Combat Center. Then Acosta felt the ship turn sharply, apparently to engage other targets, and manuals and papers throughout the Combat Center flew off the consoles and onto the deck. Each of the ship's two cannons could fire more than a dozen rounds a minute, but at the moment each gun was firing only two or three rounds a minute as they bracketed the range.

"Warning 2, Track 4131, now 35 miles out, bearing 355 degrees, closing," Acosta heard McCallahan say in a louder voice into his microphone.

"Highlight Track 4131. Comms, transmit emergency warning, tell that aircraft not to cross the 25 nautical mile radius. What's he squawking?" Captain Rogers called out, his voice rising over the noise of the Combat Center and the ship's guns.

"Sir, IFF squawking both COMAIR and MILAIR identification," McCallahan called out immediately, his voice getting louder and more strident.

All aircraft transmitted an Identification Friendly or Foe signal. Captain Rogers knew there had been several incidents of Iranian military flights broadcasting on civilian rather than military IFF modes during missions to and from Iraq, and the track profile looked as if this could be one of the F-14s recently based at Bandar Abbas. Could this be one of the provocations he had been warned about?

"Any response to our transmit?" he asked.

"No sir," the communications officer replied.

"Transmit again on both IAD and MAD," he ordered. "Issue a warning that the aircraft will be shot down if he does not change course immediately." That signal would go out over both the International Air Distress and Military Air Distress bands and should get a response—unless the aircraft was hostile, like the gunboats now threatening shipping throughout the Gulf.

Heads in the Combat Information Center were starting to turn toward the large screen displays.

"Search 1 taking fire from another group of gunboats," Acosta called out, relaying the radio call from LT Sheldon.

"Sir, the *Montgomery* reports now 5 miles from hostile group Alpha," another radio operator chimed in. "She should be engaging any moment." The *Vincennes* continued to change course sharply as it engaged the small gunboats several miles away. The lights in the Combat Center flickered every time the automatic cannons fired.

Rogers looked at the large screen display again. Track 4131 was still heading directly at his ship and he was not about to be another *USS Stark,* the Navy destroyer "accidentally" shot at by an Iraqi aircraft with the loss of 37 American lives. Not on his watch. The aircraft was flying toward the *Vincennes* at nearly 400 miles per hour and time was running out.

"What's the altitude on 4131?" he called out anxiously. The ship's guided missiles had a minimum range of 10 miles, and who knew what weapons the intruder might by carrying?

"12,000 feet sir. Maintaining bearing of 355 degrees. Range 20 miles and closing." The aircraft was heading right for them, but the video display didn't show altitude.

"McCallahan, report any change in speed, direction or altitude immediately."

"Yes sir, report any change in Track 4131," McCallahan yelled back, repeating the order. He would notice any change before it showed on the screen's track.

"Illuminate Target 4131," Rogers ordered in a loud voice. He knew they were running out of time and now seconds counted. The possible hostile was closing at the rate of a mile every 10 seconds.

Acosta noticed the change. It wasn't Track 4131 anymore; it was now Target 4131. The fire control radar was now fixed on Target 4131, which meant a firing solution had been calculated and downloaded to the missiles in about one second.

"Transmit emergency warning, divert, divert," the Captain ordered. Then he turned to his tactical operations officer. "Lieutenant Commander, I don't want to fire, but if this fucker doesn't turn away or respond within 30 seconds, I will."

"I concur, sir," his second-in-command replied. He was not about to disagree about an unidentified aircraft that failed to answer radio calls and was heading directly at them, not after what happened to the *Stark*. It was just a year ago, in a situation eerily like this one, that 37 American sailors had died when an unidentified aircraft approached an American Navy ship, ignored all radio calls, and then fired an Exocet missile from 12 miles away. Thirty-seven sailors died. Thirty-seven families had a loved one taken away. *No sir, no fucking way*, is what the TAO really thought.

Acosta and most of the Combat Center crew were now staring in the direction of the C.O.'s console. It was easy to identify Track 4131 now, the track a long red line headed directly at the *Vincennes*. The voices in the

Combat Center had quieted, but excited chatter was still coming in over the radios, they could hear the boom of the two cannons that had engaged several of the gunboats—and an unidentified aircraft was still heading at them, now closing at more than 400 miles an hour.

Captain Rogers turned the missile firing key to the activate position.

For a few moments, the room was quiet except for the occasional sound of the ship's guns firing. Then Acosta heard his buddy again, but now his voice sounded very different.

"Warning 3, Track 4131, range 15 miles and closing, bearing 355 degrees." Acosta gritted his teeth. McCallahan was usually a cool character, but now he was barking out his warnings in a loud, agitated voice. Acosta had never seen him like this before, not even during live exercises. Rogers spoke to his tactical officer again in a voice loud enough that the crew throughout the Combat Center could hear him.

"This bastard has ignored several warnings and is about to be in range to attack us." He paused for just a moment. "I am not about to let that happen," he said in a loud and aggressive voice. He knew they were running out of time and now it was seconds, not minutes.

"McCallahan, any change in attitude of 4131?"

"No change in attitude of 4131, sir," McCallahan shouted back.

"Sir, target is descending and increasing speed," someone called out excitedly from another radar console. The ship's 5-inch cannons started firing again and the lights in the Command Center flickered as the guns boomed, making the scene even more unreal.

"Negative, negative, I don't see any change in altitude on Track 4131," McCallahan yelled out, louder than before.

"I've got him descending," another voice shouted out. The unidentified voice sounded frightened.

"Which is it? Is his altitude changing? What's the range?" the Captain called out, the stress obvious in his voice.

"Sir, I've got him at 12 miles, no change in heading," McCallahan shouted back immediately.

Just then the gun crews increased the firing rate on the two 5-inch cannons and the loud, rapid-fire booming could be heard throughout the Command Center. They could smell the gunpowder now in spite of the air conditioning. The ship heeled as it continued to turn sharply to port and starboard.

Holy shit! Acosta thought. *Is this really happening?* He wiped some sweat off his forehead.

"Signals, confirm no response to emergency warnings!"

"No response, sir!" the signalman yelled back.

There were no more pauses, no more hesitations.

"Fire missiles, fire missiles," the Captain commanded in a loud voice heard throughout the Combat Center.

"Firing missiles, firing missiles," the weapons officer responded almost immediately.

The crew heard loud *whooshes* and felt the ship shudder slightly as two SM-2 missiles left the rails.

"Missiles away," the weapons officer reported a moment later.

Twenty-one seconds later the weapons officer shouted out: "Impact, impact!"

Whatever it was, Target 4131 disappeared from the screen.

That same evening
Esfahan, Iran

Eight year-old Saman Kashan was finding it difficult to fall asleep. This was the first time she had stayed overnight anywhere but in her own home, and even though she was visiting her favorite relatives, Aunt Farideh and Uncle Parham, it was still new and exciting. Her two cousins lived here, and the three of them were sharing the children's bedroom at the back of the house. Her cousins' house even smelled different than her house back in Shiraz, in the southern part of Iran. Maybe it was Aunt Farideh's cooking, or perhaps it was the smell of the jasmine that filled the back yard. Aunt Farideh claimed Saman was named after the beautiful flowers in her garden.

Saman finally fell asleep, holding onto her doll, Poupak. She was still holding Poupak when she heard noises and strange voices downstairs. Then the wailing began.

Soon the noise from downstairs wakened Ghodsi and Babak as well. Ghodsi was seven years old, and Babak only five, and they soon became upset with all the strange voices and noises. Saman was older and she tried to be brave, but soon the babble of unfamiliar voices, along with the absence of her parents and her older brother Hami, began to tell on her. She decided to find out what was going on.

Saman held onto Poupak as she went downstairs. The voices and wailing were coming from the kitchen. Aunt Farideh saw Saman as soon as she stood in the doorway to the kitchen.

"Oooh, my poor little Saman, what will happen to you?" Auntie wailed. She looked different. She was always neat and well-dressed, but tonight she was in her bathrobe, her hair wasn't brushed, and there were tearstains on her cheeks. *How strange,* Saman thought. *Aunt Farideh is usually so pretty and neat, but tonight she looks like someone else.*

Uncle Parham was usually happy and easy-going, and much more fun than Auntie, but on this strange night he looked sad and forlorn. He didn't scold Saman for coming downstairs, even when Ghodsi and Babak peeked from behind her. He held out his arms and Saman went over to sit on his lap. She could see that he had been crying as well.

"She will live with us, of course, that's what she'll do. That's what FarzAm and Afareen always said, if anything happened to them, we were to look after their children. And that's what we will do, because we promised, and because we want to."

Saman didn't understand what Uncle Parham was saying so she explained to him, "But Uncle, I can't live with you. I live with Mama and Pappa."

Uncle Parham gave her another hug and she could feel his shoulders heaving. "We'll talk about it more tomorrow, Saman. But Mama and Pappa and Hami are not coming home for a long time."

Saman didn't know it at the time, of course, but this would be a day she would remember and re-live for the rest of her life. July 3, 1988.

The day she went to visit her Aunt Farideh and Uncle Parham, never to return to her own home again.

The day she went to the airport in Tehran to say good-bye to her mother, her father, and her older brother Hami, when they left on their trip to someplace far away.

The day Iran Air Flight 655 was shot down by a missile fired by an American Navy cruiser and 290 people died.

She knew her parents and her big brother would be away for a long time. She just didn't know it would be forever.

Friday
About 20 years later

Captain Benjamin Hawkins looked over at the stack of files on a corner of his desk. Hawkins had recently returned to his office at the headquarters of the Army Criminal Investigations Command in Ft. Belvoir, Virginia. He had successfully completed his last assignment, which had taken him down to Ft. Bragg in North Carolina. The investigation had taken almost two weeks, but he had finally gotten the names and the evidence he needed to turn the case over to the provost marshal.

His work these days was easier and a lot less dangerous than his last four-month assignment. That one involved finding out how hundreds of tons of fuel seemed to evaporate from Camp Liberty, the huge Army base outside Baghdad. If you were a glass half-full kind of guy, the case showed that the Iraqis and Americans had learned to co-operate and work together. On the other hand, what they were cooperating and working on together was how to steal several hundred thousand dollars worth of fuel from the United States Army.

The American contract employees were lucky—they would be tried in the U.S. The Iraqis were less fortunate. They were turned over to the Iraqi Army, and Hawkins doubted they would be heard from for a long time. They had begged to be sent to Abu Ghraib instead, but that wasn't about to happen.

Hawkins was happy to be back stateside, but he was getting tired of smalltime drug schemes, phony check scams or whatever hustles a couple of soldiers, or the people who showed up to take advantage of them, dreamed up. Every once in a while he was handed a nice travel assignment escorting some very important person in-country or back wherever they came from—the Middle East, Japan, once even to Australia. But even that cushy assignment had grown tiresome. Now it was time to catch up on some paperwork, assign some small-time cases to junior agents—and maybe think about the couple of weeks of leave he had coming.

Captain Benjamin Hawkins had enlisted in the Army just after his 20th birthday. His old man didn't want him to go to college, saying he didn't need to spend four years not working to get a good union job down at the Baltimore docks. Ben couldn't come up with a good reason to spend four years at college either, but he wasn't interested in a lifetime at the Baltimore docks. They compromised at Ben working at the docks while attending community college.

Two years at the docks and two years at community college was enough for Ben, so he decided to enlist. He was quickly identified as warrant officer material and eventually ended up in Army CID—the U.S. Army's Criminal Investigation Command. Someone realized that he was good at police work and a few years later, when he was promoted to Special Agent, he received a full commission as a first lieutenant. The promotion was more for the benefit of his department than for him, since a lot of Army officers had trouble taking directions from non-coms and warrant officers.

Twelve years later, Ben really had no complaints. There was the occasional travel, occasionally interesting challenges, a lot of independence—not bad for a young single officer. Just a shade under six feet tall, with dark hair, nobody had ever called him "handsome," but he had a pleasant, open look about him that women seemed to like. That same look had fooled a lot of the people Hawkins had investigated and sometimes arrested over the years.

He had also found the time to finish his college degree. Funny what finding out what you were good at could do for you. Getting someone else to pay for it didn't hurt either. The Army paid for his last two years of college in exchange for a four-year Army commitment. Ben found it a lot easier and a lot more interesting when he was able to concentrate on criminal justice, with just a little liberal arts on the side. He even put in a year at John Jay College of Criminal Justice in Manhattan. The Army was happy, his boss, Major Corliss, was happy, even his old man was happy. Funny what a little success and a good paycheck could do.

Hawkins decided to start his weekend leave a little early. Sara, his fiancée of nearly a year, had plans for the evening, so he was on his own. He could head up to D.C. to see some friends, or down to Belmont Bay to check on his boat. With spring just around the corner, it was time to begin thinking about his spring launch. That meant he had to start getting things in order. He decided to stop by the boatyard.

Hawkins pushed his chair back, stood up and headed down the hall to check in with his boss before heading out for the weekend. Major Corliss had been head of the section for the past three years. A career soldier and a graduate of the Citadel, Corliss liked to keep things in order. He didn't like loose ends and he often asked Hawkins to tie up those ends before they got loose.

"Have you made any plans for those two weeks you've been talking about?" Corliss asked his chief investigator. Corliss knew Hawkins had been anxious to take some time off after his four months in Iraq. The job at Ft. Bragg had come up before Hawkins could get away.

A few of the several antennae that were part of Hawkins' personal early warning system went off. He knew Corliss really didn't care what he did or where he went on his time off. Go. Come back. Corliss was a bottom-line kind of guy. That meant he had something up his sleeve—such as, "Hawkins, here's another job for you."

"I've been making arrangements to meet up with some friends down in Florida," Hawkins answered. It was sort of true. He had friends in Florida. They always said he should come down and visit and he always said sure, he would think about it. But at least today it might come in handy.

"Where are you headed?" Corliss continued.

"They're on the west coast, down in the Ft. Myers area."

"Driving?"

"I haven't decided." Hawkins answered, starting to get concerned.

"OK, why not make it official business. Take a company car." A company car meant any car from the Ft. Belvoir motor pool, probably olive drab, a sedan, and either a Ford or Chevy. It also meant free.

"And?"

"I'd like you to swing by the Tupelo Chemical Research Center in Alabama. Follow up on an incident report and a phone call I got from the facility commander yesterday. Should be pretty straightforward, but I don't want it sitting around."

Hawkins knew he'd been had. On the other hand, he would get out of Belvoir, get some time away, and see his buddies. He could play a little golf, maybe sail out along the Gulf of Mexico or in Pine Island Sound for two or three days. It didn't really matter where he went. And at least part of it would be on Army time. Not a bad deal, he figured.

"OK, Skipper, it's a deal. Give me a day or two to get ready and I'll be on my way. What's going on at Tupelo?"

A half hour later, Hawkins left the post carrying a few notes, and a list of phone numbers, addresses and e-mail addresses. Major Corliss didn't have much background information for him. It had been a routine incident report from the commanding officer at Tupelo, if any report from a chemical munitions facility could be considered routine.

Every Army command—especially those that handle armaments, hazardous wastes and classified materials—has strict protocols for when it must file an incident report with Army CID. Every incident report has to be followed up, even if that follow-up is part of a one-week leave. And this was a report from an Army facility charged with handling chemical weapons. Hawkins would visit the facility on his way to Florida.

There was a serious flaw in Hawkins' plan, though. He hadn't said anything to Sara about a week in Florida.

Tupelo Chemical Research Center
Tupelo, Alabama

Staff Sergeant Harry McNair shifted his Mark IV forklift into gear and began moving the 45-gallon reinforced steel drum toward the assembly area. The extra reinforcement added weight and made the drum as heavy as an ordinary 55-gallon drum. Even so, McNair handled it with kid steel forks, if not kid gloves. Manufactured in 1950, this drum was older than the man handling it.

McNair was known for having "good hands," which was one of several reasons why he had been chosen for what was considered hazardous duty. He also had a wife and child, and the U.S. Army knew a family man, even a divorced one, as McNair was, acted differently than someone with less experience and less responsibility. The extra pay didn't hurt either.

There were no more than a dozen enlisted men with McNair's experience at the Tupelo Chemical Research Center. He always laughed at the name—typical Army bureaucratese, where everything had a fancy name and some kind of acronym. He hadn't seen a bit of research here at TCRC and he'd been here for nearly five years.

What he had seen was thousands of drums, shells and casings, some dating from the 1940's. There were the "little ones"—ten to hundred pounders that could be fired from field artillery. Then there were the "city killers," weighing in at over a thousand pounds, designed for long-range artillery or air drops. Big or small, any of them could very quickly kill from hundreds to thousands of people if their toxic insides ever got loose. That was the beauty of chemical weapons.

The newer weapons used VX-212, one of the best nerve agents of them all. Or the worst, depending on where you stood. VX-212 was the most lethal synthetic nerve agent ever created, thanks to the genius of the U.S. chemical industry—unless you believed the unsubstantiated stories that came out of the old Soviet Union. They had it, too, except their version was supposed to be five times more potent.

McNair couldn't help thinking about the genius that had allowed the civilized nations of the world to reach these heights. There was a whole history here—the development of gunpowder, so a man could kill from a distance. A few hundred years later, the introduction of rifled barrels, so the same man could kill from a few hundred yards. Then came automated machinery to speed the process, and then navigation and aiming devices, new explosives, delayed fuses—all designed to be more and more efficient, more and more lethal. Once you had to kill face-to-face. Now you could kill from thousands of miles away.

But these chemical munitions were technically and officially weapons of mass destruction, real live WMD's, not any imagined ones out in the deserts of Iraq. Now, thanks to the United Nations Chemical Weapons Convention that took effect in 1997, stockpiles were being systematically destroyed throughout the world. But boy, he thought, there were sure a lot of them. And they had to be handled—and destroyed—very, very carefully.

Tupelo and the two other sites in the U.S. used the CATS system, developed just a few years earlier by the U.S. Army Chemical Agency.

6

CATS—the Chemical Agent Transfer System—had been developed by an Army engineer to speed up destruction of the thousands of tons of chemical weapons. CATS was more automated, but the real improvement was in how efficiently the nerve agent and any other chemical weapons could be destroyed.

Several drums of chemical agent, or actual field weapons, weighing up to a ton each, were placed in the heavily reinforced tank. The tank—just a highly specialized furnace, really—was then sealed. Automated equipment drilled into any containers in the tank and the contents drained, while the furnace was heated to over 2000° F. Before leaving the sealed tank, the munitions containers themselves were super-heated and reduced to a decontaminated molten slag. With automation and standardized procedures, a single operator could destroy up to 10 tons of material daily. McNair's personal record, which was also the facility's record, was 14 tons in a 10-hour period.

Sergeant McNair was good at his job and he took pride in his work. He also liked that their job was to destroy chemical WMDs, not create them. He had worked at the Tupelo processing plant for more than five years, five years without an incident of any kind, despite the dangers involved in handling highly toxic materials.

Thanks to those five years on the job, McNair knew a lot about chemical weapons and how to destroy them. What he didn't know about, though, was the incident report now sitting on a desk at Army CID headquarters in Ft. Belvoir.

That same day
Dulles International Airport
25 miles west of Washington, D.C.

Elena Santana glanced around as she waited at Dulles Airport baggage carousel #5, more out of habit than any particular concern. This was her second entry into the U.S. as an exchange student from Seville, Spain, although she wasn't returning as an exchange student and she wasn't really from Seville. She wasn't even Elena Santana, but she often forgot that.

This was the part of the operation that Mahmoud was most concerned about. Customs and Immigration. Passport Control. Possibly a photograph and facial recognition scan, a check against the do-not-fly list, or worse. But Elena wasn't concerned and she wasn't nervous. It helped that she was looking forward to the operation. It also helped that she and Mahmoud had rehearsed these few minutes a dozen times, with Mahmoud playing the part of the immigrations officer, sometimes questioning her, sometimes challenging her, sometimes just stamping her rehearsal passport and waving her through.

At age 28, and with a rather vague look about her, Elena could easily pass as a younger, college-aged student, which was exactly what she was trying to do. She actually *was* an exchange student from Seville—just not Jennifer McNair, as her passport said. Her dark eyes and light olive-colored skin didn't stand out in Spain, where she had spent a considerable amount of time lately. She wouldn't stand out in the United States, either, where people might come from anywhere in the world.

How convenient, she thought. *Everyone looks as if they fit in here.* That certainly wasn't the case in her native Iran.

No, not in her native Iran, where she was Saman Kashan, not Elena Santana, or even Eleni, as she told her friends it was spelled in her parents' native Greek island of Rhodes. Neither she nor her parents had ever been in Rhodes, or anyplace in Greece, for that matter. And in the past few years Saman had spent more time in Spain than in Iran, thanks to Mahmoud Najidad.

Mahmoud had insisted that she make friends in Spain, especially American friends, and attend classes, even work part-time, although she didn't need the money. Saman had always spent time there, even as a child. Her Spanish was flawless—better than her English, which she spoke with a Spanish accent. And she had always loved the colors, the history, and the ancient sites in Spain that had been an important part of the Muslim world for centuries. She loved to visit Toledo, where 12th century Muslim, Christian and Jewish scholars had rescued the Greek classics from obscurity, providing the foundation for the European Renaissance that followed. Now she lived and studied in Seville, the once Moorish city she had come to love.

The days when Muslims occupied Spain and ruled the Mediterranean were long gone, of course, and Saman wasn't one of those crazy, out-of-touch zealots who actually believed they could re-create an empire, perhaps by blowing themselves up. Her motives were much more personal and her goals were much more specific.

She thought back to that day when her world changed forever. The day she would remember and re-live for the rest of her life. July 3, 1988.

The day she went to visit her Aunt Farideh and Uncle Parham, never to return to her own home again.

Saman was eight years old, too young, her father said, to fly with them to Dubai. Both her parents and her older brother Hami were on Iran Air Flight 655, flying from Tehran to Dubai, travelling together to a conference her father was to attend. They would be gone for almost an entire week.

She knew her parents and big brother would be away for a long time. But the week turned into forever when Iran Flight 655 was hit by a guided missile fired by the USS Vincennes as the Iranian Airbus 300 flew directly at the U.S. Navy cruiser. Her parents, her brother, and 287 other passenger and crew members died that day. Saman believed, as many of her countrymen did, that the missile attack was retaliation for the taking of the U.S. Embassy in Tehran nearly 10 years before. And nobody had made the Americans pay for it—yet.

For many years, Saman didn't know anything about flights and missiles and the confusion leading up to that terrible event. Her memories were of the noise, the crying, the strangers coming and going, and a house filled with more food than anyone wanted or could eat. She remembered that she had gone to visit her aunt and uncle and never went home again. After a while she had to concentrate even to remember what her parents and her brother Hami looked like. But that day, 20 years ago, that day she would never forget.

The details came later, when she was older and could find out for herself, since nobody at her new home would talk about it. She learned about the Iran Air flight that took off from Tehran and headed out into the Persian Gulf, flying directly at a United States Navy guided missile cruiser that was under attack by Iranian patrol boats. Why hadn't the American ship correctly identified the airliner? Why did the Americans insist on claiming the airliner's transponder didn't identify it as a civilian aircraft?

And if it was an accident, as the self-righteous Americans claimed, why had they never apologized? Did they really think that the money they sent her new family—money her aunt and uncle used for Saman to travel in Spain and to study abroad—was that supposed to make up for it?

Yes, she had been looking forward to this trip to America for nearly two years. In a way, she had been waiting for the past 20 years—ever since that day the Americans took her family away from her forever. For most of those years she had nothing but her hatred, until the day a man named Mahmoud Najidad asked her if she would like something else—*revenge*. It was an easy question.

Saman collected her bag from the carousel. Getting through customs was easy—just another American student returning home. She headed toward the *"Nothing To Declare"* lane. No, she had nothing to declare. Everything she needed was already here, including her trainer and handler, Mahmoud.

The customs agent was nice and he even smiled as he waved her through, which Saman found amusing. For reasons Saman could never understand, Americans were always so *friendly,* just as Jennifer, her fellow exchange student in Seville, had been. At least, that is, until Mahmoud's agents kidnapped her.

Later that day
Belmont Bay, Virginia

Hawkins was smart enough not to have his bags packed before he heard from Sara. He had been able to spend an hour in Belmont Bay checking on *Blue Lady*, his 32-foot Catalina sailboat. He made a mental list of what needed to be done, decided what he would do himself, and what he would ask Hank, the yard manager, to take care of. With any luck he would be back in 10 days or so and get ready for his spring launch.

It was nearly 6 p.m. when he heard from Sara. He had gotten her text message earlier telling him she would call later. As the owner of Virginia Times, an antiques shop in Woodbridge, the nearest real town to Belmont Bay, she put in a lot of hours on the job. She was also as independent as he was. Hawkins usually liked that, except when—well, except when he didn't like it.

Sara's mobile number popped up on his screen.

"Sorry to call so late. Did you get my message?" she asked him.

"Hi, sweetheart. Yes, I got your message. Everything OK?"

"Everything's fine. Just some new clients I had to look after through dinner. I'm on the way to my place now. What's up?"

Ben had no idea how she knew anything was up, but it didn't surprise him. He hadn't talked to her since getting the assignment from Maj.

Corliss. Over the past two years she had come to learn and accept what he could tell her and what he couldn't. Still, it wouldn't surprise him if Sara somehow knew when he was leaving and where he was going.

Ben had first seen Sara on the docks two years before at the Belmont Bay Marina. It was his third season at the marina with *Blue Lady*. He was sitting in the cockpit enjoying the mild summer evening when his friends Jim and Christine returned to the dock with Sara aboard their boat. He noticed how she handled the lines and stood by ready to help out while they were docking. She waited quietly while Jim and Christine finished tying up.

After everything was shipshape, they invited Ben aboard for a drink. Then it was the four of them out to dinner and before he knew it, he was seeing her every weekend, they were spending time at each other's condo, there was a trip to Bermuda, and now it had been two years. He liked it.

He told Sara about the "offer" from Corliss. He even tried to convince her to come along, or at least to catch up with him in Florida. It would be nice to spend a few days together on a beach on Sanibel or on a boat out in the Gulf. The most she would commit to was, *"We'll see"* to Florida, and, *"Sorry, can't do it"* for the drive down.

That part was no surprise. To tell the truth, he would just as soon do the 12-hour drive to Tupelo on his own. Stop when he wanted, stay wherever, and not worry about getting a place at his government rate that met her standards, which were much higher than his. But he would much rather spend a few of those days in Florida with Sara than spend the entire week with his buddies.

OK, he was all clear with Sara, pretty much squared away with his boss, and on schedule at the boatyard. Tomorrow he would throw some things together, then swing by Ft. Belvoir to pick up an Army vehicle and get a final briefing. He and Sara already had plans for that night, and he would hit the road sometime Saturday.

Friday evening
Belmont Bay, Virginia

It was after seven by the time Sara caught up with him at Antonio's, overlooking Belmont Bay. Apparently Antonio was trying to corner two markets—it was a combination Italian trattoria and American steakhouse.

Maybe you could only get away with that in a small-town place like Belmont Bay, but they actually did it well.

Hawkins was seated in the bar when Sara arrived, a Jack Daniel's on the rocks in front of him. He was keeping an eye on the front door, so he saw her as soon as she entered the restaurant. He stood up as she looked around and gave her a wave. It was still something of a surprise to him that he was with someone like Sara.

Sara was the one people looked at whether she walked into a restaurant or a museum conference room. Yes, she was attractive, but she didn't have the cool look of a model or a movie star. She was average height with slightly curly, almost black hair, but with bright blue eyes—a classic "black Irish" look, supposedly due to the friendly reception given by some of the local Irish lasses to the Spanish sailors who washed up on the eastern shores of Ireland following the loss of the Spanish Armada. There was an air about her, a warmth and openness that Hawkins was still trying to figure out. On the other hand, he wasn't in any rush.

Antonio showed them to a table in the restaurant and they ordered a bottle of Montepulciano. After the wine was served, Sara asked for the house specialty—chicken francese with artichoke hearts—while Benjamin went for a New York strip, medium rare, and a Caesar salad.

"I don't know if I can get down to Florida," Sara told him. Virginia Times had a lot going on for an antiques shop in an out-of-the-way place like Belmont Bay. Sara had worked at the Smithsonian Institute for nearly 10 years. She was considered an expert on Virginia colonial furniture and a number of customers came down from the capital area just to see her.

"It would be great if you could get away for a few days. Let Sophie take charge for a couple of days. Be good for her." Sophie had been Sara's assistant for the past five years.

"I'll try, really. But Sophie called me about a couple who want to stop by. They're setting up house in Bethesda and are interested in any 19th century furniture, especially if it's pre-civil war. They might want to commission me to search for it."

Benjamin understood, and he enjoyed this other world. It was a nice change from a world of debts, absent without leave personnel, family problems, or a list of crimes that came his way because some Army guy—or woman—was involved. It reminded him that he tended to see a pretty distorted view of everyday life.

"Well, now that we're caught up, let's enjoy the rest of the evening without worrying about next week," Sara suggested. They lingered over dinner before heading back to Sara's home, knowing they might not see each other for at least a week.

An hour later they were at Sara's, watching a Netflix movie they'd been trying to get to for a few days. They were about halfway through when Sara snuggled up closer to Ben.

"Do you really want to see the whole movie tonight?" she asked him.

Ben put the movie on hold. "We could always finish it later."

"Oh good. Later is a good idea."

Ben turned the movie off and turned to her. A week would be a long time.

Saturday

It was a bright, sunny morning, one of those early spring days that let you know there were some hot Virginia days on the way. Ben was up by 7 a.m., getting an early start on the day. He showered and shaved, got dressed, and then headed for the kitchen. While he was downstairs he could hear that Sara was up and would be right behind him.

He was up early enough to make breakfast for the two of them before heading off for Alabama and Florida. He decided to make them their usual Sunday morning favorite, something Sara called "Ben McMuffins."

After putting up the coffee, he set out some Canadian bacon, eggs, English muffins and two slices of white American cheese, which wasn't easy to find. If he timed it right, the eggs would be done just as the English muffins popped up in the toaster. A minute or two later, he put two dishes on the table just as Sara came into the kitchen.

"Something smells wonderful, honey. Could that be fresh coffee and your fabulous Ben McMuffins?" Sara asked as she came into the kitchen. She gave him a hug and a kiss. "I think I miss you already."

They had the luxury of a slow and quiet breakfast before Ben left. He didn't want to press Sara about joining him in Florida, but he was getting the feeling she would not be heading south to join him.

Hawkins was at Ft. Belvoir and picking up a car by 9:30 a.m. At least this one wasn't olive drab. As usual, he carried his own portable GPS and a satellite radio hook-up. It took him just a few minutes to set up the GPS and enter his destination. The satellite radio took a few more minutes to sync with one of the FM stations, and he was ready to go. With music to travel with—the Orioles weren't playing today—a route planned out, and his cell phone Bluetooth-enabled with the GPS unit, he could sit back and just keep heading southwest for about 900 miles.

Hawkins moved into the middle lane as he headed west on I-64. That would bring him to I-81, where he would swing southwest toward Roanoke. Maybe he would stop for lunch in Lexington and drive by the

Washington and Lee campus and VMI, the Virginia Military Institute. He had left Sara's place a little later than planned. After he told Sara—again—how great it would be to spend a few days on the beach, it looked as if she might come down at the end of the week.

The interstate followed the route of the beautiful Blue Ridge Mountains and Ben was enjoying the Virginia countryside as he headed toward Roanoke. He was a few miles north of Lexington when his cell phone rang. He saw a familiar number show up on the phone screen.

"Hello, Sara, how's everything?" he asked, as her phone number appeared.

"Fine, honey. I just wanted to see how your drive was going."

"I'm just outside Lexington. I'm going to pull off here for some lunch."

The previous fall Sara and he had spent a long weekend in Lexington attending the VMI-Citadel football game and enjoying several days of nothing to think about except each other. They promised they would return, both for the scenic countryside and beautiful campuses, and because of a wonderful B&B they both loved.

Sara remembered the weekend as well as Ben did, and she knew he was smiling.

"OK, Mr. Romantic. As I remember it, the football stadium wasn't the only place where the action was. Are you paying attention to your driving?"

"Of course. Hands free cell phone, cruise control, 72 miles an hour, 64 miles to Roanoke. All under control. Have you thought anymore about Florida?"

"Yes I have, honey. That's why I'm calling. Things went well today and I may be able to take a few days off at the end of the week. You said Thursday or Friday would be good?"

Ben figured it would take two days for the preliminary investigation at Tupelo and then he would continue on to Ft. Myers late Tuesday or early Wednesday. A day or two of fishing with his buddy would be fine, and then he and Sara could head out to Sanibel Island.

"Thursday or Friday would be great," he answered. He hadn't expected Sara to make it, but he was happy to hear it might work out.

If the demands of his work had taught them anything, it was to make sure they made an effort to make time for themselves. Ben had seen too many marriages and relationships that didn't survive the stress a few months overseas could create.

"I'm going to try to make it work, honey. I'll know better by Tuesday or Wednesday, but two or three days on Sanibel would be wonderful. Call me tonight, OK?"

"Will do. I'm at Lexington now, so I'm going to take a break. Talk to you tonight."

Ben hung up, signaled for the right lane and left Route 81 to take the state highway into town. He would make Roanoke this afternoon and then head toward Knoxville. He always liked to drive in this part of the state and he didn't feel like rushing through. He could even make Tupelo in a long push from Roanoke, so any distance he made after Roanoke was money in the bank.

Tomorrow he would put in five or six hours, arrive in Tupelo in the early evening, and be ready to go early Monday morning. He had an 8:30 a.m. meeting set up with the facility manager and the Army colonel in charge.

A few minutes later he was driving through the college town of Lexington, past the VMI parade grounds and the Washington and Lee University campus. He decided to have a quick lunch and then push on toward Tupelo and the chemical weapons facility. With any luck, he could finish the investigation by the end of the day Monday, file a report with his boss that night, and be on the road to the Florida west coast Tuesday morning. He was already anticipating a little boating and fishing with Mike and friends, and then some time with Sara when she got down there Thursday or Friday.

Ben turned out to be right about seeing Sara at the end of the week. But it would be back north at Belmont Bay, not down at Sanibel or Captiva Island.

Sunday

Ben wasn't on the road until nearly nine, but it was a Sunday with little traffic on Route 81. It was a bright, sunny spring day, with virtually no cloud cover, and he made good time heading southwest to Tupelo. Lunch was a short stop at the interstate rest area just before Chattanooga. It was late afternoon by the time he reached the Tupelo exit on Route 72, just a few miles east of Tupelo.

The two-lane road worked its way through farmland and around the Alabama hills and into Pikeville. Ben had already programmed the location of the Pikeville Holiday Inn into his GPS and he followed the directions into the parking lot.

Fifteen minutes later, he was checked in and settled in his room overlooking a wooded area in the back of the Holiday Inn. He helped himself to a Jack Daniel's from the minibar and turned on CNN News. He relaxed for a half hour before heading down for dinner in the motel restaurant.

After a pleasant enough dinner, Ben returned to his room and reviewed the incident report and background information on the Tupelo Chemical Research Center again. Tomorrow morning he would get an early start to the facility eight miles down the road. The chemical processing plant was very much off the beaten path and probably wasn't on anyone's "places to see" list. Neither was Tupelo itself.

Most people probably thought of Tupelo as the birthplace of Elvis Presley, but that was Tupelo, Mississippi, almost 200 miles to the west. This was Tupelo, Alabama, whose sole claim to fame was that it was the home of a major facility tasked with destroying the huge arsenal of American chemical weapons. The Tupelo Chemical Research Center had already destroyed more chemical WMDs than any facility in the world. It was also where several thousand tons of chemical weapons remained, waiting to be destroyed.

About the same time
Just outside Knoxville, Tennessee

Saeed had been very surprised when Najidad first contacted him about two months ago. Saeed thought his former colleagues in Iran—if "colleagues" was the right word—had forgotten about him, and about the family he left behind when he managed to leave the country eight years before. They had not. Now he was meeting with this man who frightened him in a nondescript motel room just north of Richmond, Virginia.

Najidad had told Saeed he had a simple job for him, a job he was well-suited for, thanks to his education in Iran as a chemical engineer and his work in the United States as a lab technician. There were never any actual threats at first—just a reminder.

"You have been living a nice life here in America, Saeed. But we allowed you to come here for a reason. And at least this job is something your family can be proud of."

Mahmoud spoke gently to Saeed, but inwardly he despised anyone who could leave his own country, the land of his own faith, and live in the land of non-believers. Especially in the land of the very infidels who had stood silently when such terrible crimes were committed against his people. And against Mahmoud's own father.

But today, when Saeed arrived at the tired-looking motel off Route 75, Mahmoud showed him several ominous looking canisters marked "*U.S. Army Munitions.*" Saeed's eyes widened when Mahmoud told him what he wanted him to do, and he recoiled in horror at Mahmoud's plan and out of fear at handling the deadly material.

That's when Mahmoud made a phone call and handed the phone to Saeed.

"Saeed, what is happening? Where are you? Who are these two men in our house?" his wife asked in a trembling voice. She sounded terrified, and he soon found out why.

"What is it, Laleh, who's there?"

Mahmoud took the phone back.

"I can tell you who's there, Saeed. Two men, two other soldiers fighting for our nation. Two soldiers of the Revolutionary Guards. They arrived at your house this morning, and they will leave in just a few days. They will leave as soon as you finish this job. So start transferring the nerve agent into the containers I showed you. Then we will finish our job in a few days. After that, the men will leave your home and we won't need to bother you or your lovely wife and daughter anymore."

So a terrified Saeed began the task that Mahmoud had asked of him. The transfer was not difficult if you knew how careful you had to be and had the proper tools to handle the toxin, even if you were sweating and filled with anxiety, as Saeed was. At least he didn't have to be part of the actual attack. He didn't think he had the nerves for that, even though his wife and daughter were being held as hostages.

A few hours later, while Saeed was still at work, Mahmoud went into another room and placed a call.

"Omid, all is well there?" Mahmoud asked quietly.

"Yes, Mahmoud, there was no difficulty."

"Where are the woman and the child now?"

"They are both upstairs, in the daughter's room. They are both reading, I think."

"And Heydar?"

"He is upstairs watching them."

"Then it is time to leave that place. And it is important to leave no connections to us behind for the American authorities."

"I know, Mahmoud. We will do as you instructed."

"Good, Omid. Remember, these people chose to come to the land of the infidels while you and I chose to fight for our nation and for Allah."

"Do not worry, Mahmoud. We will do our duty."

Omid ended the call from Mahmoud and pushed back from the table. He climbed the stairs and looked at Heydar, who was sitting on a chair facing the open door to a bedroom. He could hear a woman's voice, reading from a child's book.

"They have been very quiet," Heydar said, seeing Omid's questioning look.

"Good. Go downstairs and make sure we have everything ready to leave."

Omid waited until the younger man left. Then he entered the bedroom and looked at the two figures sitting on the bed. The room was painted a pale blue, and there were several dolls on a dresser in the corner. The mother, the one called Laleh, had her arm around her eight-year old daughter, who looked as if she had been crying. The mother turned to him with a questioning look.

"Don't worry, sister, we will leave you soon," he said, speaking quietly. "But you must stay in this room until we go away."

The woman looked away, sadly.

Omid left the bedroom and stood outside in the hallway. He remembered Mahmoud's words: *Yes, they had chosen to fight for their country and for Allah.* As soon as he heard the woman's voice again, reading to her daughter, he took out a .38 caliber Smith & Wesson and attached a silencer. Then he stepped back into the room quietly, aimed at the head of the larger figure and fired twice. The woman fell to the floor, unmoving. Omid heard the little girl's screams as she tried to pull her mother up. He closed his eyes for just a moment and said a silent prayer, asking for forgiveness. Then he aimed at the smaller figure and fired twice again.

He placed another phone call before he and Heydar left the house. As he and Heydar drove away, Omid could still hear the screams of a little girl reverberating in his mind.

Monday

B en was up and out of his room early. He had noticed a small diner as he passed through Pikeville the night before and he stopped there for scrambled eggs, bacon and grits, which he usually had whenever he was in the South. Thirty minutes later he was in his car and heading for the Tupelo facility, just a few miles away.

Tupelo Chemical Research Center
Tupelo, Alabama

The chemical treatment facility was located a few miles northwest of the small village of Tupelo. The plant was ringed by hills and mountains on three sides, and accessed only by a two-lane county road from the south.

The guard at the main entrance of the Tupelo Chemical Research Center was expecting him. That was a good sign. It was just after 8 a.m. when Hawkins pulled into the parking area by the main administration building. Normally, before meeting with anyone, he would do a drive-around/walk-around as soon as he arrived at an Army post. But this wasn't a typical Army post and a drive-around/walk-around wasn't going to happen at a secure facility such as TCRC.

Hawkins had reviewed the incident report again last night. The facility commander, an Army engineer named Lieutenant Colonel Girelli, had reported that some dangerous materials were either unaccounted for or actually missing. He had also reviewed the standard security measures and procedures for the two in-country chemical destruction facilities—officially known as "research centers."

Maybe someone thought that American taxpayers wouldn't be too keen on spending their tax dollars on "destruction." After all, they had spent hundreds of millions of dollars designing and building these things. Now they were spending a few hundred million more destroying them. And millions of American dollars more for other nations, such as the former Soviet Union bloc, to do the same. Hawkins wondered what the American taxpayers would think if they knew their tax dollars were being spent helping others destroy chemical weapons abroad. *Better than the alternative* was what Hawkins thought.

Hawkins had done his homework and already knew that the process of destroying hundreds of tons of chemical and biological materials had been automated and streamlined. The U.S. Army had officially halted production of chemical weapons in 1969, well before the United Nations adopted its Chemical Weapons Convention.

The 1997 U.N. Convention banned the development and production of chemical weapons and mandated the destruction of any such weapons held by the signatories. The U.S. Chemical Agency reported excellent progress toward the goal of complete destruction of all such weapons and materials. A major part of reaching that goal had been the development and introduction of the Chemical Agent Transfer System.

Thanks to CATS, a single operator could process up to 10 tons of material a day. The system was both simple and elegant. Once weaponized, even the smallest amounts of many agents, including VX-212, are extremely lethal when in direct contact. Even a few grams were lethal if airborne. But all agents can be destroyed by extremely high temperature. The challenge was to destroy both the agent and anything it had been in contact with, and that included the containers that carried them.

Part of the solution was to develop the robotic equipment to transport the many different-sized containers into the destruction chamber. The rest of the solution was to engineer automated drilling equipment that could drill into containers of any size, shape and material, while the container was in the destruction chamber. The drills and bits had to withstand the high chamber temperatures, since they also had to be decontaminated by the furnace. After that, the design of the furnace itself, capable of reaching nearly 3000° F, was pretty straightforward.

Hawkins had familiarized himself with the CATS procedures, as well as with the security measures at TCRC. He had also reviewed the personnel jackets of John Roehm, the civilian manager who ran the day-to-day operations at Tupelo, and Lieutenant Colonel Phillip Girelli, the army engineer in charge of the facility itself, including—and especially—security.

Girelli was a career officer, U.S. Army Corps of Engineers. A West Point grad, he had two tours in Iraq with an engineer battalion under his belt. It was kind of ironic. Girelli spent six months looking for chemical weapons in the Iraqi deserts and came up with nothing. He had spent the past six months in Alabama destroying tons of the kind of stuff he couldn't find in Iraq. Yes, there was plenty of it around, except it was on American soil.

The American government spent millions every year making sure weapons such as these didn't get into the wrong hands and couldn't cross the borders into the United States. The problem was that a terrorist group looking to attack the U.S. with a WMD—such as these nerve toxins— didn't have to create them or even smuggle them into the U.S. They were already here by the hundreds of tons. That's why they were so well guarded, even as they were being destroyed.

Hawkins parked his car and walked toward the administration building, past the white-painted rocks planted around a flagpole. He entered the building, crossed the lobby and introduced himself to the civilian receptionist. Her name was Sheila and she was expecting him. She offered him coffee and then excused herself to let her bosses know he was there.

He looked around the sparse reception area. It was more of a lobby than a reception area, really. But then, a fenced-in, heavily guarded facility filled with toxic chemical and biological agents probably wasn't high on anyone's "places I have to see" list. It had the standard Army decorator's taste he had seen in dozens of posts and offices—a trilogy of flags in a floor stand and framed photographs of the current commander-in chief, the Secretary of the Army and the post commander.

Hawkins hoped he could spend a day or two here, interview the key personnel, look around, and then close out the case. But he was never one to close a case until he was sure the loose ends had been made tight. That was probably why Corliss had assigned him this one.

It was Lieutenant Colonel Girelli who came out to greet him. Hawkins knew from his personnel records that Girelli was married, had two grown children, an excellent service record and was well regarded by his peers. He was an inch or two under six feet, with black and gray hair. You'd look at him and guess he was in his mid 40's, but Benjamin knew he was closer to his early 50's, with close to 30 years in the service.

"Captain Hawkins?"

Hawkins was on his feet and approached the facility's commanding officer.

"Yes sir, thank you for seeing me."

Of course, Lieutenant Colonel Girelli *had* to meet with the investigating officer from Army CID, and both Ben and he knew it, but there was still military protocol to follow. Ben might be the investigating officer, but Girelli was still his superior officer.

"Jack Roehm is waiting for us in my office. Ready to join us?"

Hawkins and Girelli went down a short hall and into Girelli's office. Jack Roehm, the facility's civilian manager, rose to meet them. He was about 6 feet tall, in his mid-40's, with thinning brown hair and about 20 pounds more than he ought to have.

Girelli did the introductions and motioned to a chair for Ben. He and Jack Roehm sat facing Girelli, who took his seat behind the desk.

"I can't say we're glad to have you here, Captain, nothing personal of course. But we *do* need this visit, so thank you to you and your boss for the quick response."

"Well, Colonel, you filed the report, so of course, it's our job to follow up. I'm just here to see exactly how much follow up this calls for. As I understand it, this is probably a record-keeping problem, but we can't afford to assume that, and your security protocols don't allow for that anyway."

Girelli started to speak, but his civilian manager interrupted him.

"That's exactly what I've been telling the Colonel, Captain Hawkins. Someone got sloppy and entered the weights incorrectly. But everything adds up, so there's nothing actually missing. This is a waste of time."

Girellli gave Roehm an impatient look.

"Yeah, Jack, you've said that, several times. But we're *required* to make that report, and CID is *required* to investigate. Other than that, you're probably right. I certainly hope so, because I don't want to think about the alternative."

They spent about an hour going over the incident report Girelli had filed two weeks ago. As they talked, Hawkins picked up on the tension between Girelli and Roehm. It was clear that Roehm didn't think an incident report was called for. But Girelli was regular Army, and an engineer at that, so everything was by the book. Hell, Girelli had helped write parts of the book—the section on incidents as they related to "dangerous materials."

As Jack Roehm had said earlier, the incident in question had to do with some numbers that didn't add up. Hawkins was a quick study, but he also believed in being prepared. He was already familiar with the types of incidents that a place like TCRC had to report, and this one fit in—sort of. Maybe Girelli was right to report it. Maybe Roehm was right that he didn't have to. Or maybe Girelli was wiser in the ways of Army CYA.

The numbers that didn't add up had to do with the weight of materials—the chemical or biological agents and their containers—before and after destruction. These weights, and the gases produced by the CATS equipment, were carefully measured using very precise calibrated equipment. Each batch was weighed both before and after destruction. It seems that the numbers *did* add up—but in several instances not quite in the right column.

Girelli had found the discrepancies. In about a half dozen instances over the past two months, the total weight was on the mark, but the breakdown between the non-lethal gases produced by the process and the superheated container materials was a little off. Less inert gases, more leftover, decontaminated metal slag. A few ounces here and there on a few runs, but over a two-month period it added up to almost four pounds of missing material. Missing decontaminated gases that were once lethal VX-212.

OK, interesting enough. Certainly enough for an incident report and a follow-up from Army CID. Hawkins was beginning to think the few days in Florida might not happen after all.

Monday afternoon
Tupelo Chemical Research Center
Only a half dozen of the army specialists stationed at Tupelo were certified to handle and process the hazardous materials. Each of the specialists had started out with a military occupational specialty in shipping and handling and moved up from there. At a minimum, each had several years of handling other hazmat, such as ordinance, hospital waste or decontamination equipment. And each had taken and passed a 12-week training course and was certified as a G-4 handler. That meant handling materials beyond hazmat, beyond explosive and beyond toxic. G-4s were the only ones certified to handle lethal. Lethal as in WMD lethal.

Over the years, Hawkins had developed his own way of handling interviews and investigations. He liked to be prepared and he liked to know as much as possible before poking around. That way he could concentrate on what was happening in front of him, whether it was a scene or a person.

Hawkins also had a remarkable talent for knowing when a person was lying. And the witness or suspect he was questioning—or, as he preferred to think of it, having a discussion with—soon realized this. In the recent Ft. Bragg case, the suspect had voluntarily taken and passed a lie detector test. During his discussion with Hawkins, though, he eventually admitted his role in the phony check scheme, and Hawkins was able to turn the case over for prosecution.

He spent the rest of the morning going over the personnel records of the six G-4 handlers. Lieutenant Colonel Girelli had arranged preliminary interviews for the afternoon. Five of the six specialists were available. The sixth man, Specialist 4 James Hartman, was out, halfway through a two-week leave.

Hawkins spent the afternoon with the five materials handlers. Obviously they knew something was up, which was fine with him. These men were used to very tight security measures and knew they had a serious and dangerous job.

There was no *"Eureka, I have found it"* moment that afternoon, but Hawkins learned a lot about the actual handling procedures. For one thing, driving the articulated Mark IV forklift wasn't as easy as it looked. A handler would bring the Mark IV forklift into a secure weapons storage area to pick up a load of chemical weapons ordinance, such as a batch of cluster bombs, or mortar or artillery shells. The drums, filled with VX-212 or some other chemical agent, were handled one at a time. After weighing out and signing for the material, the handler would take the load over to the ultra high-temperature furnace.

After the entire load was delivered and sealed in the furnace, the internal pressure was lowered to a half atmosphere to prevent any gas leakage, and then everything—metal casings, drums, shells, liquids and anything else—was super-heated to nearly 3000 degrees Fahrenheit. The heat destroyed the nerve agent and turned any of the munitions casings into a decontaminated molten slag.

After cooling, the gases within the furnace were bled off and the slag removed. Both the gases and slag were weighed. Even a non-engineer Army investigator like Ben could see that the beauty of the system was that there was no direct handling or transfer of open containers or materials. Neither of the two facilities in the country had had a serious incident in more than three years of operation. Until now.

Hawkins also learned about the men themselves. Apparently, Specialist 4 Rivera was the best handler and Samson was something of a goof-off. McNair was the senior member of the group both officially and unofficially. The men seemed to like each other well enough and occasionally got together for a beer after work or on the weekend. Hartman had another week of leave, and at 26 was the youngest of the handlers.

"So what's this all about, sir?" Specialist 4 Rivera asked Hawkins during their question and answer session.

"Just a routine security check. Something we're supposed to do periodically," Hawkins answered without enthusiasm.

"Yeah, right, sir." the enlisted man answered. "So how come CID has never been here before?"

Ben paused for a moment before answering.

"It's a new security requirement. You know how everything's changed after 9/11." For now, Ben thought that was enough of an answer. He didn't think Rivera believed him, and he really didn't care. None of the other handlers seemed to believe him either when they asked the same question and got the same answer. It was just as well if they were concerned. Everyone else was.

"So doesn't it worry you, handling stuff that could kill you and maybe a few million others if you dropped a 55-gallon drum of it?" he asked each one at some point. He liked to keep his questions simple and he didn't mind if he sounded simple himself.

There were a few variations on their responses, but basically they all seemed to like the job, and believed it was important to destroy the VX-212 and the dozen or so other agents they handled. Most had gotten into it for the extra pay, though.

They were also used to handling and living around lethal chemical agents and they took pride in their training and skill at handling the hazardous material. They were also proud of their unit's safety and performance records, which were impressive, at least until a week ago.

Ben gave each man his card with his CID office and his cell phone number in case they thought of anything else.

There was a lot more background work Hawkins could do, but he was still trying to get a handle on the actual problem. He had two experts here. Girelli was concerned, but Roehm didn't seem to be. Roehm thought it was a record-keeping error. Whichever it was, Ben was beginning to think that this was not something he was going to straighten out in a day or two.

Was material from some U.S. Army chemical weapons actually missing? Hawkins decided that he needed someone with far more expertise to look at the problem before he started looking at financial trails, interviewing neighbors, studying movement history, or anything else, He would spend another day looking around at the Tupelo facility, get a little more insight from the facility commanding officer, and then he would lay out a plan for bringing in some experts. Whatever the next steps were, he wouldn't be heading down to Florida while a lot of unanswered questions hung around here. Not when terrorists had tried shoes and who knew what else to get lethal weapons into the U.S. And these lethal weapons were already in the country.

It was late in the afternoon when he called Major Corliss at Ft. Belvoir and gave him an update. Corliss didn't sound surprised when Hawkins told him there were as many unanswered questions at the end of the day as there had been at the start. Hawkins gave him a heads-up about calling in some outside help.

"Do you want me to call you back after I see Lieutenant Colonel Girelli?" Ben asked his boss. The facility commander had asked Ben to see him at the end of the day.

"No, Ben, not unless something new turns up, which I doubt. Keep me posted after your next round of questioning tomorrow." Hawkins had already scheduled some additional interviews for his follow-up visit to Tupelo the next day.

It was a few minutes after 5 o'clock when Hawkins returned to the administration building where Lieutenant Colonel Girelli was waiting impatiently. Girelli was hoping to find out how seriously CID was taking the incident report and how they would handle it. He didn't seem to have a lot of faith in a young officer who was more investigator than engineer.

"How's your investigation going?" Girelli asked, even before asking Ben to sit down.

"Not bad, sir. I talked to most of the G-4 handlers, learned more about how you run things in the CATS shed. Is there anything you want to add about the men?"

"I'd like to hear what your impressions are. But I'll tell you, these are good men, they're well trained, and they take their work seriously. These are E-4s and E-5s who handle material everyday that could eliminate half the people in the state of Alabama."

"Fair enough, sir. Of course, they get paid extra for it," Ben said. He'd learned long ago how to get people to talk and he wasn't here to make new friends.

"Sure they get paid extra, and they deserve it," Girelli shot back. "And if that's why they took this job, that's fine with me. But as I said— they take their work seriously and they do it well. And not that it matters, but I don't think most of them took the job for the extra pay."

"What makes you say that?" Ben asked.

"Because the money isn't enough to take this job unless you think it's important work. Each one of those men volunteered for this work. You don't just get assigned here. It's too important and too dangerous."

Whatever, Ben thought to himself. He had pressed Girelli and Girelli had stood up for his people. That said something about his people. Or maybe it said something about Lieutenant Colonel Girelli.

"Captain, do you know what the stuff these men handle can do? What VX-212 is?"

"I know that it's a very lethal nerve agent. That's about it."

"Yeah, very lethal. You could say that. You could also say it's the most lethal synthetic nerve agent ever developed. Are you familiar with the term LD50?" Girelli asked the CID investigator.

"No, Colonel, I'm not."

"LD50 refers to the dose that will kill half of the population exposed to it. VX-212 is rated at an LD50 of 10 mg by direct contact, 40 or 50 mg if inhaled. Do you have any idea what those numbers mean?"

"Well, I know that 10 mg isn't very much."

"No, Captain, it isn't. It's a few hundredths of an ounce. A drop of two. Let me put it in more familiar terms: four pounds of VX-212 could kill more than 100,000 people if someone delivered it very efficiently. Oh, but maybe only 10 to 20 thousand if someone just dispersed it in the air."

"OK, sir, I get the point. The material is very, very dangerous, and your men volunteered to handle it." Ben had already made a mental note that all the handlers had volunteered to be assigned to Tupelo. Interesting. "It's a good thing stuff like this has never been used."

"Actually, Captain, it has. With the intended results. But only on a few people."

"Really? Who used it?"

"Do you remember about 10 years ago that subway attack in Japan by members of some cult? That was Sarin—not nearly as deadly as VX-212. Somehow they figured out how to make it themselves. That attack killed a dozen people and seriously injured another 50, and they only had a few ounces. VX-212 is a lot more potent. A *lot* more potent."

"At least there weren't more killed." Ben answered.

"That's true enough, although that might not matter if you're the one killed. And it's a nasty death. The toxin paralyzes your entire muscular system. A little twitching, then paralysis. Including your respiratory system, which shuts down, and you can't breathe. You lie there helpless, you can't move, you can't breathe, and you slowly suffocate. And die."

"OK, Colonel, I get it. Very nasty stuff. And we're destroying our last stockpiles of it. And anyone handling it deserves to get hazard pay. No argument here. What can you tell me about the civilian, Jack Roehm?" he asked Girelli, getting back on track.

The Colonel was a little vague about how Roehm, a civilian, got along with the enlisted men, or with Girelli himself. As far as Hawkins could tell, Roehm wasn't quite as professional, not quite as dedicated as Girelli thought he should be.

On the other hand, Girelli wasn't at all vague about how serious he thought the incident was. Girelli was all for calling in Homeland Security and had said so to Major Corliss from the get-go, which was news to Hawkins. And he thought Hawkins' visit was just slowing things down.

"This is probably just a paperwork error. I sure as hell hope so. But I told your boss and I'm telling you that I want this looked at from top to bottom. And I want that on the record."

Hawkins knew Girelli had already conducted his own investigation of sorts. Then he filed the incident report with CID. Either he was very cautious, or very concerned about covering his own ass. Either one was OK with Hawkins. He agreed with Girelli about calling in some specialists to begin looking over the facility, the procedures, and the men. Maybe they could clear up the discrepancies tomorrow and he could still head for Florida.

Unfortunately, things didn't get any clearer the next day.

Tuesday

Hawkins spent the next morning looking over the chemical decontamination facility from a secure observation area. The men working the forklifts were aware of him, which was fine. He saw that Rivera and Patterson were working the forklifts and the front of the CATS, while McNair and Samson were handling the treated materials.

The men showed up for work in their regular army combat uniforms. Those assigned to actually handle the materials or work with the CATS system were required to wear an orange coverall over their army combat uniforms, or ACUs, both to protect themselves and to identify the personnel who were handling the chemical munitions.

Today Rivera and McNair were handling the Mark IV forklifts. One forklift operator would pick up 45-gallon reinforced drums of chemical or actual chemical munitions and place them in hardened tungsten-steel handling tubs. The second operator would pick up the handling tubs and move them into the transfer area. From there, the tubs, essentially oversized cooking trays capable of withstanding extremely high temperatures, were moved into the furnace.

After the material was in the furnace, the system was fairly automatic, including the drilling into munition casings and the 60 minutes of blast furnace time at those 3000° temperatures. After cooling, the handling tubs and whatever metal slag remained were tested for complete decontamination, then moved out of the furnace and weighed. Then Patterson and Samson, working on the other side of the CATS system, moved the slag to a storage area outside and the steel tubs were returned to the staging area for re-use.

He had seen enough by the end of the morning and went up to the main administration building. Sheila, the administrative assistant he had met the day before, found him some desk space.

"How do you like your coffee?" She asked him.

"Black, one sugar, but you might as well show me where it is. I'm going to be here for a while, so I'll need a few refills."

Sheila showed him where to find coffee. After he was all set up, she left him alone and he began going over the CATS records and the personnel records.

Hawkins compared the dates of the weight discrepancies with duty rosters. It took some time, since he essentially was creating a spreadsheet by hand, but a pattern showed up by the time he was halfway through. Then all he had to do was to see if the pattern held up for the rest of the dates. It did.

It seems that only two of the G-4 handlers were on duty on every date that a weight discrepancy had occurred. Hawkins had interviewed one of them yesterday. The other one, Specialist Jimmy Hartman, was still out, with another week remaining on his two-week leave.

Hawkins was reminded of what a former defense secretary once said—sort of. He knew enough to know that he didn't know enough. But he sure couldn't close out this case with the weight discrepancy still unresolved, and he was pretty sure he wasn't heading to Florida anytime soon. What he did need was a lot more help.

By late afternoon, Hawkins was on the phone to let his boss know what he had found. After the preliminaries, which took about 15 seconds, Corliss got to the point.

"So what have you got?"

He filled in Major Corliss with what little he had found and what his concerns were. He also outlined the steps he recommended for finding out more about the two G-4 handlers. Getting authority to look into financial records and phone logs took someone with higher rank than captain. He didn't mention that one of the handlers happened to have a daughter studying overseas.

"OK, Ben, do your debrief with the facility commander tomorrow morning, and then head back here. I'm going to start making some calls and get some more support for the investigation."

"What about my trip to Florida?"

"Unless you get some answers at your debrief tomorrow morning, I'm afraid you're gonna have to put that off until this investigation is put to bed. This one is too serious to have anyone out of the loop."

Ben had been waiting for that shoe to fall.

"And what do you want me to tell Lieutenant Colonel Girelli?"

"Exactly what you told me. The records don't jive, the personnel don't have an explanation, and you can't rule out a breach of security. We're expanding the investigation, unless he can give a reason not to. I don't think he'll be surprised."

It occurred to Ben that Corliss didn't sound too surprised himself. He was beginning to think he'd *really* been had.

"Next question, boss. What kind of support? This is supposed to be a highly secure facility and they're handling some very dangerous materials—some of which *may* be missing."

"I'm gonna kick that question upstairs, Ben. I agree we need technical support, of course. Probably someone from the other chemical processing center, and a chemical munitions specialist. But either we get some answers real fast, or we're going to be calling in some high level security, too. That will be General Flanagan's call."

That meant General Coleen Flanagan, the one star general who was director of Army CID.

The Alabama sun was still bright when Ben went in to the commanding officer's office to review his findings with Girelli and John Roehm.

"You were right to call us in. I can't rule out a serious breach here." Benjamin told the two men.

"So what's the real problem?" asked Roehm. "OK, some numbers don't match up. Somebody put down too much weight for the handling tubs and not enough for the residual slag."

Girelli looked a lot more concerned. For Roehm it had to do with his job at Tupelo. For Girelli, it had to do with his Army career. Whether it was sloppy records or a breach of security, it didn't look good. On the other hand, Girelli had called in CID as soon as the apparent breach was found. And he understood just how dangerous the threat could be.

"Look, John, we're not talking about maybe some missing equipment or motor parts—we're talking about a very lethal nerve agent. Probably nothing is missing. But if we can't account for all the VX-212 run through CATS, we don't know for sure there *isn't* some missing."

"That's precisely the point," Ben said. "As you know, the records indicate more residual slag than there should be. About four pounds' worth.

But the totals are right. Which tells you what?" Ben asked, looking at both men.

Roehm looked away while Girelli spoke up. "It could be that we're four pounds short of gasses. Which means four pounds short of nerve agent."

"How can you end up four pounds short of VX-212 if everything is super-heated and destroyed by the CATS system?" Ben asked, pretty sure all three of them already knew the answer.

It was Girelli again who spoke up. "Only one way I can think of. Four pounds of it never went in." The room went quiet. Then Ben spoke again.

"OK, a few more questions. I saw Rivera and Patterson handling the front end of the operation and McNair and Samson handling the back end. Do the men always have the same job, or do they rotate?"

"They rotate. That allows us to keep working with any four men on the job, plus it keeps the work more interesting," Roehm, the civilian manager offered, involved in the discussion for the first time.

"Any four men? It looked as if a single operator could handle any of the jobs."

"Army regulations. We need at least two men working at each end. It's a security requirement."

The meeting broke up a few minutes later. Now that he couldn't rule out a serious problem, Benjamin knew it was time to call in some serious help. No way he was heading south.

Ben was in his car and on the road by 6 o'clock. It was a 13 or 14-hour drive back to Ft. Belvoir, so he wouldn't make it tomorrow, but he could put enough miles behind him to be able to report in Thursday morning. While he was heading north he would be on the phone with Major Corliss, reviewing their plan of approach.

That night
Near Chattanooga, Tennessee

Ben made it to about an hour south of Chattanooga before he pulled off Interstate 59. His GPS unit told him there was a Hampton Inn about a half-mile west of the interstate and he had called ahead for a reservation. Twenty minutes later he was checked in and ready to call Sara.

"Well honey, just thought I'd warn you—I'm heading north, not south."

"What happened to Florida?" she asked him.

Ben gave her a vague rundown on what he had found at Tupelo. "We don't know if we have a recordkeeping problem, or if some Army property is missing. But it's a serious breach of security and we're going to have to put a team together."

Sara didn't have security clearance, of course, and Ben wasn't about to go into specifics with her. She had come to understand when he could talk and when he couldn't. On the other hand, Sara knew he had gone to a chemical processing facility. Army facility, chemical processing, and CID investigation—she had probably put 2 + 2 + 2 together already. She also knew when not to ask questions.

"Did you call Mike and the guys down in Ft. Myers?"

"Damn!" he thought. He'd been so busy trying to get a handle on the problem at the Tupelo facility that he had completely forgotten about the friends who were expecting him in a day or two.

"Jeez, Sara, thanks for reminding me. I'll call Mike tonight." He would have to cancel without going into any details, of course. *"Army business"* would have to do. Mike would complain, but he would understand. He had worked with Ben for two years before giving up an Army career for civilian life.

Sara told him about her time with the couple from D.C. Both were attorneys for a lobbying firm in town and they had the interest and the money to be serious about decorating a three-story brownstone in Georgetown. That meant they might commission Sara to find some major pieces.

She and Ben made plans for Thursday night. Neither of them knew Ben would be turning around and heading back to Tupelo in just over 48 hours.

Wednesday

Saman was at a shopping mall in College Park when her cell phone rang. Only two people had her cell number. She was expecting the call.

It was Mahmoud Najidad, as she expected. He had only contacted her once since she arrived in the U.S., right after she cleared Customs and Immigration. She hadn't seen him since he visited her in Spain three months ago.

"I'm glad you arrived safely," she heard Mahmoud say, without bothering to identify himself.

"There was no problem," she answered. "You know I look like her, I know where she's been studying. I even know her."

Mahmoud was concerned about Saman and her tendency toward recklessness. Her desire for revenge was a powerful motivator and was the main reason he recruited her, but he knew it could also lead to carelessness.

"As you know, her father was very cooperative. But things are happening a little faster than we expected," he told her.

"What's happening faster?" Saman asked.

"Jennifer's father called yesterday. He says the Army has started inspecting the facility. He can't help us anymore."

"Will that be a problem?"

"Not at all. We have what we need. We expected the Americans to catch on, just not so soon. Everything is fine," Mahmoud reassured her. Everything was not exactly fine, but Saman didn't need to know that. Mahmoud had planned to kill the American soldier when he finished turning over the nerve agent, but now someone was inspecting the facility and the sergeant had disappeared.

Actually, he was almost relieved. The operation to kidnap the daughter and coerce McNair had gone better than Mahmoud had expected, and he always knew there would be a narrow window to collect enough nerve agent before the theft was noticed.

Saman had faith in Mahmoud's assurances. It was all part of the plan. And everything was happening just the way Mahmoud said it would when he first told her about it six months earlier. That was when he promised her they could make the Americans pay for what they had done that day 20 years ago. He just didn't like sharing all the details with her. He said it was safer that way.

Her first assignment had been to befriend Jennifer McNair, which she had done easily enough. Her second job was to lead Jennifer to a small villa a few kilometers outside Seville, supposedly to spend a few days with some of her Spanish relatives. She timed the visit just at the start of one of the many university breaks, when many of the exchange students liked to travel around the continent. She wouldn't be missed for at least two weeks.

Mahmoud told her they wouldn't hurt Jennifer. They were just going to hold her for a few weeks, long enough to let Jennifer's father know they had her. And long enough to get Harry McNair's cooperation.

Saman hoped the people in Seville wouldn't hurt Jennifer—she liked her. She wasn't really convinced of that, though, and for good reason. She knew firsthand that Mahmoud didn't mind hitting women.

Mahmoud had recruited her two years ago. During one of their political discussion sessions, Saman made the mistake of asking him about his father. She watched in morbid interest as Mahmoud gradually grew enraged as he talked, the memories of his father's sufferings coming back as if he were still alive.

"My father was in the Revolutionary Guards, and fought in the struggle against the Iraqi invaders," he told her. "The war lasted more than eight years, and it almost bankrupted the Republic. You remember, it was Saddam and the Iraqis who invaded *us* and killed hundreds of thousands of our revolutionary fighters. And it was the Americans who supported our enemy, even when they used chemical weapons against us. Where was their righteousness about chemical weapons then?" Najidad asked Saman.

"And what happened to your father?" she had asked.

"Our Islamic Republic stood alone against the nonbelievers," he continued, referring to Saddam and the rest of the Sunni leadership of Iraq. Najidad didn't mention that Iran's greatest source of military hardware and technology was their other great enemy, Israel, who saw Iraq as a greater threat than Iran. Israel's assistance had been invaluable to Iran—but that was then and they had their own agenda, didn't they?

"And your father served in the Army?" Saman asked again.

"He volunteered for the Revolutionary Guards," Mahmoud answered with pride. "He was there when we fought and defeated the Iraqis at Basra. But then they used their chemical weapons again, and still the Americans supported and helped them. My father was injured when the Iraqis gassed our revolutionary forces at Basra, and he was never the same. He suffered for many years."

Saman could feel the heat rise in her face as she remembered how the Americans had killed her own family.

"And why do you blame the Americans for what happened to your father?" she asked without thinking.

"How can you even ask that?" Mahmoud answered angrily and he reached across the table and slapped her. She was more shocked than hurt, until he hit her again and she fell off her chair.

Mahmoud seemed to be someplace else, as he remembered the many years his father suffered. He had grown up watching and hearing his father live every day in pain, the wracking cough, the visits to the hospital, the drugs, the years of agony before he died at the age of 42. And then there was the final letter his father left for him, trying to make his son understand, not wanting his son to become another casualty in the war against Iraq:

"My son, we know we must all end our journey in this world. It's just the timing we don't know. I have decided it will be a time of my choosing. I hope someday you will understand."

Had he lived, the father would have been disappointed. Mahmoud only understood the hatred that stayed and grew within him. He continued his rant.

"The Americans knew the enemy was using chemical weapons, but they said nothing. They didn't go to the United Nations then, or ask for inspectors. They *knew*, and still they helped our enemies, with money and equipment and information they used against us."

Mahmoud seemed to be re-living his father's daily struggle after the gas attacks at Basra. Then he focused on Saman again.

"And then we hear them preach against weapons of mass destruction in Iraq?" he asked harshly. "The Americans helped pay for them! And who has the most such weapons in the world? The Americans! So perhaps it's time for them to know what it's like to be on the receiving end."

That was the first time he hit her. It wasn't the last, but what difference did it make? They had to do what they had to do. And Mahmoud's plan *could* work. They would teach the Americans what it was like to be afraid. To wonder if something awful could strike them at any time. Out of the blue, just as it happened to her parents and to Hami.

Saman looked around her, making sure none of the people strolling about the shopping mall could overhear, as Mahmoud continued. "We need to make sure he doesn't talk to the police or the FBI, or anyone else. I'll call our friends in Seville."

Thursday

*T*he scales were completely unbalanced, with a large, four pound sack on one pan, while the other pan was completely empty, and then there was a loud, insistent buzzing. Ben rolled over and the dream faded away. *Four pounds*, he thought. Then he rolled over again and looked at the nightstand. His cell phone alarm was buzzing, just as the first streaks of dawn were lighting up the eastern sky. *Oh yeah*, he remembered. *Need to get an early start.*

He was out of his room and on the road by 7:30. He picked up a large coffee and two doughnuts before getting on I-81. It was about a three-hour drive to Belvoir, and he wouldn't have time to stop for breakfast. His boss would be waiting for him. He set the cruise control at 74 mph—not quite fast enough to interest the state highway patrol—and settled in for the drive.

Four pounds short. Four pounds short. The phrase kept running through Ben's mind as he headed northeast back to Ft. Belvoir. But Roehm said they *weren't* four pounds short. Someone had just recorded it wrong, put the numbers in the wrong column. McNair? Hartman? They were both on duty on the days the numbers didn't add up. *Actually, they did add up,* Ben told himself. *They were just in the wrong place.*

Four pounds short. Four pounds in the wrong column. Which was it?

But Ben knew how the Army worked, especially when military ordinance was involved. And this was some ordinance. They would have to *prove* where the error was, or at least prove they weren't actually missing four pounds of a lethal nerve toxin. Although he understood the need to expand the investigation, he just couldn't accept that four pounds of VX-212 could have actually disappeared. It's not as if some terrorists had been hanging around Tupelo, Alabama, or had been found taking pictures of the nearby secure and well-guarded Army facility.

On the other hand, Ben had only talked with the Army personnel at the chemical treatment facility. He hadn't talked to any of the locals, and wasn't about to. That was a job for civilian police, or even the FBI if they got called in. For all he knew, unknown persons *could* have been hanging around Tupelo, taking pictures, planning…planning what? To infiltrate a guarded military facility and steal military ordinance? Undetected? It didn't make sense.

Someone put some numbers in the wrong column. That number adds up to four. Right?

There was little traffic, and by mid-morning, Ben was just a few miles from I-95. He figured he had time for a short break. Twenty minutes later he was back on the road, heading due north.

Weekend traffic on I-95 hadn't started to build yet and Hawkins continued to make good time. He was back at Ft. Belvoir and in CID headquarters by noon. He was in his boss' office when the office phone buzzed. Corliss picked it up.

"Yeah, he's here." Corliss answered. Then his eyes opened and a worried look crossed his face.

Corliss hung up. "Looks like we definitely have a problem. Lieutenant Colonel Girelli just called from Tupelo. Sergeant McNair never showed up today. Girelli sent base security out to his place and there's no sign of him."

"*Holy shit,*" Hawkins thought. He had just talked with McNair a few days ago. Then he remembered about McNair's daughter, Jennifer, who was studying in Spain. McNair hadn't mentioned anything about her during their interview, but then, it was an interview, not an in-depth interrogation, so that wasn't surprising. Ben thought someone should try to contact the daughter or some other family member. He told Corliss about Jennifer.

"OK, we'll try contacting her. But it's time to call in some troops here, Ben. This has gone from an investigation into improper record-keeping to a high risk alert. That means I'm going to contact the Director and she's gonna want to bring in some help from outside our division, and probably outside CID. And that means someone from outside the Army."

"You mean FBI?" Ben asked.

"That's up to the Director, or maybe her boss, the Secretary of the Army. But I wouldn't be surprised if the FBI gets involved real soon, and maybe Homeland Security, too. *Real* soon."

That was alright with Ben. They both knew he was out of his league in terms of the technical part of the investigation. He was an investigator, not an engineer. But the disappearance of G-4 handler Harry McNair had raised everyone's anxiety levels. In a world where fundamental terrorists had already proven they would—and could—go to extreme ends to harm the U.S., bureaucratic jealousies and inter-agency competition were generally a thing of the past. Generally.

That afternoon
Ft. Belvoir

Hawkins was back in Corliss' office, but this time two FBI agents were there as well. He knew things could get complicated now that the FBI was involved. Ben wondered how long it would remain an Army case.

On the other hand, things were already complicated, with several pounds of VX-212 possibly missing and a person who handled it definitely missing. But was McNair responsible for the unaccounted material? What exactly had he handled, or mishandled? It was going to be tougher to find out from a missing suspect, so Hawkins knew he would have to deal with the FBI agents sitting in the room with him. It was the ones he couldn't see who concerned him.

"OK, let's start with a full financials investigation," the senior FBI man, an agent by the name of Rawls, started. "We'll also interview all his neighbors, the men he worked with, visit the local shops, pull his phone records…."

Hawkins spoke up. "I already spoke to four of the five guys he worked with. The other one is out on leave."

"That was before their buddy turned up missing. We—or you— need to interview them again. And where is this guy who's out on leave? This is a federal criminal investigation now."

Rawls was right, of course. While Army CID could put several more investigators on the job, the FBI could put on a dozen or two, plus a lot of other resources, such as their national crime lab at Quantico and their forensic accounting people. Plus the rest of Homeland Security, and wasn't this the new world? Inter-agency cooperation. Solving the crime. Forget the jurisdiction.

Corliss was already calling it a joint Army/FBI team investigation, although technically, CID was still the lead agency. The FBI would access any electronic records they found at McNair's, but they would share the data with the rest of the team.

Hawkins had already given Major Corliss and the FBI agents his impression of McNair from the half hour interview he had with him.

They decided to have Hawkins do the follow-up interviews with the other G-4 handlers after all. That would put him on-site in Tupelo to coordinate the investigation with Lieutenant Colonel Girelli. An hour later, Hawkins and the two FBI agents were leaving Corliss' office.

Although they would call it a CID/FBI Task Force, the FBI would coordinate the overall investigation and do the bookkeeping, as Hawkins called it—and he was pretty sure they wouldn't limit their financials investigation to McNair. They would be looking at all the G-4 handlers, as well as Roehm and Girelli, the people in charge. Hell, they would be looking at Hawkins' bank records before they were through. FBI agents would also canvas the neighbors and anyone else in the community around Tupelo who might have had contact with McNair.

They also set up a forum website accessible to all the team members. There would be no more, "Nobody shared that info with me," not after a few critical memos seemed to have gone unread before 9/11. All team members would send whatever they found to the site at least daily, and any electronic input could be tagged to go out immediately to designated e-mail addresses. Army CID would manage the site—encrypted, of course—and keep the data organized.

Later that night
Belmont Bay

Hawkins was actually feeling better about the investigation, despite the news about the disappearance of Army Staff Sergeant Harry McNair. Putting together a plan with Corliss and the FBI agents had something to do with it. So did having dinner with Sara.

Sara was in Washington, meeting with clients at the Smithsonian. Originally Ben was going to meet her at the Capitol Grill, a spot in downtown Washington that was popular with a lot of legislative people and the lobbyists they often dined with. The dark paneling and long history made almost anything you were talking about seem important. But the day's events and the outcome of that afternoon's meeting meant Hawkins was heading back to Tupelo in the morning.

Normally he wouldn't mind heading up to Washington to have dinner with Sara, even though they would then turn around and drive right past Belvoir on the 45-minute drive back to Belmont Bay. But tonight she was just as happy to head back home and not have him put in any unnecessary drive time. They agreed to meet at Antonio's again.

She called him when she was about 10 minutes out, so he had a very cold vodka martini waiting for her and a Jack Daniel's on the rocks in front of him. It had been a week since he had seen her.

"There you are, good-looking," he heard a familiar voice say. He assumed it was Sara behind him, but you never knew.

He stood up, gave her a hug and something between a peck and a real kiss. It had been a while, but he did have a lot on his mind. She held him for a moment and then sat down.

"So you thought you'd be heading for Florida by now. What happened?"

Hawkins hadn't given her any details. She just knew he had hurried back to Belvoir and wasn't heading to Florida soon. But Sara was smart, and she had been a help to him before, security clearance or no security clearance. He considered the matter and decided he needed her help. He filled her in about the weight discrepancies and McNair, skipping over the details about exactly what kind of materials were involved—and how lethal they were. Not surprisingly, she saw the problem pretty quickly.

"So you don't know if it was even stolen. Or misplaced. Or how. Or even by whom, although this guy McNair taking off seems to fill in that blank."

That was exactly the problem. If it was McNair—which was an assumption, but a logical one at this point—why did he take off? That had certainly drawn all the attention to him.

"How long will this trip be?" she asked.

"It's really not up to me," he answered. "We'll be co-coordinating through the FBI and it may depend on what they come up with. My job is to get face-to-face with the Army personnel I spoke to earlier this week, but now I'm going to press them much harder."

"But I thought you don't know yet how much stuff was stolen?"

"That's true. At least, we don't know for certain. But Lieutenant Colonel Girelli thinks he found about four pounds missing—at least, *maybe* missing."

As Ben expected, Sara put the pieces together pretty quickly. "Four pounds of some material *might* be missing and there's a big investigation starting up? And the FBI has gotten involved? That must be some material. Chemical research, huh? Sounds like chemical weapons to me."

In the past two years Ben and Sara had reached an unspoken understanding about what he could tell her and what he couldn't, and she had come to trust that understanding. When Ben did give her details, it was usually more for his benefit than for hers. Her thoughts and perspective had been very helpful on several of his investigations.

"Let's just say the Army facility I visited has the responsibility to destroy a lot of materials we no longer need. Outdated weapons."

"Outdated weapons being destroyed at a chemical facility and now the FBI is involved in an Army matter. Still sounds like chemical weapons to me—but hey, don't tell if you can't."

So much for trying to keep the information vague, Ben thought.

"Nobody ever said we made nice weapons. And they didn't used to be illegal, but now they are since the U.N. passed a resolution in 1994 banning them. And we supported that resolution. Anyway, the container and the chemical agent are both supposed to be destroyed. And they're supposed to keep track of both."

"And?"

"Well, the good news is that the Army has been making great progress destroying these stocks—hundreds of tons of this stuff."

"And the bad news?"

"They keep very good records. Except in this case, there's the matter of a little discrepancy."

"Benjamin, I don't think there's such as thing as a *little* discrepancy when you're talking about some kind of chemical weapon. Isn't that the kind of thing we were looking for in Iraq?"

"True enough. We went into Iraq to find and destroy their chemical weapons. It just turned out that didn't have any. But *we* do—or at least, we *did*—have a few thousand tons of it over here. The funny thing is, this is stuff we made all by ourselves."

"So what's the 'little' discrepancy?"

"It seems the totals add up—but there's about four pounds too much leftover slag."

"And that's a problem because…?"

"Four pounds too much slag could mean four pounds too little of the bad stuff destroyed. The slag is the container material."

"I see what you mean. But couldn't that be a recordkeeping thing? How could you steal some kind of nerve gas or whatever it is from an Army facility? I assume that stuff is tightly guarded."

"Sure it's guarded, and remember, we don't even know if it *was* stolen. That's what we're trying to find out. Maybe it's just bad recordkeeping."

"And now the FBI is involved. Like I said—sounds like very dangerous stuff."

Ben shook his head. It amazed him how much she had put together on her own. "Look, you can't say anything about anything to anyone, Sara."

"Yeah, I think I got that, Captain. Let's hope someone doesn't get the idea to attack us because *we* might have weapons of mass destruction."

"Maybe they're about to." *There's a real conversation-stopper,* Ben thought, as both he and Sara grew quiet.

Once dinner came, they talked about what Sara had been up to the past week, and how the world of antiques was faring. He didn't know much about that world, but he was learning, and he found it interesting. Besides, the details of his work usually weren't a good topic at the dinner table.

They were finished before 9 o'clock and headed to Sara's place just a few blocks from the boatyard in Belmont Bay. Ben could swing by his place in the morning and grab a few things. This time he would be flying down to Tupelo. Tomorrow was going to be a long day.

Friday

It was another rise and shine morning for Benjamin. He wanted to be on the road by 7 a.m. That would give him plenty of time to stop by his place, drive up to Reagan National, and catch the 9:30 morning flight to Huntsville, about 40 miles west of Tupelo. He would pick up a car and be at the Tupelo chemical facility by noon. He'd already programmed his handheld GPS with the local addresses of the Army enlisted men he would be visiting.

Sara had coffee ready when Ben came downstairs. She already knew pretty much what he knew, including that he had no idea how long he would be in Tupelo. She poured Ben a cup of coffee and he could tell the case was on her mind.

"Benjamin, however this turns out, this is different than anything you've handled before."

'Yeah, I know—even though we're still not sure that we're not facing anything other than sloppy record-keeping, and now a missing person case that may or may not be related."

"And maybe some killer nerve gas." Sara added.

"Well, that's the whole point. Nobody is going to mess around if three or four pounds of nerve agent is missing. That's probably enough to take care of all of D.C."

"So now you've got not only Major Corliss and the commander at Tupelo involved, but the FBI as well."

"Yes, but that's the good news. There's gonna be a lot of legwork here, and the FBI can help with that. I can concentrate on the people at Tupelo."

"And if anything happens, nobody wants to look back and ask 'why didn't you follow up on the warning signs'—like that mislaid FBI memo before 9/11." Sara said.

"Right. But it's not just CYA for these guys. We know bad stuff can happen and it's their job—our job—to make it *not* happen. And something else—I've already said too much, but this stuff is strictly between you and me right now." Ben still wasn't used to the idea that his investigation might have to do with a terrorist attack rather than some stolen Army goods, or some Army man or woman arrested for DUI, which was the kind of case he was used to talking to Sara about.

He finished his coffee, kissed Sara and headed out the door. In a few hours he would be back in Girelli's office to continue the investigation at the Tupelo facility. All this—CID, FBI, plus the local police in Tupelo—for four pounds of material that was either not properly accounted for, or was actually missing. True, it was because the case involved the highly toxic nerve agent VX-212 that the alarm bells had gone off. But it was the disappearance of Harry McNair that had really turned up the volume.

That afternoon
Tupelo Chemical Research Center

It was just after noon as Hawkins approached the gate at Tupelo Research Center and he heard his cell phone ring. He pulled over before the gate when he saw it was his boss calling.

"I just got a call from someone at the FBI who introduced himself as Assistant Director Donniger," Corliss started. You're going to want to go over to McNair's place and see what they've pulled off his home computer."

"Why don't you just tell me, sir?"

"Well, the gist of it is a couple of e-mails that look as if they came from his daughter overseas. And they're sending his answering machine to their forensics lab at Quantico to see if they can recover any messages from the past couple of months."

"OK, great, we get to put the FBI lab people on it. That was one of the reasons to get them involved."

"Well, since you mentioned it, I have some other news for you, and you may not like it. Our Director just kicked this up to Homeland Security. It was just a matter of time, and I think it's a good call—except that they've already made the FBI the lead agency."

Benjamin knew they had to bring in other investigators, but there was a lot that just didn't feel right. This was still an Army case, no matter who ran the investigation and he would be seeing the Army chemical munitions handlers again today. This time there would be interrogations, not interviews.

But Ben understood that nobody was going to tread lightly when several pounds of VX-212 were unaccounted for. Army CID, FBI, and now Homeland Security and probably the Justice Department's Counterterrorism section—all of them would be trying to get a handle on what might have happened. He really didn't care who was the lead agency, as long as they stopped whatever was going on. He had learned long ago you could accomplish a hell of a lot more if you didn't worry about who got credit for it.

He pulled into the parking area in front of the administration building. He was meeting Lieutenant Colonel Girelli to bring him up to date, at least in general terms. Girelli wasn't under investigation, at least by Army CID, but he wasn't exactly in the clear either. But he was still the official commanding officer of the Tupelo facility, so the team decided to keep him in the loop, at least in terms of the general investigation. They wouldn't be sharing specific information with anyone not on the investigating team, though, and Hawkins would make that clear to Girelli.

Girelli's administrative assistant, Sheila, was at her desk in the outer office when Ben arrived. Ben declined her offer of coffee. She buzzed her boss, said a few words and hung up.

"He's ready for you," she told the CID investigator.

Ben walked down the short hallway and entered Girelli's office.

"Good morning, sir," he started, and sat down in the chair Girelli indicated. Girelli didn't look good, and seemed to be watching the door into his office.

"I can't say it's good to see you again, sir," Ben started out.

Girelli didn't waste any time. "This is a nightmare. McNair was one of the best. Good, solid record, very dependable. He's missing, and that means we have to assume the VX-212 is missing."

"Yes sir, that's our assumption. And because of that, we've put together a team to handle the investigation. This is way beyond my pay grade. And a lot more serious than we thought."

"Who's on the team?" Girelli asked.

"Homeland Security and the FBI are involved now. They're looking at bank records, computer files, phone records, neighbors, everything. The FBI will be the lead agency. Who knows how long until a few other federal agencies with initials we know—like NSA and CIA—will be involved."

"I suppose you'll be looking at me, too," Girelli said.

"That's not my call, sir—but I think you can pretty much count on it. Jack Roehm, too."

Girellli leaned forward. "Look, whichever way this turns out, I assume my career is over. I won't be here much longer. But this is much bigger than me or Roehm, or you either, Captain. They can investigate me up the wazoo, but they're not gonna find anything. Just let me know what I can do."

"How bad could this turn out? Let's say McNair made off with, say, four pounds of VX-212. What's the worst-case scenario?" Ben asked.

"Like I told you the other day, it could make 9/11 look like a warm-up round. This is very, very lethal stuff, the most toxic we have, maybe the most toxic in the world. Just one pound of it dispersed the right way, some kind of airborne release, could kill 5,000, 10,000 people. And it's not easy to clean up."

"Colonel Girelli, I'm sure you already know that CDC will be involved to deal with the aftermath if an attack actually occurs. They have the communications in place to alert medical facilities across the county. I'm here to find out whatever else I can about McNair from the other men at the plant. And to let you know that other than cooperating with us fully, you are not a part of this anymore—for now."

Part of Hawkins' assignment on this trip was to give that message to Girelli. He didn't think Girelli was surprised by it. Hawkins knew that other experts were already drawing up worst-case scenario response plans. He had learned that the Centers for Disease Control and Prevention in Atlanta had already developed a series of contingency plans following the Tokyo subway attack.

CDC had been working for years with emergency responders and local health agencies to prepare for a possible attack on U.S. soil. Their plans included prevention of a bacteriological or chemical attack, but prevention was up to the CID and FBI now. They would also play a major role recommending and monitoring medical treatment in the event of an actual attack.

After a very unenjoyable lunch, Hawkins began his round of follow-up interrogations of the Army personnel who handled the VX-212. He had already spent several hours with them the previous week, and nobody pretended anymore this was routine. A fellow worker who had disappeared, a CID investigator hanging around, and now the FBI asking questions in their neighborhoods. No, it sure wasn't routine.

He didn't turn up much during the follow-up interviews, except for something from staff sergeant Hector Rivera. Rivera had been at Tupelo for just over two years and had a good service record. He'd also been friendly with McNair. Last week Rivera hadn't volunteered anything and seemed to resent Hawkins. But that was before his buddy took off—or was kidnapped. He was a lot more talkative today.

According to Rivera, McNair had seemed different the past month or two.

"What do you mean by 'different'?" Hawkins asked him.

"I don't know. He was kind of distant, not so friendly."

OK, that was pretty vague, Hawkins thought. Out of touch. Not so friendly. Which led to an obvious question.

"Any idea why, what was up with him?" he asked Rivera.

"No, he said everything was OK. I thought maybe something with his daughter or his ex-wife. But he never said anything."

"You didn't say anything last week."

"What was I gonna say, sir? 'Hey, Captain, my friend Harry hasn't been so friendly the last coupla weeks.' But now I'm thinking maybe that had something to do with his taking off."

Benjamin sat there wondering if Rivera had known McNair might go into hiding or had any idea where he was. He asked him both questions, along with a few others. Was there anything different about Mc-Nair's work, did he get phone calls, was he irritable? There wasn't anything specific Rivera could point to, and he claimed he had no idea why or where McNair had run.

By 6 o'clock Hawkins had finished talking with the four handlers again, including going back to each of them to talk about what Rivera had said. There wasn't much more. He knew the FBI investigators were checking into their credit card and bank records even as he met with them, but they didn't have to know that. The FBI had taken care of getting broad coverage search warrants the night before, and those warrants included searching the electronic universe that everyone inhabited.

Hawkins was staying at the same Holiday Inn in Pikeville as earlier in the week. He was back in his room and had a secure online connection to the team's clearinghouse website when his cell phone rang. It was Major Corliss back in Virginia.

"Hawkins, how did it go today?"

Benjamin filled his boss in, which didn't take long.

"So McNair might have been acting a little different. Did you see that info on the website about his e-mails?" Corliss asked him.

"No, I haven't gotten there yet. I was just starting to look over the website."

"Well, as I told you this morning, they found a whole series of e-mails from overseas—you remember, his daughter was studying someplace in Spain."

"Sure, I remember. I mentioned that at the meeting yesterday. Seville I think it was. Somebody was gonna track her down."

"Well they haven't succeeded. They ran down a cell phone number in Spain, but no answer. The phone seems to be turned off—at least, we're not able to locate the phone by the GPS chip, so either it's off or someone disabled it. And get this—her e-mails to good old dad pretty much stopped about two months ago."

"What do you mean 'pretty much'?"

"There was one more about two weeks ago, but the FBI tech thinks it was mailed from a different IP, maybe even originated here in the U.S."

While Ben was thinking about that, Corliss told him about the other FBI suspicion.

"The FBI linguistics expert thinks the recent e-mail was written by someone else, not the person who had been writing to McNair for the past several months. In other words, not his daughter."

"They can tell who wrote the e-mails?"

"No, but apparently they can get a pretty good idea about who *didn't* write them. The linguistics guy says the language structure, the tone, the length of sentences, and I don't know what else. It's different, and he's 90% sure the last one was not written by the daughter."

Ben was quiet for a few moments.

"What about the earlier e-mails? Anything there?"

"Nothing the FBI could put a finger on. They're posted on the website for you to look over. But they didn't see anything funny except that there were two or three e-mails a week for the past six months, and then, like I said, about two months ago, they stopped."

"What about the phone records?" Benjamin asked.

"They were able to pull logs of calls from Spain for the past couple of months. Maybe one every week or two. And then about two months ago they dropped off, too, except for one a few weeks ago."

"OK. I know they're putting all this in an algorithm, looking for patterns, but there's a pretty obvious one here, don't you think?"

Corliss paused. Yeah, it was pretty hard to miss and you didn't need multi-variable analysis to pick it up. About two months ago, e-mails stopped. About two months ago, the phone calls dropped off. And about two months ago funny things started happening at the Tupelo Chemical Research Center.

"Hey, Boss?"

"Yeah, Ben?"

"What do you want to bet they don't find anything in McNair's financials?"

"You're thinking...."

Neither of them wanted to say it. *They have the daughter, they don't need to offer money.*

After finishing his conversation with Major Corliss, Benjamin put in a call to Sara. They chatted for a few minutes about the shop and a lead Sara had on some early 19th century Virginia furniture. There wasn't much that had survived the Civil War, let alone the 20th century, and most of that was in museums. Sara had opened up a new world to him when she brought him to some of the smaller museums around the state. Her previous status as assistant curator at the Smithsonian made her something of a minor celebrity at local and university museums and he had come to enjoy the visits.

"Alright, sweetheart, I'll see you sometime after lunch tomorrow," Ben said after they were all caught up. He planned on catching a plane out of Huntsville in the morning, putting him into Washington National well before noon. If the meeting with his boss and the investigating team were only an hour or two, maybe he and Sara could salvage a few hours out of what was supposed to be his week's leave.

Then Ben realized it had been only a week ago that he thought he was heading off to Florida. Instead of thinking about fishing or sailing, now he was wondering if there were a few pounds of VX-212 someplace out there, a homegrown American WMD, capable of killing thousands of Americans.

The irony of the WMD scenario hadn't escaped Ben. He knew the United States monitored chemical, biological and radiological WMDs all over the world, and spent millions of American taxpayer dollars to help other nations destroy them so they wouldn't be hijacked and used against the U.S. or anyone else. We had even gone to war with Iraq over them, although they turned out to be phantom WMDs.

But we didn't put together a CID/FBI Task Force to look for a WMD smuggled into the country, Ben thought, and he smiled grimly. *We put it together to locate and recover our own, made-in-American WMDs, and make sure they aren't used against the people who made them.*

The same afternoon
FBI Headquarters, J. Edgar Hoover Building
Washington, D.C.

Assistant Director Tom Donniger felt like a quarterback running the team offense. He had played football at Northwestern University, but as a defensive lineman, not a quarterback. Actually, that was more like what they were trying to do now—run a good defense. Know your opponent, know their strengths and weaknesses, work harder than they were willing to, and never, ever, ever quit. The problem was that they didn't know who their opponent was, so none of the rest of it fell into place.

Donniger had been here before and his experience told him they were well past the "Do we have a problem?" stage and well into the "Let's solve the problem" stage. That meant deciding what information you need, figuring out where to look for that information, and then mobilizing your resources. You send those resources into the field—or the lab, or the internet—to get that information. And that was the easy part. The hard part was making sense of the information they collected.

For the past three years, Donniger had been assigned to the Weapons of Mass Destruction Directorate, part of the FBI's new National Security

Branch. Part of NSB's job was to coordinate FBI counterterrorism efforts with other federal agencies, such as Army CID.

Donniger spent two years as the WMD field office coordinator in Baltimore before his promotion to national coordinator of the Directorate. Over the past three years he had worked with many of the field office co-ordinators, investigating and occasionally preventing relatively small scale and poorly organized attempts. But even small scale attacks could create widespread havoc, as the anthrax attacks of 2001 had demonstrated. He had also worked with a number of scientists, academics and state and local government officials helping to organize and prepare local defenses against WMD threats.

This case was unique, though. Fortunately. Donniger had never seen a case with a potential threat as great as this one. He had already received a briefing on VX-212, which the chemical engineer had described as "100 times more potent" than anthrax.

The involvement of a secure Army processing facility was just as disturbing. That's where these chemical weapons were supposed to be destroyed, not let loose on American soil to be used against American citizens. Someone with the intelligence and capability to penetrate a supposedly secure military facility had to be very determined and very good. They were also either very foolish, or very dangerous.

The joint CID/FBI Task Force was reconstructing McNair's activities from his banking, credit card and phone records. Nothing had turned up on the financials of any of the six handlers, or on the facility's commanding officer or civilian manager. Donniger thought both Girelli and Roehm needed to be interviewed again, but he wasn't sure that Army CID was the best outfit to do it. He didn't know the CID investigator who had opened the case, a Captain Hawkins, and he wasn't sure if the young officer had enough experience for the job.

And where was the daughter? Jennifer McNair, age 20, junior at University of Alabama, a good student who was on a semester study abroad program in Seville, Spain. They had found her cell phone number, a local phone purchased and activated in Spain. They were working on getting the phone logs from the Spanish national police, but that might take a few days.

According to McNair's answer machine records, he had gotten calls from her pretty regularly. He had registered for international calls to Spain and had a pattern of calling his daughter about once a week. Donniger had an agent going over the long distance phone carrier's logs right now.

The CID investigator, Hawkins, had filed an update report a few hours earlier. His day at Tupelo hadn't turned up anything specific, but you had to cover the bases. Donniger put more faith in the records search, but that would take awhile. He also had field agents interviewing the neighbors of all six materials handlers. Then there was the one handler they hadn't located yet—Specialist Hartman, who was still out on leave and who wasn't answering his cell phone.

Donniger was also smart enough and experienced enough to be careful about fixating on a target. Sure, everything pointed to this Sergeant McNair—his turning up missing was an obvious red flag, and the change in the pattern of phone calls and e-mails was important. That's why earlier in the day he had contacted the National Security Agency. International calls meant satellite transmission and they were considered fair game for NSA listening even before there were any warrants. And they recorded a lot of them.

He looked over their forum website for another half hour, looking at reports and data input by more than a dozen investigators and technicians in the past 48 hours. Then he logged off and called it a day. They had another meeting scheduled at Ft. Belvoir for tomorrow at noon. Maybe that sixth handler would report in. Or McNair would show up. Maybe NSA would have something. Maybe...but he doubted it.

Saturday

It was just after 11 a.m. when US Air Flight 3114 out of Huntsville touched down at Washington National Airport. That put Hawkins on the right side of the Potomac to head down to CID headquarters at Ft. Belvoir and then to his place on Belmont Bay. He turned on his cell phone as the plane taxied to the gate to send a text message to Sara and saw he had a voice message. He sent the text message to Sara first and then called in for his message, hoping there was a break in the investigation. No such luck—it was just a reminder from Major Corliss about the meeting in his office at Ft. Belvoir at noon.

Ben picked up his car from short term parking and headed south to Ft. Belvoir. He would just make the meeting at noon, although they could certainly start without him. He didn't have much to offer, and what information he did have he had already posted online at the task force website. These meetings were usually about brainstorming and planning, not reporting.

He thought about how different it was from the old days—only a few years ago—before the FBI, CID and other federal agencies initiated a major effort to incorporate up-to-date technology into their information management and sharing. The Department of Defense alone had spent more than a billion dollars upgrading their IT equipment and programs.

Five years ago, the meeting would have been about finding out what everyone else had done, who had what information and what the information was. It was data-sharing, something like comparing notes. Now, when you walked into a meeting, everyone was expected to be up to speed on the data itself, and ready to talk about what the data meant, compare possible scenarios, and then be prepared to move on to planning.

Reagan National Airport to Ft. Belvoir is about a 20-minute drive, most of it along Route 1. It was just before noon as Ben turned onto Belvoir Road, and was waved through the entrance gate by one of the MP's manning the entrance gate. A few moments later he was parked in the lot in front of the CID headquarters building.

Corliss had moved the meeting to a mid-sized conference room, although only a half-dozen people were present. Ben didn't recognize several of them. Several flat screen monitors were mounted on the walls around the conference room.

Introductions were made and Benjamin learned that the National Security Agency was now part of the task force, with two of their people present at the meeting. The woman, Emily Olstadt, would share whatever she could from NSA. Her colleague called himself an information technology expert, which Hawkins took to mean computer geek. The assistant director of the FBI had come down from Washington, along with another FBI agent, a tall, austere looking man who was coordinating the fieldwork. Several of his field agents were still out in the field around Tupelo, interviewing neighbors and friends.

"Alright, ladies and gentlemen, let's begin," Corliss said, to get the meeting started.

"I want to remind everyone that we're investigating the *possibility*—this is unconfirmed, so we're still talking *possibility*—that up to four pounds of a nerve toxin called VX-212 has been stolen from the Tupelo Chemical Research Center in Tupelo, Alabama, sometime in the past four to six weeks. In the wrong hands, a pound of this nerve agent could cause anywhere from 20,000 to 100,000 deaths, depending on how the nerve agent is delivered."

"Now, I said '*possibility*,' but as we'll be discussing today, while several pounds of this nerve agent may or may not be missing, a United States Army non-commissioned officer who was closely involved in handling this material disappeared two days ago. The name of this individual of interest is Sergeant Harry McNair and his whereabouts are still unknown. He disappeared shortly after one of our senior investigators, Captain Ben Hawkins, who is present today"—Corliss paused and looked over at Ben, who nodded in return—"questioned him during an inspection tour of the Tupelo facility."

"The reason you're all here is that—until confirmed otherwise—we are required to treat this as an actual event. So let's get started."

Corliss went on to review the security protocols for the investigating team. All information was to be shared on the secure project website. All phone calls were to be made using task force cell phones that would be issued at the end of the meeting. No use of flash drives, CDs or any other portable data media storage, even if encrypted. Homeland Security and the Department of Defense had made portable data media off limits after several leaks from a secure facility at Los Alamos. There would be no more talking over the case with Sara.

Then Assistant Director Donniger spoke up and it became clear that pretty soon Donniger was going to be the task force leader, even though CID had not yet officially turned over the investigation. That seemed OK with Corliss, and it was certainly alright with Hawkins. He would ask Corliss about it later, but for now they had some decisions to make.

"Alright, as you know from our collaborative website, we don't have anything new on McNair's whereabouts, or on the guy out on leave," Donniger started out.

"Let's go over what we know about this Sergeant McNair first, and see if we agree that he's our only identified person of interest right now. Captain Hawkins, what did the other handlers have to say?"

Ben went over Staff Sergeant Rivera's comments that McNair seemed different in the past month or two, but he knew he was telling everyone something they already knew. He reminded everyone in the room of his initial finding that McNair had been on duty for each shift when there were some discrepancies in the reported weights of the gasses and slag after decontamination and destruction of the chemical weapons.

The accounting forensics specialist was next, presenting information everyone had already looked at, but putting it into an organized picture. The banking records didn't show anything unusual. McNair's Army paycheck was deposited automatically each month, he paid his bills by paper check and there was a clear trail. There wasn't any unusual activity or change in the pattern of money moving into and out of McNair's account over the past year, except that six months ago he began sending an online transfer to an account registered in his daughter's name. He had three credit cards and was pretty careful about them. He was paying off a mortgage on his house, but his car was paid for. Nothing unusual at all.

The FBI woman who had gone over the land phone and cell phone records was more interesting than the accountant, and she was nicer to look at. Thanks to a broad federal warrant, she had been able to put together a matrix of incoming and outgoing calls to McNair's home phone and cell phone. She had plotted both landline and cell phone activity on a timeline and the pattern jumped out when it was displayed on the large video monitor in the front of the room.

"You can see here that the incoming landline calls from Spain dropped to zero about two months ago. Prior to that, there was a pattern of weekly calls from several different phone sources, all in the Seville area."

Hawkins spoke up. "Well, remember he has a daughter studying abroad in Spain. My guess is she was calling home using an international phone card, so she could also use almost any phone. That would explain the calls originating from various locations. And obviously, something changed two months ago."

"You may be right, Captain. I'm just looking at the pattern of calls. I'll leave it up to others to figure out the meaning. I also want to point out the pattern of outgoing calls from our person of interest *to* Spain. Outgoing calls also decreased about two months ago, but they didn't stop altogether until about six weeks ago. But for two weeks, the pattern was very different. During that period, they were short calls, much shorter than the previous pattern. Two or three minutes at most, all of them to the daughter's cell phone.

The cell phone pattern was a little different, and Hawkins had to admit that the graphic was very helpful. The cell phone calls had also changed about two months ago, but unlike the landline calls, they hadn't stopped. In fact, the calls had increased to two or three a week, but they were also much shorter than before

The information from the IT specialist was also interesting, chiefly because the pattern of e-mails followed the phone call pattern. There were regular e-mails between McNair and his daughter until about six weeks ago. Then there was an obvious drop-off, although the e-mails were a little more regular than the phone calls. But the IT man had kept an ace up his sleeve.

"Something else showed up as we started tracing the incoming e-mails," the IT technician said about ten minutes into his talk. "For the past six months, the e-mails from Spain came from the same IP address. The last ones were the same IP address, but we traced it back to a different routing. I'm not sure where they originated, but I *am* sure that it's different from the earlier ones."

"What does that mean—a different routing? A different computer, a different location—what?" Corliss asked.

"A different computer, very likely. A different routing, definitely. What I mean is, for all we know, those e-mails could have originated from a neighbor across the street from the sergeant, but then routed through the original IP address."

"OK, back it up a minute. You mean we don't know who sent them or even where they were sent from?" Donniger cut in.

"That's right." The guy was trying to be patient without being condescending. He succeeded at the patient part. He was in his late 20's and probably knew more about computers, internet providers and routing addresses than the rest of them in the room put together. After all, the rest of them had learned this stuff on the job. The IT specialist had grown up with Gameboys, iPods and cell phones, and had a degree in computer science. Ben knew most of the senior agents at both the FBI and the CID had been slow coming up to speed with 21st century technology, even if their agency had not.

By the time the information specialist was finished, it was clear why Harry McNair was their leading person of interest, even if another one of the handlers was unreachable. McNair was missing, and six weeks ago something had changed dramatically in the communications between McNair and his daughter. Donniger reminded everyone that both Interpol and the Spanish national police were searching for the daughter, but without success so far.

The meeting got even more interesting when Emily Olstadt, the NSA analyst, spoke up. The NSA woman was a youngish, scholarly looking woman who started by giving them a sketchy introduction to some of the NSA capabilities on monitoring, intercepting and decrypting microwave transmissions.

"You mean listening in on phone calls," Benjamin broke in. He never understood why some people just wouldn't speak plainly.

"That's right," she said patiently.

"International phone calls, you mean?"

"Almost all international calls are microwave transmission, so yes. But many—maybe even most—domestic calls also involve ground-to-air and air-to-ground microwave transmission, so no, not just international calls."

"Like cell phone calls"

"Sure."

"So you can listen in on all the international phone calls and all our cell phone calls as well," Benjamin asked.

"We can, and so can some other people. But it doesn't mean we do."

"Because?" Benjamin wasn't sure if he was pressing to get clarification or if it was because the NSA woman irritated him.

Donniger broke in brusquely before it went much further. "Let's not get bogged down here. If you have some more background we need, fine. Otherwise, do you have something for us?" he asked.

"Yes, we think we do," the NSA analyst responded patiently. "But to answer the Captain's question, it's a question of legality and resources. The domestic calls are off-limits without judicial clearance. And even if we wanted to, we just can't monitor the millions of calls that take place every day. So we work just as hard at designing programs that help us figure out which calls could be significant as we do actually monitoring calls."

"OK, so what have you got?" Donniger broke in again.

"Well, we have programs that latch onto a phone call based on geography—we monitor a lot more calls going into and out of Iran and Pakistan than we do calls from Portugal. And of course we have certain phone numbers that trigger automatic monitoring and review, and a list of high risk names and words that can set off an automatic monitor. Certain phone numbers, of course, get full-time attention."

"You mean if the caller says, 'Hi, this is Mr. Bin Laden calling with a special offer,' that phone call is snatched up automatically and recorded, whoever made the call?" Major Corliss asked.

"Absolutely. Or a call using words such as "satan,' 'Allah,' 'security,' and about a thousand other words can also trigger a monitor."

"We're with you so far, and I take it someone connected with this case made a call like that," Donniger said.

"Bear with me a little longer, please, Assistant Director Donniger. Seville is not a high risk site and the name McNair isn't—or at least, wasn't—on our list at all. Both have been tagged now, of course. But in the past few years we've been able to identify another variable that has been very helpful—something called *prosody*."

"Which is...?" Donniger jumped in, trying to get her to move on.

"Prosody is the tone or style a person is using. Yelling is different from talking, and it's considered a strident prosody. Prosody looks at whether it's fast speech, excited speech, angry speech and so on. The speech recognition programs have gotten sophisticated enough that they can detect whether the person speaking is angry, excited, afraid, and so on."

"Alright, Ms. Olstadt, so tell us about the angry caller, or whatever, that you picked up and how it's connected to this case," Donniger asked. He assumed the background lecture on linguistics and prosody was leading somewhere.

"We looked back over calls that happened to be pulled out over the past two months originating from the Seville area and with anything unusual in the language or the prosody. We found one call that qualified and it was made to the Alabama area—to Sergeant McNair's landline in fact."

"And I'm guessing the caller was McNair's daughter," Hawkins said.

"We think so, but we can do a spectral analysis to compare it to any recording you have of her to make sure. We only got the tail end of the conversation. I can send over a transcript, but basically she was pleading to someone—presumably her father—to do whatever they asked."

Donniger spoke up. "OK, we can send you an audio file of a call she made to him a few months ago. Something we picked up off his home answering machine. Anything after that? Did that phone number or that area get monitored more?"

"No, I'm afraid not. And we wouldn't have found this one if you hadn't asked us to look. You can tag and record a lot of calls—the problem is, you just can't actually listen to most of them," the analyst said.

Donniger looked around the small group. They all had pretty much the same information now, and probably each of them had reached the same conclusion he had. He didn't want to limit other possibilities and ideas, so he kept his opinion to himself for now and asked each person present to offer a scenario.

"Before we start talking about where we go from here, I want to remind everyone in the room that this is an Army CID case—or at least it started out as one," Major Corliss started.

"But my boss, General Flanagan, has made it clear that although we consider this an Army responsibility, in no way does that affect how this investigation will be handled. CID is co-operating fully with the FBI and all other agencies involved, and we agree and support that the FBI is the proper agency to head up this Task Force."

Good for you, boss, thought Hawkins. True, it had already moved way beyond an Army internal investigation, but that's because CID had asked for the help. Corliss probably wanted everyone to remember that it was CID who first identified the potential problem and there was no stonewalling here.

The room was quiet. The IT guy dealt in information and he had already provided it. The Olstadt woman from the NSA was quiet too. It was Cooper, one of the other FBI agents, who finally spoke up and said what everyone was already thinking.

"I think it's pretty clear that until we know better, we have to act as if there are several pounds of this stuff out there and that this Sergeant McNair is our chief suspect, so we need to focus on anything to do with him. Any phone records, bank records, credit card activity, computer files, and especially any phone numbers connected to him, incoming or outgoing," Cooper started.

"Yeah, that's pretty clear," Donniger agreed. "So what are some possible scenarios that got us here?" he asked again.

Benjamin had spent the past week trying to answer that question, and he knew no one knew the answer yet. But he had some ideas at least, so he spoke up.

"What we know is that McNair was on duty during every shift when there were recordkeeping discrepancies, he's missing, and as far as we know, so is his daughter. He got regular phone calls and e-mails from her until a few weeks ago and now they've stopped. So both he and his daughter are involved," he started.

"You think his daughter is part of it?" Donniger interrupted.

"I said 'involved'," Benjamin answered. "Everyone at Tupelo, from Lieutenant Colonel Girelli to every one of the other handlers, said he was a great father, that his daughter Jennifer was everything to him. Plus he's got an excellent service record, and he's got 15 years in. I don't see someone like that getting his little girl involved in hijacking several pounds of nerve toxin. I think if his daughter *is* involved, it may be that she was used to blackmail him into doing something."

"Maybe so. I don't care about the 'whys' right now. The point is, do we think this all revolves around McNair and his daughter?" Donniger asked.

"I disagree—I think the 'whys' may be important. And the point is, if the daughter is involved, and was used to coerce McNair into hijacking the VX-212, that might be the route to investigate." Ben wasn't known for being subtle and he wasn't sure Donniger would get it.

"OK, Captain, you made your point. But I'm not hearing any disagreement about concentrating on McNair. We're not gonna forget about the guy out on leave, Specialist Hartman, but that avenue should clear up in a day or two and we have two agents watching his condo. But for now, everything else centers on McNair until we hear a reason to do otherwise. I'll get back to each of you about how we go from here."

After a pause, Donniger continued, "And we have a lot of work to do canvassing the local area. We concentrate on McNair, but for all we know, there could be outsiders involved, with or without McNair. Civilian investigation is outside Captain Hawkins' jurisdiction, of course, so we'll use FBI agents to talk to the locals in the Tupelo area."

Ben noticed how Donniger, the senior FBI agent present, had already taken over. He also knew about Donniger's training and experience in counter-WMD work, so it made sense to him.

It looked as if the meeting was about to break up. It had run an hour longer than Hawkins had expected, but he could salvage the rest of the Saturday afternoon. He heard a quiet humming and saw Donniger look down at his Blackberry. He studied it for a few moments and then surprised everyone.

"That missing daughter, Jennifer? Well, INS may not be the quickest bunch, but they *are* thorough. They say Jennifer McNair entered the country last week."

That evening
Belmont Bay

Benjamin sat across his kitchen table from Sara. So much for saving at least part of a Saturday afternoon. With the news of Jennifer McNair apparently entering the country a week before, the task force meeting had continued on for another hour to map out strategy. If the daughter had returned to the U.S., and McNair had gone missing at about the same time, what did that mean? Were they both in on it after all? It just didn't sit right with Benjamin.

He hadn't gotten back to his place until nearly six. At least Sara had volunteered to stop at the grocery store on her way over to his place.

"So what's next?" Sara asked, as she prepared a salad.

Benjamin was mixing a sauce for the fish he was about to grill. "The Task Force decided to concentrate on McNair and his daughter Jennifer. We'll keep a couple of agents around Tupelo, continue talking with neighbors and workers. And we're looking into anyone who had any contact with McNair in the past two years or so."

"But you don't agree with them...."

Sara was right. He couldn't disagree with Donniger's reasoning, and he had no better alternative. But he had met McNair and he had talked to several people who knew him. He just didn't seem like a guy who would involve his daughter in something like this. And there was no history leading up to it, no complaints filed, no gripes with the Army, no meetings with radical groups, no middle-age conversion to Islam. There was no sense to it—except that everything seemed to point to it.

"The daughter Jennifer seems to be the key," Sara thought out loud. "So let's suppose you're right. She's not part of it. Why did she go quiet for more than a month? Why did she disappear? And why would she come back to the U.S. and not call her father? She was already back when you talked to McNair last week. That doesn't make sense."

Ben was weighing how much more he could discuss with Sara when something she said hit him. Supposedly Jennifer had returned to the U.S., but there was no sign that she had seen or even called her father. Sara was right—it didn't make sense, not for someone who called or e-mailed every week. But in fact, they *didn't* know Jennifer was back in the U.S. All they knew was that someone had entered the country using her passport.

Sunday

Benjamin was at his desk by 9 a.m., even though it was a Sunday. He grabbed a cup of coffee and began writing up the scenario. He wanted to run it by Major Corliss and then post it on the website for the other members of the task force to consider.

Major Corliss was just coming into the office as Benjamin was finishing.

"Morning, Boss. Not much of a weekend, huh? Hey, I've got something I'd like to run past you."

"Sure, Ben. Come on in."

Ben grabbed his coffee and went into Corliss' office. He outlined his thoughts about McNair and his daughter.

"So you think Jennifer is gone, run away someplace. And that wasn't her who came back two weeks ago," Corliss summarized.

"It's certainly possible. All of a sudden they stopped writing or phoning for six weeks—or at least almost stopped. All the communication changed. And she comes back to the U.S. in the middle of her semester abroad and doesn't contact her father? Doesn't make sense."

"OK, that's one idea. A possibility. Post it on the website so everyone can think about it. And I'll ask Donniger to send some agents around to the University to see if the daughter showed up there."

"I've already got something ready to go, but you know that Donniger has already made up his mind. He's after McNair and his daughter, and I don't think he's gonna look at anything else."

"So where are you in your investigation?" Corliss asked Ben. "Doesn't seem like you have a lot else to do right now."

That was true enough. He had done what he needed to do at Tupelo, and with the FBI and Homeland Security involved, now there were specialists looking at bank records and phone logs and computer drives. His job was to concentrate on Sergeant McNair and Jennifer McNair. The only problem was, where was the trail?

The same day
Knoxville, Tennessee

The Iranian agent known to Saman as Mahmoud Najidad, and to Harry McNair as Joseph, was in his motel room an hour north of Tupelo. Saman Kashan sat in a chair near him.

Mahmoud's last direct contact with his commander in Qazvin had been two days ago, but that wasn't unusual. Some of their communication was through message drops on various websites, hidden in blog entries and chat rooms. Their primary contact, though, was through the Facebook page of a fictitious grandmother from Pennsylvania. Grandma's photo had been picked randomly from an online site.

On the other hand, the last message from Qazvin had been unusual. Posted yesterday, it said essentially, "Hold tight." The message concerned him. Major Heidari had approved the whole plan and everything was working perfectly. Saman had entered the country without incident. They had the material. What was "hold tight" supposed to mean?

The message had also asked for confirmation that Saman and Mahmoud had covered their tracks and their identities well. Well, that was all part of the plan, wasn't it? Why were the people back at Qazvin asking about that now? Was Major Heidari getting nervous?

Mahmoud believed there were people who *planned*, and people who *did*. It was the rare individual who could do both, and Mahmoud considered himself one of those rare individuals.

Mahmoud had a satisfied smile on his face as he thought back to the first days of this operation more than two years ago. He was the one who had sold it to the action group of the Quds Force, now headed by Major Heidari.

Mahmoud was also the one who had recruited Saman from a group of radical students. Not the radical students who wanted to change the Iranian government and give new "rights" to the people of Iran. No, he found Saman in one of the smaller, harder to find student groups who still believed in the ideals of the revolution, or at least wanted to prevent Western notions about women and freedom and worship anyway you wanted from poisoning their Persian culture.

Saman had come to his attention because of her morbid interest and obsession with the United States. It didn't take long to hear her story and to see the hatred she had for the people she blamed for destroying her family. After several months of observing her, Mahmoud was ready to approach her.

"Saman, I know you believe in the Revolution and the future of our nation," he had said to her.

Saman had looked at him warily. She had seen him at several meetings. He was older than most of the group and had spoken very little. He had always seemed to her more of an observer than a participant of the group.

"Of course I do. You have heard me talk about the important role the Islamic Republic is destined to have."

"But most people just talk about it. Do you just talk about it too?"

"I am just a student, and a female student at that. But someday I will do more than just talk about it."

"What if that day came sooner rather than later?" Mahmoud asked her.

An antenna went up in Saman's brain. Some members of the group suspected that Mahmoud worked for the government, maybe even kept an eye on them for the government. That was OK with her—she just hoped they kept a close watch on the real radical student groups, the ones that were always talking about marching in the streets.

At one time, all students in Iran were subject to *gozinesh*, the government program that screened all students for moral behavior and loyalty both to Islam and the revolutionary regime. *Those days were long gone, and now look at what went on in the streets of Tehran and other cities!* Saman thought to herself.

"Someday I hope to see the arrogant Americans put in their place. They think they can go anywhere they want, and cause trouble for us just because they are so powerful. You know what they did to my family...."

Indeed he did, which was the reason he talked to her that day. He knew the details of that terrible day in 1988, when more than 200 airline passengers died at the hands of the American Navy. In fact, he knew many details that Saman had no idea about, such as why the Revolutionary Council allowed a civilian airliner to fly out of a military airfield and over the Persian Gulf, even while Iranian patrol boats were attacking American ships in the same area. But Saman didn't need to know those details.

The talks continued for several weeks, until Mahmoud was sure she was right for the job he had in mind. Since that day, she had never wavered, not even when he ordered her to change her identity and enroll in a foreign university in Spain. She chose the name Elena because it sounded familiar, almost like her real name.

They had also been lovers, if only briefly. Mahmoud grew to care for the dark-haired Saman, but he was careful not to let any feelings for her get in the way of the plan he had spent almost a year perfecting, and would spend another year putting into place. No, even their relationship was part of his plan, another way to make her dependent on him.

He also told her his own family story. He wanted her to identify with him, to see him as a fellow sufferer, not just her leader. Whenever he told her about his father and his injuries from the Iraqi chemical attacks, though the memory of his father's sufferings came back as if he were still alive.

And so Mahmoud and Saman began their journey. Now, almost two years later, everything had fallen into place. He and Saman just had to finish the job.

Mahmoud wasn't sure he ever truly believed they could succeed. But now they were very, very close. They *could* succeed. The Americans would know what it was like to suffer from those terrible, evil weapons, just as his father had suffered.

It would happen in just a few days, and it didn't matter whether the Americans accepted their ultimatum or not. That was just to give them some hope, make them imagine there was a way out. Make them believe they could bargain their way out of this, the way they always tried to. And if Major Heidari was nervous about "deniability" back at Qazvin, so be it. Of course they had covered their tracks.

Mahmoud had fully considered the matter of how the U.S. would respond to their demands. He didn't expect the Americans to accept them, of course, but it made it easier to recruit Saman when she believed the Americans would be humiliated. Mahmoud fully intended to go ahead with *his* plans regardless of what the Americans did.

Now Mahmoud and Saman were having their second face-to-face meeting since she had entered the country. Mahmoud had instructed her to make the 10-hour drive from Virginia so they could go over the final details of the operation. Until today, Saman had known very little about the actual attacks, which was fine with her. He had told her a year ago that it would be safer if they each operated separately. She was the ace up his sleeve.

If he failed—and even if he succeeded—the next blow would be unexpected and it would be even more devastating than Mahmoud's attack. His attack was against a facility, a physical plant, although a few hundred people might die in the process. Her attack would be against human beings, directed at the Americans and whoever kept company with them. He expected the death toll to surpass that of the World Trade Center victory, and he would be remembered throughout both the western and Muslim worlds.

"I present you with four pounds of an official, American-made weapon of mass destruction," he pronounced formally, trying to make light of the moment. They were coming to the end of two years of planning and preparation.

"And you are sure this is real? Jennifer's father gave you the real nerve agent?" she asked again.

"Absolutely sure. One, do you think McNair would risk his daughter's life? Well, maybe. But two, our engineer friend Saeed tested it in his lab. It's VX-212 alright."

Saman didn't know Saeed, or how he had access to the equipment and instruments to handle a deadly nerve toxin. Mahmoud had always assured her that handling the material would not present a problem and apparently it hadn't. He hadn't told her how he used Saeed's wife and daughter to guarantee his cooperation, or that he had ordered Omid to murder the little girl and her mother.

"And our canisters are guaranteed?"

"Yes, Saman, Saeed has promised me they will work fine. But you are correct to be very cautious, so you will appreciate the little test I have planned."

Mahmoud proceeded to tell Saman how they would make sure the nerve agent was lethal, and mislead the Americans at the same time.

"And these are for you," Mahmoud added, handing her two aerosol cans. He neglected to tell her about the other surprise in each of the cans, the small explosive that would be set off when the can was activated. He had to be sure no one could question his prize agent and possibly trace the plot back to their nation. He felt she would understand.

She looked at the two aerosol cans. Each was the size of a can of household air sanitizer and looked liked something you would pick up at your local grocery store. She read the label: *"Kills odor-causing bacteria in the air."*

"That's funny, don't you think, Mahmoud? *Kills odor-causing bacteria in the air.* Don't the Americans insist on truth in labeling? Maybe we should change the label to read *"Causes death when introduced into the air."*

Mahmoud looked at her and suddenly reached over and slapped her hard across the face. She fell against the desk and landed on the floor, too shocked to cry out, a bright red mark on her cheek.

"You think this is funny, Saman?" he said harshly. "This is for real. Now let's go over your plan one more time. Then it will be time to go."

He didn't want to start worrying about her now and for the past year she had given him no reason to do so. But he had people counting on him back in Qazvin, even if they hadn't answered his last posting.

An hour later, they were finished reviewing the details of Saman's operation. As they were about to leave the motel room, Mahmoud stopped at the door and looked at Saman. Perhaps he had been too harsh.

"You have done very well, Saman. Remember all our work and planning. And remember that our people are counting on us."

Saman certainly did remember. Mother, Father, Hami, and everyone else on Iran Air Flight 655. She was sure they were all counting on her.

Monday

Colonel Arash Kashani was sitting behind a desk in a small office located in an administration building at the Borj-e Milad Sharif University of Technology. He drank some of the strong tea he had brought in with him. Two other men sat in chairs in front of the desk. Kashani had arranged the meeting, and it was the first time the three of them had met together.

Colonel Kashani monitored the activities of a small group of Iranian agents within the Ministry of Intelligence. He also kept track of the intelligence activities of the Revolutionary Guards, although that could be a challenge. The Revolutionary Guards had a record of pursuing its own agenda, and often acted independently. Their independence and their recklessness often created serious problems for the Supreme Council, as each acted on its own agenda.

Kashani reported directly to General Hamid Gulab, the security advisor to the Supreme Council of the Islamic Republic of Iran. He thought it was wiser to meet with these men away from their own military facility and away from any eyes that might be trying to follow the activities of the Revolutionary Guards. Kashani knew he tended to be paranoid—that was the nature of his business, and might be one reason why he was so good at it. But he also knew that didn't mean there *weren't* spies, both from within his own government and those the Americans might have recruited.

The two other men in the room were members of the Revolutionary Guards, intelligence agents attached to units of the Quds Force stationed in Qazvin. Kashani hadn't met these agents before, and he had been sent to find out what they were up to. His boss had been getting some unexpected inquiries from some of his contacts in Europe. Unexpected and disturbing.

This was a particularly sensitive time, with the U.N. and especially Europe and the United States considering—once again—ratcheting up the trade sanctions against his country. Their own president, the belligerent

Ahmadinejad, wasn't exactly helping their cause with his threatening rhetoric and hostile challenges.

Kashani often wondered why the United States and its allies hadn't taken stronger actions already. He knew that even their fellow Muslims in the Arab world across the Persian Gulf would be more than happy if the United States or Israel took military action against his country to prevent them from becoming a nuclear nation. Arab solidarity trumped Muslim brotherhood. The so-called Arab leaders just wouldn't risk saying so in public.

Qazvin was a good place to house a small group of dedicated servants of both God and the Iranian Supreme Council. Located about 100 miles northwest of Tehran, near the Elburz Mountains, the mountain range that ran between Tehran and the Caspian Sea, the city was small enough to not rate a lot of attention, but large enough to have the facilities the group might need. Thanks to the significant military presence in Qazvin, the activities of a small group of agents didn't stand out.

"Tell me more about this group. What is their assignment?" the colonel asked the senior of the two men, a major by the name of Heidari.

"Our man is working with a female agent we placed in Spain. He has a plan to bring great harm and embarrassment to our enemies."

Kashani had little patience for the Revolutionary Guards and their notion that they ran the country, but he knew better than to challenge them head-on. Kashani was a senior officer in MOIS, the Ministry of Intelligence and Security. MOIS controlled the Iranian secret police and national intelligence operations, both domestic and abroad. But the Revolutionary Guards ran their own operations independent of MOIS, and rarely shared information. They didn't seem to understand the broader implications of their actions. They could think tactically, but not strategically. Colonel Kashani doubted these officers understood the tremendous strain the country was under as it forged ahead with its nuclear development program despite continued international condemnation and isolation.

"And what is it these agents of yours hope to do?"

Kashani knew it might take awhile to get the full story from the two men, but he would keep them here until he had it. Apparently there were some alarms going off in the U.S. and Europe, and that meant alarms had gone off within the Supreme Council.

Kashani himself wasn't concerned about the European agencies or the nations they represented. In his experience, they would talk and talk and talk, but they wouldn't do anything, not without the United States behind them. And the Americans wouldn't do anything unless someone forced their hand.

After all, the Iranian Defense Ministry had been developing nuclear capabilities for more than 20 years. The Europeans and Americans had issued vague threats and imposed embargoes for several years, but that hadn't stopped them. It just made the Iranians play a carefully orchestrated public relations game. India and Pakistan had developed these weapons. So had Israel. *So why not the Islamic Republic of Iran?* their reasoning went.

It was the Shah himself who had started them down the road to nuclear power. After the Shah was deposed, the nuclear program got little attention during the turmoil of the first years of the revolutionary government.

The next few years were still chaotic, with reformists and conservatives fighting for control of the country. When Muhammad Khatami became president, the western powers were pleased to see a reformist, someone who believed the Republic should make an effort to co-operate with the world of nations. But he was still Iranian. That meant he believed in Iran's historic role to control the region—and that meant he believed in nuclear weapons.

The eight-year war with Iraq demonstrated how pivotal such weapons could be. Iraq had chemical weapons. Iran didn't. And when Iraq used their chemical weapons in nerve gas attacks against Iran, against their armies, against their people, and against their cities, Iran had no response. Thousands of Iranians, both military and civilian, died from the chemical weapons Saddam used at places like Susangerd, al-Basrah, and the battle for the Al Faw peninsula—and the world was silent.

No, Iran had no response, and neither did Europe or the Great Satan. And even when the United Nations finally condemned Saddam for his massive use of chemical weapons, the United States voted against the resolution. Where were the Americans then with all their talk about outlawing such weapons?

Oh yes, the war with Iraq had made it very clear that those who didn't possess the terrible weapons were at the mercy of those who did.

And then the game had changed. The Americans and their allies invaded Iraq. With Saddam gone, and Iraq in chaos, there were many voices in the Supreme Council saying that it was time for the country to reclaim its historic role.

And who stood in the way of the Republic's march to control the region? Years ago it had been Iraq and that fool Saddam. Today the obstacles were Israel and the United States. Everyone knew Israel had its own nuclear arsenal. Without a similar capability, Iran would always be a second-rate power, at the mercy of anyone who had that capability, as they had been at the mercy of Iraq and their chemical weapons.

Experts from Pakistan and North Korea were more than willing to provide technological knowledge and assistance. There were scientists and engineers from the former Soviet Union who were willing and able to do anything if the money was right. The Russian government was usually cooperative, too, especially after the two governments signed several multi-billion dollar trade agreements.

But how much more time did they have? The western powers might do something eventually, but Colonel Kashani was just as concerned about the pressures from within his own country. The counter-revolutionaries were getting stronger and stronger every year. The protests at Tehran University had gotten particularly ugly. These young students seemed more interested in western technology and western ideas than in the ideas he and his generation had struggled for. They didn't get it—and neither did the religious zealots. It was Persia that counted, and this ancient nation could reclaim its rightful place in the Middle East and the rest of the world.

From what Kashani heard, the nuclear engineering people needed only another year or so to produce a low-yield nuclear device. After that, they wouldn't have to worry about the Americans or the Europeans anymore. Even Israel would be a different story.

Funny how the foolish Americans had gone after Iraq, claiming it was about those so-called weapons of mass destruction. If that were the real reason, why hadn't they come after Iran instead? Now the Americans wanted to increase the pressure on his own country, but they would be too late.

But what the high-ranking security officer heard in Qazvin during the next half hour took him by surprise. It was worse than he thought—much worse. These fools had started by helping the Iraqi insurgents with supplies and equipment for building more lethal IEDs. OK, one enemy fighting another enemy, and let the Iraqis do the dirty work. We would settle with the Iraqis later anyway. As far as Kashani was concerned, Iraq was supposed to be governed by his own people anyway, as it had been for centuries.

But these fools had gotten ambitious. They didn't just want to damage a few Humvees around Baghdad or Fallujah, or kill a few American soldiers. They had an ambitious plan to make the Americans pack up and leave. Ambitious—and very dangerous.

"You see, Colonel," Major Heidari, the senior Qods Force officer explained. "We'll turn their own weapons against them. We'll use their own WMDs, the kind of weapons they are so righteous about, to make them leave Iraq. Then we can do whatever we want there, not just smuggle in materials and equipment for a few insurgents."

"What about deniability?" Kashani asked. "Can the Americans trace this back to us?"

"No, Colonel, that will not be a problem. When more than a dozen Saudis attacked the World Trade Center and their Pentagon, did the United States attack Saudi Arabia? No, because these were individuals who merely happened to be Saudis. They were acting on their own, or so it appears. They had no connections to the Kingdom or to the family of Saud, so why would the Americans attack Saudi Arabia? And they didn't, of course."

Kashani persisted. "But this man Najidad is connected to us. He's connected to you and to the Revolutionary Guards. Surely the Americans are likely to discover that."

"We took very careful steps to prevent that," Major Heidari countered, but he was becoming uncomfortable with the challenging questions. He had expected the Revolutionary Council to be very pleased with the operation, and he was already thinking of the rewards that might be in store for him.

"Almost two years ago, after Najidad came to me with his plan, he and I worked on the details for several months. Only then, when we were completely satisfied that it could work, did I have him discharged from the Guards, with discipline. He left in disgrace, with an unsatisfactory record, discharged for stealing from his own men. He lost his position, his benefits. Even his family was ashamed of him."

"He accepted this? How did he deal with it?" Colonel Kashani wondered, unable to imagine the hardship and disgrace of being discharged from your unit "with discipline"—the same as a dishonorable discharge.

"He accepted it as a true believer. Not in the religious sense, for he is not particularly religious. But as a soldier in the Revolution who is proud to do his duty," Major Heidari answered proudly.

"Colonel," he continued, "he even applied for several jobs, including one at the University of Tehran, knowing he would be turned down once they saw his record. So who is this Mahmoud Najidad? If the Americans do capture him, he is merely a disgraced ex-Revolutionary Guard, unable to gain employment except for the most menial of jobs. A man who, in his misguided way, perhaps sought to regain a sense of self-importance or self-redemption by an act of madness. Madness, Colonel, but the madness of an individual, not a state government."

Colonel Kashani actually admired the plan and how well the group had done. A supposedly rogue agent placed in the United States, and the coerced co-operation of an American soldier to help them steal an American WMD, or at least a very lethal nerve agent from the Americans' own chemical weapons. Carefully implemented steps so their own government could not be connected to the act. Impressive. It would be a shame to arrest these men for actions deemed dangerous to the Republic. He complimented them, and both agents looked pleased with themselves.

"Now tell me how you contact this Mahmoud Najidad and this Elena Saman in the United States," he instructed Major Heidari.

Over the next few hours, Kashani learned the operational details of the plan, along with information about the types of facilities the agents would target. He also learned how Heidari contacted his senior agent, Mahmoud Najidad, in the United States.

Yes, Colonel Kashani was impressed, but neither he nor the people he reported to were willing to risk exposing his country to the anger of the United States and putting their entire nuclear weapon program, and the Islamic Republic itself, at risk. The foolish Taliban had done just that and look where they were—driven from power and hiding in the mountains and caves of eastern Afghanistan. The egomaniac Saddam Hussein hadn't learned that lesson and he ended up with a noose around his neck.

Kashani had more tea and several light dishes brought into the room. He wanted to relax with Major Heidari and his assistant, Captain Ashkani. He listened to them talk excitedly about how well their plan was working. Once he felt there were no more details to learn, he got ready for the 100-mile drive back to the capitol.

Before leaving the university grounds, Kashani placed several calls, including one to the Iranian Embassy in Madrid. He also issued an order to Colonel Backhi, head of security for the Revolutionary Guards and a man he had worked with previously, reminding the Colonel that he, Colonel Kashani, was there on the authority of the Supreme Revolutionary Council.

"Alright, Ahmad," he told his driver. "We're heading back to Tehran."

During the two-hour drive, the very concerned security officer worked out his travel plans. They were about halfway to Tehran when he looked out the window at the Elburz Mountains looming in the darkness to the north. On the other side was the Caspian Sea, an area Kashani and his family loved to visit. He wouldn't return home for at least a week, if all went well. If it didn't—well, he might not return at all.

Colonel Backhi was surprised at Kashani's order. Major Heidari and Captain Ashkani were even more surprised on their return to the Revolutionary Guards base when Colonel Backhi and two guards escorted the two intelligence officers to secure officers' quarters.

"Don't be concerned, gentlemen, but for security reasons, I am placing you in protective custody, at least for the duration of this operation," Backhi told them. He didn't tell them that Colonel Kashani had said "house arrest," not protective custody.

"I will need your cell phones," he added. The two security officers looked concerned, but they had no choice but to dig out their phones and give them to one of the guards.

"You understand, Major Heidari, this is only temporary. Security precautions."

Colonel Backhi left the secure area, knowing he had no idea how long "temporary" would be. Backhi was more concerned with his own health and wellbeing being right now. He had signed off on the operation more than a year ago and he had decided then to keep the operation strictly in-house, not wanting to involve the political figures and bureaucrats in Tehran. The appearance of a senior intelligence officer from the Supreme Council and his unusual order to detain two officers made him realize that might have been a foolish decision.

Minutes later, the Revolutionary Guards officer was back in his office. He had a second order from Colonel Kashani, one he didn't understand either, but he was not about to question someone from the Supreme Council. He sat at his computer, composed a brief message, and pressed "Send." His two agents in Seville would get their new instructions in a few seconds.

That same day
Belmont Bay, Virginia

Ben rolled over and looked at the clock on the nightstand. It was 7 a.m. Normally he would be up and getting ready to head in to the CID office at Ft. Belvoir. He had been on the clock for almost two weeks straight without a break—so much for his week's leave enjoying the sun and the Gulf waters off the west coast of Florida.

Major Corliss gave him a lot of leeway when he was working a case, and this was some case. He was used to working solo, but on this case, there was plenty of work being done without him, thanks to the resources of Homeland Security and the FBI. Corliss had suggested he take a day off just to clear his head, and report back in on Wednesday.

That left Ben with a day on his own and nothing in particular planned. Sara would be heading into her antiques shop later in the morning. Ben decided he would pick up where he had left off with *Blue Lady*. What better way to kill some time then around a boatyard? He could talk with Hank, the yard manager, take the winter cover off *Blue Lady*, and begin to clean her up in preparation for her spring launch. His day mapped out, Ben rolled over and went back to sleep.

That afternoon
Belmont Bay

It turned out to be a glorious spring day for working outside. A sunny day, temperature in the mid 80's, it was almost too warm for hard work. With the help of one of the yard hands, Ben had gotten the canvas cover off *Blue Lady*. He was looking her over as she sat in the yard, supported by jackstands. She looked like a duck out of water, but she was still beautiful. Ben had a list of items he needed to complete before *Blue Lady* could be launched in a few weeks. He was about to call it a day when his cell phone rang.

"Captain Hawkins?" he heard.

"This is Captain Hawkins," Ben answered.

"This is Sergeant McNair. I spoke with you down at Tupelo."

Ben paused, wondering whether his phone was being monitored.

"What can I do for you, Sergeant?" he asked. Ben had learned long ago when to ask specific questions and when to let the other person direct the conversation. He also wasn't ready to let the sergeant know how much Army CID knew about him.

"There are some things I need to tell you, but I also need your help," McNair answered. "But it would be better to talk face-to-face."

"I'm back at Ft. Belvoir, Sergeant, so perhaps you can tell me over the phone." *That wasn't quite accurate, but no need to let Sergeant McNair know exactly where I am,* Ben thought.

"I'm not in Tupelo, Captain. I can meet you anyplace outside Ft. Belvoir tomorrow, but I'm not coming into any Army facility. I think you know why."

"What I know, Sergeant, is that there are some people who want to talk to you. And right now, you're AWOL, so it's not your call when or where we meet. I'm ordering you to report in to Ft. Belvoir." Hawkins was getting angry and that wasn't good—*but Christ, stealing a toxic nerve agent from the U.S. Army, and then demanding a secret meeting?*

"Yeah, I'm AWOL, and a lot worse than that, so screw your order. Forget about Belvoir. I have some information that's important to you and a lot of other people, too, but I need some help. If you can help me, fine. If not, you won't hear from me again."

"Help you? Are you kidding me?" Ben said, his voice rising. "You stole highly sensitive U.S. Army property, you're AWOL, and you want to bargain with me? Why would I do that?" Ben asked.

Then McNair proceeded to tell him, as Paul Harvey used to say, the rest of the story.

Tuesday

Hawkins was back in his office at CID headquarters in Ft. Belvoir. He was logged in to the investigation website, reviewing entries made in the past 24 hours. FBI agents were still talking to neighbors in the Tupelo area and at the University of Alabama in Tuscaloosa. NSA didn't have anything new, but they had raised the surveillance level for calls originating or terminating in Spain, and the Seville region in particular. They had also raised the alert level for monitoring chatter on more than a thousand internet sites NSA kept an eye on both for content and for pure volume of activity.

Hawkins was particularly interested in two aspects of the website information. Nobody had commented on his theory suggesting that McNair and his daughter were not running an operation—they were being used. And if McNair and his daughter were being used, the task force needed a different approach trying to locate them.

Only Donniger had commented on the idea: "*First find them, then we'll worry about how they're involved,*" he had written.

That's a big help, Ben thought.

But there was another entry from an agent specializing in accounting forensics, and it might explain Donniger's reaction. The FBI had just found an account in a small local credit union in Jennifer McNair's name. It wasn't a big account—$9,500 had been deposited to open the account a month ago, just enough not to trigger any reporting requirements. McNair hadn't said anything about it during the phone call the day before.

McNair's phone call had put Ben in a difficult position. By all rights, he had to report the call, and then find McNair and bring him in. Donniger wasn't being unreasonable: first find McNair, then worry about how he's involved.

But what if bringing in McNair put the investigation at risk, rather than moving it forward? And if McNair were telling the truth, that's exactly what could happen. Donniger and about a dozen agents would grab McNair, scare off anyone else, and the link from McNair to whoever was behind this would be broken. If McNair were telling the truth. And if not? There was still the matter of several pounds of VX-212 out there, and now Ben knew it wasn't a possibility, it was definite.

Ben wished he could have recorded the call from McNair. For all he knew, maybe someone had. He remembered the conversation almost word for word. The call had come in just as Ben was finishing his work on *Blue Lady*.

"Where the hell are you, Sergeant?" he had asked McNair.

He remembered his first meeting with McNair in an office at the Tupelo processing facility. It seemed like yesterday, but actually, more than a week had passed. Two weeks ago there was the possibility of a record-keeping error. Today they were facing the possibility of a major terrorist attack—and Sergeant McNair was at the center of it.

"I'm not gonna tell you where I am, and I'm gonna keep this call short, just in case you're trying to trace it. They've got my daughter and I'm trying to keep her alive."

"Who's got your daughter?"

"I don't know who. The first time they contacted me was almost two months ago. Some woman called me, said she was a friend of Jennifer's. Some friend. She knew all about her, though. She told me what I had to do if I didn't want them to hurt her."

"Look, McNair, no matter what you think or what they've told you, you can't handle something like this alone. This isn't just the United States Army anymore. The FBI and the rest of Homeland Security are involved too. We can handle this better than you can."

"Maybe so, but I'm guessing everyone there is interested in only one thing: getting those canisters back. Getting Jennifer back isn't high on their list, is it?"

Fair enough, and how could it be any other way? Thousands of possible casualties—thanks to his help—compared to one person's life. Ben thought it prudent not to say that out loud.

"McNair, you don't even know what's going on. Interpol is looking all over Europe for your daughter. We're monitoring internet sites all over the world, international phone calls. And by the way, someone came into the country a few days ago on your daughter's passport. Could it have been her?"

"If she were on her own, she would have called me. Last I heard from her was more than two weeks ago, and that was through this woman—she called herself Elena. And they told me—I go to you, they kill Jennifer."

"We're her best chance, Sergeant. Let us help out. And we need your help finding the VX-212."

"That stuff is gone. They had me drop off the canisters about two weeks ago. So here's the deal...."

"There are no deals, here, McNair. You're only making it worse."

"There *better* be a deal here, Captain. There may be a way to contact these people. But no FBI, no Homeland Security. They couldn't care less about some army enlisted guy. You and me. Think about it. I'll call you again tomorrow."

And that was it.

Ben was still at his desk when the second call from McNair came in, just before lunch.

"Are you going to help me, or you still trying to get me to come in?" McNair asked as soon as Ben answered the phone. McNair was using the number Ben had given him the day before, a direct landline into the CID office. Ben didn't know who might be listening in on the team cell phones the task force members were using. He figured it would be less risky to have McNair call him on his regular office phone.

"Would you come in if I asked you to?" Ben responded.

"No way. You wouldn't hear from me again."

Ben wasn't using a team cell phone, so it probably wasn't monitored. That didn't mean Ben couldn't record it, just in case, which is exactly what he was doing. He thought working with McNair instead of against him was the best chance to track down the VX-212. Somebody else might not see it that way, though, and just because you think you're doing the right thing doesn't mean you don't cover your ass.

"Alright, what do you want?"

"I want help finding my daughter. You and all those agents poking around Tupelo just want to find the VX. As soon as I come in you'd stop looking for Jennifer, wouldn't you?"

That was probably true enough. The daughter wouldn't know any-thing. The terrorists, or whatever they were, had just used her to force Mc-Nair to co-operate. The FBI and Homeland Security wouldn't have much interest in her once they had McNair.

"You may be right. But right now the Spanish National Police are looking for her in Spain, Interpol is covering the rest of Europe and the FBI is looking for her here in the States. Where are you going to look for her? And how?"

Aye, there's the rub, Ben had thought after McNair's call the previous day. Homeland Security had the resources to look for Jennifer, but they might not have the motivation once they had McNair in custody. McNair had the motivation, plenty of it—he just didn't have the resources. That's what Hawkins was counting on.

"That's what I want to talk to you about, Captain—but it would be better face to face."

"Tell me where and when," Ben answered. "But it can't be down around Tupelo. I can't disappear for that long."

"No problem," McNair said. "I know where you are and I couldn't hang around Tupelo anyway. I'm actually not far from you right now."

Somehow Ben wasn't surprised by McNair's revelations that he was in the area. The two men talked over possible meeting sites and they agreed to meet later that afternoon at a restaurant Ben knew off Route 123 in Woodbridge, about 10 miles south of his office at Fort Belvoir.

They hung up and Ben thought about McNair and his kidnapped daughter. He was thankful he hadn't been in McNair's position and only hoped he would have made the right decision. He just wasn't sure what the right decision was. *But Christ, four pounds of VX-212 out there in who knows whose hands? Your daughter...or twenty thousand other lives?*

That afternoon
Outside Ft. Belvoir

Ben left to meet McNair earlier than he needed to, but he wanted to grab a bite to eat outside of the office. He couldn't get his satellite radio to play through the FM setting he usually used, so he turned it off. He drove off base to Sam's Place, a pub he liked on Route 642. The place was just a few miles south of Ft. Belvoir and on the way to Woodbridge. He usually ended up there with some friends or co-workers, but today he was working solo again. He thought he was doing the right thing—dealing with McNair on his own—but he knew Donniger and maybe even his own boss wouldn't see it that way. Doing the right thing was important to him, but that didn't mean you didn't worry about the consequences.

He was heading back to his car after lunch when he noticed the grey Ford in the small parking lot on the other side of Route 642. Well, that was one of the reasons he had stopped here on the way to meet McNair. Just to make sure, he headed west on Route 642 for about a mile, and then turned off the highway into a Shell station. He pulled up to an inside pump, putting the gas pumps between him and Route 642. That gave him a nice view of the grey Ford as it passed the station and then pulled off the road about a half block further west. Now he knew the FBI was following him, probably just on general principles.

Ben finished up at the gas pump and got back in his car. He continued west on Route 642 until he came to the Lorton Shopping Mall, one of those huge complexes surrounded by several acres of parking lot. After pulling into the south side parking area, he found a spot that wasn't completely surrounded by other cars. The car would be visible and very easy to watch.

He took his time getting out and headed into the mall. He didn't think the agents would risk following him, and they didn't need to if his car was transmitting his location. They had probably installed a GPS transponder—a custom-made Lojac system. Maybe that explained the problem he'd had with his satellite radio/FM station connection. They could just sit and wait for the signal to move, which is exactly what he was counting on them to do.

He entered the mall complex, which had almost a hundred shops and restaurants. OK, his car was Lojacked, possibly his phone bugged. He didn't want to risk using his personal phone, so he strolled past the shops until he saw two teenage boys standing outside the Banana Republic store.

"Hey buddy, can you help me out?" he asked the nearest one.

"What's up?" the teenager asked. The kid didn't look too edgy—no tattoos and only a single earring.

"My phone battery is dead and I need to make a quick call to my wife. Can I borrow yours for a second? I'll be happy to pay for it."

"No problem, dude. Just don't make it too long."

Ben dialed Sara's number at her antiques shop.

"Hi, sweetheart. Hey, I need a big favor."

"Sure, if I can," Sara answered. "What is it?"

Ben told Sara what he wanted, but without explaining why. It was better if she didn't know.

A half hour later, Sara pulled in front of the north entrance to the mall. Ben saw her immediately, walked out and got in the passenger side.

"Are you going to tell me what this is all about?" she asked him.

"Let's just say I didn't like the car I was driving. Let's drive back to your shop and I'll drop you off."

A half hour later, Ben said good-bye to Sara and headed south to meet McNair in Woodbridge.

That evening
Belmont Bay

It was close to 7 o'clock by the time Ben got back to his own place. His cell phone rang just as he was pulling into his parking space.

"Ben, this is Corliss."

Ben had been expecting the call. What he didn't know was how much anyone had figured out yet.

Ben had met with McNair for nearly two hours. Then he had returned to Sara's shop and asked her to drop him off at the Lorton shopping mall. By the time he bought a shirt at Brooks Brothers—more for the shopping bag he would be carrying then for the shirt—he had been parked for nearly four hours. He didn't really expect the two FBI agents tailing him to buy it, but at least they would have to wonder.

"I just got a call from Assistant Director Donniger. He wants to know why you're going on a shopping spree in the middle of a very sensitive investigation."

"What's his problem?"

Major Corliss proceeded to describe how two FBI agents had spent several very warm and boring hours parked in a shopping mall in Lorton. And Donniger wanted to know what Hawkins had been up to.

"Boss, if the Assistant Director of the FBI wants to go shopping with me, maybe he can give me a call. We could have lunch, spend some quality time together. But I want to know how he knows where I was. And why he cares."

"How do you think he knows? Apparently he has a couple of agents following you."

"And what the hell is that all about? I thought we were on the same team."

"Yeah, we're all on the same team. But we're not all playing by the same rules. Now don't get all high and mighty on me. You and I know this isn't the first time you played by your own rules."

Yeah, Ben knew it wasn't the first time, and it wasn't the first time Major Corliss had reminded him either. Corliss, who was a combination of boss, mentor and maybe even surrogate father, had made it clear that the only reason Ben had been passed over for promotion to major the year before was his habit of working outside normal Army channels. And that was despite Corliss' endorsement of his junior officer as "highly qualified."

"Ben, are you there?"

Ben realized he hadn't been listening to his boss, which was never a good idea.

"Donniger is on to you, so I hope it was worth it."

"It was definitely worth it. I'll come in to talk to you about it. But this being tailed by a couple of FBI agents pisses me off, so screw Donniger."

"Like I said, don't get too high and mighty on me. For whatever reason, he doesn't trust you. Now he might not know it yet, but you know and I know that in fact, he was right not to trust you. You went behind his back."

Hawkins didn't want to argue the point, mostly because he knew Corliss was right. Donniger *couldn't* trust him—but that was only because Donniger was being an ass. And a close-minded ass at that. The only reason Donniger couldn't trust him was because he thought Donniger's way was going to get a few thousand people killed by some hijacked VX-212. Other than that, Hawkins didn't have a problem with him.

Ben told his boss about the phone calls from McNair and the meeting he'd just had.

"All Donniger was going to do was haul McNair into custody and start interrogating him. He wouldn't have gotten anywhere."

"Yeah, well, maybe so, maybe not. But you said it was worth it, playing this by yourself, so fill me in."

"OK, your office in an hour?" That would give Ben a chance to grab a sandwich at home before returning to Belvoir. Might as well lead the agents who were following him back to the home office.

"Sure. See you about 8 o'clock." Major Corliss hung up his office phone.

He placed another call and in a few moments he was speaking to Assistant Director Tom Donniger. "See? I told you he would produce."

Monday (the previous day)
North of Richmond, Virginia

Staff Sergeant Harry McNair looked at the bedside clock in his motel room. It read 5:30 a.m., an hour before he had set the alarm. He wasn't sleeping well these days.

McNair was staying in a motel about a mile off I-95, halfway between Richmond and Washington. He might be just a highly trained forklift operator, a non-com with no special training, but he wasn't stupid either. He knew the FBI and CID would be looking for him, so a week ago he had visited Randy Searlon, an old fishing buddy. Searlon gave McNair his credit card, no questions asked.

The nightmare had begun about two months ago. It started when he opened what he thought was an e-mail from Jennifer, one of the one or two she sent every week from Seville. She had been in Spain for almost three months by then and her semester abroad was beginning to wind down. But the e-mail wasn't really from Jennifer, although it had her address on it. And the world changed for Staff Sergeant Harry McNair when he clicked on the e-mail:

> *To: ssmcnair102@hotmail.com*
> *From: jmcnair0595@hotmail.com*
> *Re: Your daughter*
> *Sergeant McNair:*
> *Your daughter is good. She will be good as long as you do what we tell you to do. Do not contact anyone, not the police or the army, or anyone else. Check for e-mail every day by 9 pm your time. We will contact you again. When you do what we tell you to do, we will let your daughter go.*

He insisted on a phone call from Jennifer. The people holding her, whoever they were, readily agreed. Jennifer assured him she was alright. But she was frightened, understandably so. She wasn't able to tell him anything other than that she had been held for three days and she either didn't know or couldn't say where.

After that, he received e-mails about every other day, sometimes from the people holding Jennifer, sometimes from Jennifer herself. Jennifer would describe something she and her father had done together so he would know she was the writer. The other ones, the ones from the people holding Jennifer, told McNair what they wanted from him.

That's when the nightmare got worse. At first, McNair thought they wanted money. Then he got the e-mail, again with Jennifer's e-mail address, but signed by someone who called himself "Joseph."

To: ssmcnair102@hotmail.com
From: jmcnair0595@hmail.com
Now you have talked with your daughter and you know she is OK. She will be OK as long as you do what we say. We are not bad people and we don't want to hurt her. But it is up to you.
Soon someone will call you. He will arrange to meet with you near your home. You are to follow his instructions. Then your daughter will be allowed to leave.
Joseph

Two days later, McNair went to a Holiday Inn on the outskirts of Tupelo and met a slender, dark-haired man in his late twenties who called himself Joseph. He spent two hours with Joseph, first not believing what he wanted, then arguing with him, and finally realizing he had no choice if he wanted to see Jennifer again. And what guarantee could Joseph give him that Jennifer would be released?

"The only guarantee I can give you is what will happen to her if you don't do everything I have told you to do," was Joseph's answer. "Besides, what do you care? We don't have these terrible weapons in our country, and we can put them to good use there."

What they wanted was unbelievable. McNair debated whether he could do it, but there seemed no way out. That's when the rationalization began.

All he had to do was to play a shell game at the Tupelo facility. The chemical plant processed and destroyed hundred-pound, five hundred-pound and even one-ton shells and bombs. Usually, though, they processed the thousands of small, one-pound and two-pound canisters, each containing from four ounces to a pound of VX-212 or some other chemical agent.

Joseph had a general idea of the procedures at the Tupelo processing plant. He wanted several pounds of nerve agent, and he was very specific: VX-212. He also had some ideas about how to obtain it.

McNair was to substitute a one-pound metal slug for one of the one-pound canisters. The metal slug would go through the CATS system, ending up as molten slag, along with the other processed materials. The stolen canister would go into a fanny pack he had taped to his mid-section under his ACUs, replacing the one-pound slug he had brought in. Then he would bring the canister home and wait. They would tell him when to start, when to stop, and when they would pick up the canisters.

Did he have a choice? He thought about going to his C.O., Lieutenant Colonel Girelli, but they said they would kill Jennifer if he talked to anyone—and they were watching him. Besides, they said they were shipping the nerve agent back to their own country. What did he care? At least, that's what he told himself.

He remembered the day he crossed the line. He did a dry run first. Before he left for work, he duct-taped an empty fanny pack around his waist. It didn't look too noticeable in his bathroom mirror. Then he headed for the treatment facility.

Once at the Tupelo chemical plant, he went into the equipment area and found the Mark IV forklift he usually ran. He climbed onto the forklift seat and got ready to move into the transfer area. His buddy Hector Rivera called out to him.

"Hey Harry, you putting on a little weight?"

"Very funny, Hector."

McNair shifted the forklift into forward and moved into the transfer area, where he picked up a bin with several dozen one-pound and two-pound canisters. He moved the bin into the CATS processing area and lowered it into the furnace containment basin. Then he went back to the transfer area for another pick-up. He continued moving back and forth throughout the day, just another typical day destroying chemical weapons at the Tupelo Chemical Research Center, except that this day he happened to be doing his work while he had an empty fanny pack taped to his belly. It would be hard to explain if someone noticed it, but it wasn't a violation of Army regulations or federal law—yet.

By the end of the day, Harry had helped process about three tons of chemical weapons, and nobody, including Hector Rivera, seemed to notice anything different. He was surprised how easy it had been. Would it be as easy when there was one pound of VX-212 taped around his waist, and he was actually stealing a weapon of mass destruction from the United States Army?

It was. Rivera never said anything more and no one else noticed anything, even when McNair was carrying a one-pound canister inside his work clothes. The actual exchange of the metal slug for a weaponized canister took less than 30 seconds and he found he could do it just by stopping the Mark IV between the transfer area and the CATS room for a few moments.

Over the next two weeks Staff Sergeant Harry McNair removed six canisters filled with VX-212 from Tupelo. He turned the canisters over to Joseph at his second and last meeting with him. As soon as he had the canisters, Joseph disappeared.

The e-mails and phone calls continued for another week, filled with warnings that he keep quiet. Then the e-mails and phone calls stopped. A week later, when it was already too late, the guy from Army CID showed up, and McNair knew it was only a matter of time. That's when he decided he couldn't risk returning to the job site at Tupelo.

A few days of hiding out, though, convinced McNair that he wasn't cut out to be a fugitive. What he really wanted was help getting his daughter back safely to the U.S., and he had no idea how to do that. Between a rock and a hard place, burn your bridges behind you, look before you leap—there were probably a few dozen more words of wisdom he could think of, all equally helpful. That's when he decided to contact the young CID officer who had come to Tupelo.

"Where are you, McNair?" had been the CID investigator's first question when McNair reached him by phone. But Hawkins had agreed to meet him without calling in anyone from the FBI.

They had met last night. "Why did you take off?" was the first question Captain Hawkins asked.

"Because sooner or later you were going to take me into custody. I know you figured out about the missing materials. And then who was going to look for Jennifer? You? The FBI?"

Captain Hawkins was silent for a while. "Okay, Sergeant, so an agent or a team of agents targeted the Tupelo Chemical facility, fingered you for some reason and kidnapped your daughter to use as their leverage. They wanted several pounds of VX-212 and now, thanks to you, they have it."

"That's about it. Nothing I'm proud of," he had answered.

"What did this Joseph say about when Jennifer would be released?" the CID officer had asked.

"He said she would be released after I got them the six canisters. That was three weeks ago and I haven't heard from them since."

"We've got the Spanish national police and Interpol looking for her right now. There's no reason for them to harm her once they got what they wanted."

McNair wondered if the Army investigator actually believed that.

"Tell me more about this Joseph. What he looked like, how he sounded," the officer had asked McNair.

McNair told Hawkins all he had seen in his half dozen meetings with Joseph. Mid-twenties, dark hair, spoke English with a definite accent. Always polite, but very clear about what would happen if McNair didn't co-operate.

"Middle Eastern? Saudi? Iranian?" the CID man had asked.

"He could have been Iraqi or Saudi or Iranian. Definitely Middle East and Muslim."

"How do you know?"

"He used the name 'Allah' pretty often, so it wasn't too hard to figure out. And by the way, I'm pretty sure one time he got a call from a woman."

"How do you know that?"

"He just took a different tone. Not like the other calls he got. Very polite, but also kind of condescending, you know? Now, I'll tell you everything I know, but I need to know you'll help get my daughter back."

"Yeah, well, I'd like to feel sorry for you and for your daughter too, but I'm more concerned about the four pounds of very toxic material that some dangerous people now have their hands on. At least two suspects, one possibly a woman. Your job now is to help us find them and the material."

And that's when he came to an understanding with Captain Ben Hawkins of Army CID. No plea deal or bargain, but he would provide whatever help he could about "Joseph" and anyone else who contacted him, and Hawkins would make sure the feds would continue to search for his daughter.

Tuesday evening
Ft. Belvoir

Pretty good plan, Ben acknowledged to himself after Sergeant McNair told him the whole story. Planned in detail. Organized carefully. Executed flawlessly—so far. The only bad break for whoever was behind it was that the theft had been noticed sooner than the operatives expected, but so far that hadn't made any difference.

Who *was* behind it? More importantly, what was next?

Ben had learned years ago to put aside the "what ifs" and concentrate on the "What next?" *What if the daughter had escaped? What if McNair had refused to steal the VX-212? What if Lieutenant Colonel Girelli had noticed the theft after only one or two canisters had been substituted?* None of that mattered because none of that happened. What counted was...*what's next?* Nobody collected VX-212 as a hobby.

Ben was back at CID headquarters in Ft. Belvoir and both Assistant Director Donniger and Major Corliss were present. Ben had asked that Donniger be there, but he was pretty sure the lead agent in charge would have been there even without his personal invitation.

"So let me get this straight," Donniger started off. You intentionally shook off the FBI agents who were assigned to follow you?"

"Let me get this straight first," Hawkins shot back. "We're doing a joint investigation about a possible pending terrorist attack and you're using manpower to follow me—the guy who was first on the scene. Is that right?"

"Apparently that was a good call, because the first thing you did was to shake them off and then arrange a secret meeting with the guy who stole the material in the first place!"

"That's exactly right. Because it was either gonna be a secret meeting with me, or no meeting at all. And remind me how much success the FBI had in locating McNair anyway."

"OK—so where is he now? I want him in custody."

"I have no idea. I didn't bother asking and he didn't offer. But I know he'll come in as soon as we find his daughter."

"That's not how it works. Now we have an arrest warrant and he doesn't get to pick and choose when he comes in."

Corliss decided to put a stop to it. "Are you two finished? Because I figure we have three or four pounds of nerve agent out there in the hands of someone who couldn't care less about what you two did or didn't do. Do you think we could get to work on that?"

Ben wasn't really all that worked up, and he didn't think Donniger was either. They were both staking out some boundaries, but now it was time to do something more productive.

Ben filled in the two men on his meeting with McNair. The ransoming of McNair's daughter, the meetings with Joseph, the phone calls and e-mails. Then Donniger, who seemed to have cooled off, offered some information of his own.

"We found several items of interest last night. We retrieved the e-mails from McNair's daughter, or whoever was using that address, and his e-mails back to her. We also found another bank account with his name on it. Someone deposited $50,000 into it a week ago. Are you sure this is still about his daughter?"

Hawkins thought it over. It was a fair question, one he'd already asked himself. But why would McNair have contacted him if he was in on it? And why would he hang around now and offer to help out?

"That sounds too easy to me. He's gonna end his career, deal with terrorists and turn over a deadly toxin for $50,000? And since his daughter *is* missing, she would have to be in on it. It doesn't add up."

"Yeah, I agree," Donniger answered. "Too pat. Not that it changes anything with McNair—we still want him and we want to do the questioning, not you. There's too much at stake here. And if you meet with him on your own again, I'm going to charge you with obstruction and lying to a federal officer."

"Look, the goal is to get information, and I can get it better than you. He contacted me and he'll co-operate as long as we keep looking for his daughter."

"That's not his choice anymore—never was. But that's the other news I've got for you. We found Jennifer McNair."

Wednesday

Colonel Kashani was dressed in dark slacks and a sports jacket as he sat in one of the Terminal E waiting areas at Charles DeGaulle Airport. He had flown from Tehran to Madrid on Iberia Airways, using a diplomatic passport. In Madrid he had been met by a member of the Iranian embassy staff who gave him a different passport and a roundtrip ticket to Paris on Air France. Kashani wouldn't use the return portion if he changed his identity again, but he would attract far less attention with a roundtrip ticket.

He had thought about traveling by train from Madrid to Paris, but time was a factor. These days there were serious security precautions on trains, too, especially after the train attack in Madrid itself, so there wasn't much to be gained.

Kashani was met by another agent at the terminal in Paris, an Iranian who had been a naturalized French citizen for more than 10 years and who occasionally travelled to the U.S. on his French passport. The Americans were unlikely to make any connection between the traveler getting on an Air France flight to New York's JFK airport and a government bureaucrat who had entered Spain yesterday.

The ticket transfer was surprisingly easy since air travel security procedures are directed at travelers *entering* the system, not leaving it. Kashani simply met the local Iranian agent at one of the many bookstores located within the secure terminal area, after the man had already gotten his boarding pass and gone through security. He and the agent exchanged tickets and passports and the man left the terminal with Kashani's ticket from Madrid in his pocket.

Kashani found a nearby men's room and entered one of the stalls. He looked at the passport and boarding pass that had been handed off to him. For the next few hours he would be Georgios Vassilis, a French citizen. Apparently Greek by birth, but nowhere was that indicated, since in France even the French State Department couldn't legally ask for or identify the applicant's ethnic background. He was already checked in on Air France Flight 12 to New York's JFK airport. The checked luggage receipt was stapled to it and there was even a photo of the single bag that would be waiting for him at the luggage carousel. Seat 15H, window seat. Excellent.

He was among the last to board. He handed his boarding ticket to the agent at the boarding gate and held up his passport, knowing she wouldn't look at it.

"Oh no, sir, you won't need that until you arrive in New York," she said.

After boarding the aircraft and taking his seat toward the front of economy class, Kashani buckled his seatbelt and began looking through the flight magazine. He stopped reading to listen politely to the attendant's safety instructions. Fifteen minutes later they were airborne. Colonel Kashani put on his headphones, selected "Classical" from the list of music offered by the onboard entertainment system, and leaned back. A few minutes later he was asleep with Mozart in the background and didn't wake up until they were over Newfoundland, less than an hour from their arrival at JFK.

The same morning
Seville, Spain

Jennifer woke up early, a habit she had developed during her enforced stay in the small villa north of Seville. There wasn't much to do, with no access to her phone or the internet, and her two watchers constantly about. Her small bedroom and sleep were a welcome refuge.

But something was different this morning and she sensed it immediately. *What was different? What was it?*

Then she realized it was sound—the lack of sound—that was different. It was quiet, very quiet in the house.

Jennifer looked into the small living room and kitchen areas. Empty. The bathroom and laundry areas. Empty. She ran upstairs. There was no one else in the house.

Jennifer hurriedly finished dressing. Ten minutes later she had her small backpack on and was out the front door.

OK, I know what to do. I remember where the American consulate is. They'll help me contact my father. And then I'm going to find Elena.

That same day
FBI Headquarters
Hoover Building, Washington, D.C.

The day was overcast and cool as Ben entered the Hoover Building by the Pennsylvania Avenue entrance. There wasn't much of a lobby any-more—after 9/11, most of the space was taken up by a new and imposing security system. The days of public tours were long gone and few people visited the small FBI museum anymore. The photos and newspaper stories of past exploits by criminals like John Dillinger and Baby Face Nelson seemed quaint compared to the threats the FBI dealt with now.

He gave his name to one of the security guards stationed behind a heavy glass window. The guard checked his list and found his name. He made a brief phone call and then handed Ben a temporary identity card.

"Please wear this while you're in the building," the guard said pleas-antly. "Someone will be down to escort you upstairs in a few minutes. You can have a seat over there," he said, pointing to some chairs in a small wait-ing area. The area—more of a large glass-enclosed cubicle than a lobby—was completely sealed off from the rest of the FBI building and Hawkins noticed the several video cameras in plain view.

It was just two or three minutes later that a man who looked to be in his early 30's entered the waiting area from a locked side door and ap-proached Ben.

"Welcome to FBI headquarters, Captain. I'm Special Agent Bartels. I'll be escorting you upstairs. You'll have to go through here, though," he said, motioning toward the metal detector area.

Ben placed his briefcase on the conveyor belt and walked through the metal frame of the detector. He had left his personal weapon secured at Ft. Belvoir since he didn't want to check it at the FBI building.

Ben and his escort took an elevator to the fifth floor, exited the eleva-tor, and walked down a corridor to the conference room the team would be using. Along the way, Bartels explained the security procedures everyone had to follow within the building.

"You know how it is these days, Captain. Used to be people could just wander around here, tours went through, drop-in meetings. No more, as you could see downstairs."

Ben knew how it was. Just another one of the hidden costs 0f 9/11—security checks, metal detectors, pat-downs at the airport. It was a brave new world. Or at least a security-conscious one.

"All your Task Force meetings will be in a SCIF—a Sensitive Compartmental Information Facility. Pretty much just a highly secured conference room. There are about a dozen of them within the building. We've arranged your SCI security clearance already and you'll get an ID card at the meeting today. After today, you'll have to swipe that to get inside the building, and again to enter the SCIF. And no recording devices allowed inside or anywhere within the building—no audio, no video, no phones, no cameras. No data storage devices, either—like flash drives or CDs."

"OK, I think I got it," Ben answered. "No copying the data."

"Maybe you get it, Captain, and no disrespect, but let me go over the cyber protocols very specifically. Our networks are attacked literally every day, and we have level five firewalls in place. But you walk in here with a flash drive with who knows what on it. We're more concerned about what you might put *into* the system than what you might take out. So let me stress what I said about storage devices. No laptops, no flash drives, no thumb drives, no CDs, no data storage devices of any kind are allowed through the door."

"Right, Special Agent. No data storage devices."

"And you have none on you now, sir, is that correct?"

"That is correct."

"And just so you're not taken by surprise, you—and everyone else entering the SCIF—will have to sign a statement to that effect every time you enter the room."

"Every time?"

"Every single time you walk into the room."

"OK, I can handle it, Special Agent."

"And when you leave."

"I have to sign off when I *leave* that I still don't have any recording or storage devices? You know, the ones I didn't have when I entered the conference room in the first place."

"That's right, Captain. Look, I know all this may sound paranoid, but there are people—and organizations and agencies and other countries, as a matter of fact—that try to break into the Bureau's computer networks every day. And into lots of other national security networks too, including yours, I assume, Captain. And not just to steal information. We're just as concerned about what they might try to put *into* our network, maybe a virus or a worm that works its way through our system, doing who knows what kind of damage. That's why there's no...."

"Yeah, no storage devices, portable or otherwise. I think I get it. Really."

The agent held out a clipboard with a form attesting that Captain Ben Hawkins had been briefed on the security protocols of the FBI SCIF room, with several boxes for him to check off. Ben checked and signed.

He followed the agent into what he called a conference room and what the FBI called a SCIF, said hello to Tom Donniger, and took a seat at one end of the conference table. He looked around at the other members of the task force. It was hard to believe they had first met at Ft. Belvoir just over 72 hours ago. Everything seemed to move in slow motion at first and then it hit the fan. Like yesterday's phone call from their missing suspect, Harry McNair. And then the news that his daughter Jennifer had surfaced.

Ben had called Sergeant McNair as soon as he found out from Donniger that Jennifer was alive and well and safely in American hands in Spain. She had never re-entered the U.S. at all. According to Jennifer—who was now at the American consulate office in Seville and talking to FBI agents from the FBI Legal Attaché office in Madrid—she had been held at a farmhouse several miles north of Seville for several weeks. But yesterday, when she got up, everyone was gone. She had simply walked out of the farmhouse and found a bus back to Seville and the university. Her advisor contacted the Spanish police, who escorted her to the American consulate.

"She's alive? She's OK? You're not just setting me up, are you?" McNair had yelled into the phone.

"No—she's fine, and none the worse for wear. Apparently she's angry—angry at her friend, someone called Saman, who set her up for the kidnapping, and angry about being held hostage for two weeks. But she's fine."

"When do I get to talk to her?"

"As soon as you come in for questioning."

"Now it's sounding like a set-up. How do I know you're not screwing around with me?"

"I figured you might think that. Call back in 10 minutes and we'll put her on the phone. But after that, the next conversation has to be at CID headquarters at Ft. Belvoir. My boss made that very clear. And the FBI wants to talk to you, too.

It was exactly 10 minutes later when Harry McNair was finally able to talk to his daughter for the first time since his nightmare had begun. It was after midnight in Seville.

"Jennifer, Jennifer, are you alright?" the sergeant, WMD handler and soon-to-be military prisoner said into the phone.

"Yes, Dad, I'm here. I'm OK, everything is fine. Are you OK? Are you in some kind of trouble?" his daughter asked.

"Don't worry about it. I have some things to do with the Army investigators—but you're sure *you're* OK? They told me they were holding you."

"I'm fine—they didn't hurt me. I'm safe now, Dad."

Then Jennifer's voice was cut-off and the next voice McNair heard was one he knew well by now. Captain Ben Hawkins had cut in.

"Alright Sergeant, now you know that your daughter is safe. She's with two FBI agents from their Legat office in Madrid. They'll arrange her flight back to the U.S. You can talk to her again from FBI headquarters in Washington. It's probably better if I bring you in."

And that's exactly what they did. Hawkins, accompanied by two Army MPs, met his man at the motel where he was staying in Dumfries, a small town in Virginia about 30 miles south of Washington. An hour later, Hawkins was back at Ft. Belvoir with his new prisoner, where they were met by Corliss, Donniger and two other FBI agents, and an officer from the Judge Advocate Corps. The two MPs remained outside the interrogation room as Corliss began the initial round of questioning. "Sergeant McNair, before you're processed into the detention facility, we're going to ask you some questions. Captain Perzanski from the Judge Advocates Corps is here as your legal counsel," Corliss began.

"Sir, I don't need any legal counsel. Captain Hawkins says you found my daughter, she's safe and she's coming home. That's true, isn't it? Nothing personal, sir," McNair said, looking sideways at Hawkins.

"Yes, it is, Sergeant. Two FBI agents are with her, but she's still in Spain. They're arranging her return flight here. Are you ready to answer some questions?"

"Yes, sir, I'll tell you everything I know. That was my deal with the Captain, and I'm here to co-operate. I'm not proud of what I did. In fact, I feel pretty shitty about it, but you have to understand, sir, they had my daughter. They said they would kill her."

"Well, she's safe now. At this point, we need to find out everything you know about these people, exactly what you did for them, and what their plans are. We want to know what they looked like, what they sounded like, how many are involved. The JAG officer will remain during the questioning. But you know better than any of us here just how dangerous the material they have is. And that's thanks to you, Sergeant. So let's get started."

And so the long night began. Corliss and Donniger asked most of the questions, while Hawkins, the two other FBI agents, and Perzanski, the JAG officer, sat and listened. The questioning lasted until about midnight, and then McNair was processed into the post stockade.

Now, less than 12 hours later, Donniger and the two CID officers were meeting with the other members of the task force. Only now, the task force meetings had been moved to FBI Headquarters in Washington.

Donniger took a seat at the other end of the conference table, cleared his throat, and began the meeting.

"You all know Major Corliss and Captain Hawkins who are here from Ft. Belvoir."

Donniger looked over at the Army officers, who nodded.

"Major Corliss and Captain Hawkins are still part of the investigation, but because of the expanding scope of this case, the FBI has become the lead agency now. That decision was made by the Secretary of the Army and the Director of Homeland Security, and with the full support of CID. Isn't that correct, Major?" Donniger asked, looking again at Corliss.

"Yes, that's correct, Tom. In fact, Captain Hawkins and I recommended that action, I think for obvious reasons. This has gone way beyond an Army investigation."

"Thank you, Major. Before we get to the investigation itself, let me update everyone on information sharing," Donniger continued. "Now that the FBI is the lead agency, we'll be using our Sentinel case management system to manage the investigation and case information. We'll brief the non-FBI people on our IT procedures at the end of the meeting."

"OK, let's go over what we know." Donniger was looking a little tired, but a lot happier than he had been. Having one of their main suspects in custody helped make up for a few hours of the sleep he had lost. Maybe they were on the road to finding out exactly what—and who—they were up against. Maybe.

"We now know it was Sergeant McNair who took what looks like four pounds of VX-212. That number agrees with Lieutenant Colonel Girelli's number. McNair turned it over to a guy called Joseph. Middle Eastern, and apparently there's at least one other person in the U.S. working with him, a woman who uses the name 'Elena.' McNair is in custody and we're still going over the events."

"Middle Eastern. Which Middle Eastern?" the NSA analyst, a middle-aged guy named Kemp, asked. He was accompanied by Walter Phillips, the president's national security advisor. Phillips and Kemp were sitting together at one end of the conference table in the sealed FBI security office.

"We don't know, so we'll come back to that later. These people have a cell working with them in Seville, Spain. They were able to locate and identify McNair's daughter, who was in a student exchange program over there. We assume they sought her out because somehow they knew her father handled chemical weapons. And they managed to lure her to a location outside Seville and hold her there for several weeks."

Ben interrupted Donniger's presentation. "But they had someone in place to befriend her—which means they planned this several months ago."

"That's right. McNair's daughter, Jennifer, told us that the girl who lured her out to this house was supposed to be a friend of hers—someone she had known for about two months. Someone by the name of Elena."

"Where is Jennifer now?" Ben asked. He had little sympathy for McNair, given the problem they now faced, but they might get more information with McNair and his daughter together.

"She'll be on a plane back here in a few hours. She understands the best thing to help out her father is to come to FBI headquarters and continue to help us. Plus she's mad as hell anyway."

"Obviously it wasn't Jennifer who entered the country last week," Donniger continued. "We have a photo taken in the customs area at Dulles. Not a very good one, but we sent it over to Seville and Jennifer thinks it's Elena. So now we're looking for this Joseph and an accomplice, probably this same woman named Elena."

"We have several good photos of this Elena. Here's one we found in the school records." Donniger passed around a passport-type photograph of an attractive woman, apparently in her early 20's, with olive complexion, black hair and dark eyes.

"The people who were holding Jennifer took away her cell phone and camera. We haven't recovered the cell phone, but we got a break. Jennifer stored several dozen photos on Shutterfly, one of those online photo shops. Here you are—a whole bunch of shots of Elena, some with Jennifer, and several with other girls from the school." Donniger passed around several photos, including one showing only the woman in question.

"And what did Jennifer tell you about this Elena?" Corliss asked.

"She really didn't know a lot about her, except she thought she was Greek and had family living there. She couldn't be any more specific. She did say her Spanish and English are both excellent. Our agents are looking through the school records in Seville now."

Kemp, the NSA agent spoke up again. "But she's probably not Greek. You said 'Middle Eastern.' I'm thinking Iranian and we have some reasons for thinking that, unless you have some other information."

"We're still trying to pin it down. We're running some language samples past McNair. He says this Joseph occasionally broke into a Middle Eastern language, so maybe he can identify the language or accent. But why do you say Iranian?" Donniger asked the NSA agent.

"We picked up some chatter in the past two months, plus some of our contacts within the Iranian government, saying something is going on, something they seemed to be real concerned or excited about."

"You don't believe the Iranians would actually sponsor a terrorist attack against the U.S., do you?" Donniger asked Kemp.

"No, I don't think their government would sponsor any action inside the U.S. They save that for Iraq. But there's something going on

108

within the Iranian government, special attention being given to some kind of event or activity going on here in the U.S. It's pretty hard to categorize since the Iranians always have a lot of concern about us, given their nuclear development program. There are people over there who expect us to attack any day.

"But they've been involved in covert activities within our borders in the past," one of the other FBI agents interjected.

"You mean that episode up in New York a few years ago?" Kemp responded.

"That's right. As I remember, several of their embassy personnel were declared *persona non grata* after they were caught doing surveillance and collecting videos at Grand Central Station and JFK airport."

"You're right. Three of their embassy people ended up being deported. No, we don't doubt that there are groups in Iran who would try to do whatever they think they could get away with. But that's different than a direct confrontation, and especially a direct attack within the U.S. That would be a game-changer and they know it."

"Even with Ahmadinejad and the other zealots in charge right now?" Corliss asked.

"You're correct that there's a very reactionary and anti-American group in power now. We thought their anti-Americanism would begin to ease up a few years ago, but instead, a group of hardliners came into power. Ahmadinejad is more of a mouthpiece than a power source, but he seems to have the support of their supreme leader Khameni and others."

Donniger spoke up. "All our agents got from Jennifer McNair so far is that it was a group of four "Middle Eastern" people, three men and a woman, who kept her under guard in Seville. We'll do some facial profile and ID work when she gets here. So for now, maybe Iranian, maybe not."

"But that's not gonna help much over here." Hawkins said. "We're looking for at least two people—"Joseph" and Jennifer's impersonator, Elena, or whatever her real name is. And they're hanging out someplace with four pounds of VX-212. We need to know how many others, where they are—and of course, what they plan to do."

"We've pulled in nearly a hundred agents from around the country," Donniger told the six people sitting at the conference table. "And we've set up ongoing communication links with the security chiefs of more than a dozen cities we consider high risk. We've also alerted the Centers for Disease Control in Atlanta, in case we can't prevent whatever it is they're planning."

Phillips, the president's advisor, was next.

"The president is going to want to know about possible targets and the worst case scenario if it hits the fan. What does he need to know?"

The group quickly compiled a list of specific high risk targets for four pounds of nerve agent. Then Donniger reviewed the responsibilities of each member of the group. Two of his own agents would handle media and internal communications, including contact with the state, local and facility security chiefs who had already been alerted.

Brett Alexander, the two-star sitting in for the Joint Chiefs of Staff, would be the liaison for any military action either within the country or overseas.

The Army chemical munitions expert would work with CDC in Atlanta. VX-212 wasn't a disease, or communicable, but CDC had the resources and know-how to deal with an outbreak of thousands of sick and dying—or quickly dead—civilians.

Donniger made it clear that Hawkins' work was essentially done. His job was to babysit McNair for the interrogations that would continue. Other than that, his work was finished. He was an investigator, a detective, not a counter-terrorism expert, and he certainly didn't know anything about nerve agents or foreign terrorist cells.

As he headed back to talk with McNair again, he called Sara at her shop. It had only been a few days since he had seen her, but it seemed like a few weeks.

"How about dinner tonight?" he asked her.

"Sure. Antonio's?"

"You're on. How about 7 o'clock?"

That evening
Belmont Bay

Ben looked across the table at Sara. Less than two weeks ago he thought he was going on a routine check at an obscure Army facility on the way to a few days of R&R. A lot had happened and the CID/FBI Task Force had learned a lot—but there were still several pounds of very dangerous stuff out there, and they were no closer to recovering it.

"So are you better off or worse off than a few days ago?" Sara asked after the waiter left menus for them.

Ben had already outlined the situation for Sara without going into the details. He found she often helped him think through a problem facing him.

"A little better off, but potentially a lot worse off," he answered.

"You understand that makes no sense at all to me."

"Well, we were able to find out more about what the problem actually is. It's just that the problem could be real bad."

Sara sat quietly for a few minutes as she looked over the menu. She didn't need to read the menu since they were at Antonio's a few times a month, but it allowed her mind to wander.

"What's your job now, then?" she asked Ben.

"My job is pretty much done. I investigated, I interviewed. I even delivered the perpetrator, McNair. The rest is up to the FBI and Homeland Security people."

"And where is your 'perpetrator' now?"

"He's in the stockade at Belvoir and he's not leaving any time soon. And when he does leave, it'll be for about 20 years at Leavenworth."

"Can you tell me exactly what he did? And why?" Sara asked.

Ben told her what he could, including the kidnapping—and escape—of McNair's daughter. He didn't have a good answer when she asked him if he would have done anything different than McNair. It didn't matter. Four pounds of nerve toxin could do more damage than the attack on 9/11, and knowing about it in advance might not make one bit of difference.

They didn't talk much through dinner. Ben couldn't accept that his role in the investigation was almost finished. He would continue to question McNair and he would be on call for the rest of the team until "the incident," as they were calling it, was over. Maybe going out for dinner hadn't been such a good idea after all.

Thursday

Ben was sitting across the kitchen table from Sara when the call from Assistant Director Donniger came in. Ben had spent the past hour reviewing the team website, reading notes posted from all over the country. Possible sightings, several surveillances, dozens of interviews. The FBI had been criticized for compartmentalizing information before the attack on the World Trade Center towers. Now it seemed there was so much data that you had to spend valuable hours reviewing what everyone else had done, and most of it wasn't helpful.

"I wanted to give you a heads-up before we posted it on the team website," Donniger told Ben. "We got a call from someone calling himself Joseph."

"Our man?" Ben asked, and he was beginning to think that at last the investigation was heading someplace.

"Oh yeah. He told us he's got the VX-212 and what he wants us to do. Or else, of course."

"And what does he want?"

"A public statement that we'll start a withdrawal of all U.S. combat forces from Iraq within 90 days."

"What's the 'or else'?"

"He wasn't too specific about that, unfortunately. Just that he would use the VX within the U.S."

"So is this guy Iraqi after all? Not Iranian?"

"We don't know. We got a good voice print. We'll run the audio file by the voice and language analysis people, but I want you to be here when McNair listens to it."

"You want to make sure it's the same Joseph.

"Right."

"And you have McNair's description of him."

"Yes. By the way, he's here at FBI headquarters now, released to our custody early this morning at the request of the FBI director. We're not trying to take over, but I wanted to get a photo generated. He's been look-ing at a few hundred shots of various agents we know around the world. Nothing yet."

Ben decided to ignore the middle-of-the-night move Donniger had made to get McNair into FBI custody.

"Composite photo or drawing?"

"We don't do drawings anymore. C'mon, this is the 21st century. We take the photos of anyone McNair says looks something like our Joseph and then the computer generates a few thousand mixes and matches and the judge—McNair—tells us if we're getting closer or not. Actually, it goes a lot faster than you would think."

"Any luck?"

"Yes, we generated a photo your sergeant says is a pretty good match. But both we and NSA ran it through our facial recognition programs and neither of us was able to match it to any known agent in our files, foreign or domestic."

"Still, it's something. At least we know what they want."

"Something, but not much," was Donniger's answer. "Look, I want you to talk to McNair again, see if you can get him to remember anything else."

"You think that will do any good?"

"Probably not, but we don't have a lot of leads and we want to nail down the ID on Joseph. That's why I asked your boss to remand him to our place to be closer to some of our specialists."

Ben knew that "our place" meant FBI headquarters in Washington.

"I'll be there in 45 minutes," Ben answered and hung up. He hadn't bothered to ask about any response to the terrorists' demand. Their job was still to find and kill or capture Joseph and his friend Elena, and recover a few pounds of some very nasty stuff. But something about the whole opera-tion was bothering him. It was surprising enough that these people knew that McNair handled chemical weapons, but how had they made the con-nection to his daughter studying abroad? And how is it they were in place and prepared to befriend the unsuspecting daughter? But most of all, after all the groundwork, why did they release the girl before the operations was completed?

Sara was getting herself a second cup of coffee.

"Look, honey," Ben said, sitting at the kitchen table and looking out the alcove window. "Maybe it would be a good idea if you didn't go into D.C. until this is over."

FBI Headquarters
J. Edgar Hoover Building
Washington, D.C.

Ben sat in a secure conference room at the FBI offices with former staff sergeant and current Army prisoner Harry McNair. McNair wasn't actually "former" yet, but he would be soon.

He had made sure he wasn't carrying any flash drives or other memory devices. As promised, he had been required to sign another statement acknowledging that fact before an agent took his card, swiped it through the reader next to the door of the SCIF, waited a moment for a series of recognition beeps, and then admitted him into the conference room.

McNair was already in the room. Corliss had explained that McNair would be transferred back to the Army stockade at Belvoir later in the day. A dishonorable discharge would be the least of his problems, not when he was facing 20 years at Ft. Leavenworth.

"How'd it go with you daughter?" he asked McNair. McNair had been allowed to see his daughter early that morning.

"She's alive and well and back in the States, so it went great. She's real tired from the whole thing and the overnight flight, but she's OK. Thanks for letting me see her, Captain."

Ben had seen on the team website how Jennifer had escaped, if "escaped" was the right word.

"She tell you how she got out of that house in Seville?" he asked.

"Yes sir. Kinda strange. She got up Wednesday morning, looks around and there's nobody there."

Ben knew the story from the posting on the website. Jennifer had been interviewed for several hours by two FBI agents from the FBI Legat Office in Madrid.

Jennifer told the agents she got up Wednesday morning, expecting to see her holders as usual. Instead, the house was empty. She described simply walking out of the house and catching a bus to go the 15 or 20 kilometers back to Seville. She had the sense to go to the American consulate, which she knew from having visited it to update her student visa. Eight hours later she was on a plane to Andrews Air Force Base.

"Well, we had a deal. I know you're co-operating with the FBI. They just want to make sure we're not overlooking something."

"Look, I screwed up, and I'm not making any excuses," McNair said. "But I had to make sure the Feds would protect Jennifer. Now that she's safe, I'm all yours. No bargain, no deal. I'll do whatever I can."

"Well, it may be a little late for that, seeing as how they have all that VX-212 you gave them," Hawkins shot back. He had tried to be sympathetic, but they wouldn't' be wondering about the lives of several thousand people if McNair hadn't co-operated with them, daughter or no daughter.

McNair sat silently. Ben sat silently. *Well, this isn't helping anyone,* he thought to himself.

"OK, let's go over each of your contacts again, especially the last phone call."

Hawkins and McNair spent the next two hours reviewing every Joseph contact, but there wasn't anything new. But later, looking back, Ben had to wonder. Why hadn't Joseph told McNair they would be releasing Jennifer? Or more to the point, why let the girl go before their operation was finished? Joseph and his friends had the VX-212, true enough, but surely they knew McNair would talk as soon as his daughter was safe. Something didn't add up. They were missing something....

Friday

It was early afternoon on a beautiful sunny spring day, and Ben was at the boatyard looking over *Blue Lady* when his cell phone rang.

Both Donniger and Major Corliss had suggested he take a few hours off, but he was still on call while the task force kept trying to track down Joseph and the woman who had entered the country using Jennifer's passport.

"Hawkins," he answered.

"As in Captain Hawkins of United States Army Criminal Investigation Command?" asked the voice on the other end.

"Yes, that's right. Who is this?" Ben replied, noticing the slight accent. He pressed "record," but he didn't bother to tell his caller that it was for quality or training purposes. It wasn't.

"For now, consider me a good friend of yours. And I may have some very valuable information for you."

"Really? OK, let's have it."

"It's about some materials missing from one of your chemical facilities. You know, the kind of materials that you Americans insist no country should possess. The ones you were looking for in Iraq."

Ben inhaled sharply and hoped his caller hadn't noticed.

"Alright, you have my attention. But I don't know what materials you're talking about."

"By now, Captain, you've noticed that I'm not a native speaker of your language, although I like to believe that I speak your language well. And by now you have probably started to record this call."

For all Ben knew, this guy was a reporter from the Washington Post, trying to pin down some gossip he had heard. How long could anything remain a secret in Washington? But he wasn't about to help the guy out.

"And why would I do that?" Ben asked, wanting to prolong the conversation.

"Captain Hawkins, this call will last precisely 30 seconds longer. You may trace it, but that doesn't matter. And I hope you *are* recording it. You're looking for some missing VX-212. Several pounds of it. It is missing from your Tupelo facility. I tell you this so you know I have credible information, and so that you place close attention when I call again. That will be very soon. Oh, and you can call me...oh, I don't know, how about 'Julian'."

"OK, Julian," Ben answered, but Julian had hung up.

So much for his afternoon working on *Blue Lady*. Ben put in a call to Assistant Director Donniger.

Later that afternoon
FBI headquarters
Hoover Building, Washington, D.C.

Ben sat in the secure conference room at FBI headquarters that the agents had started calling the "Game Room." A tired-looking Tom Donniger sat across the conference table.

Hawkins knew his only assignments were to keep tabs on Staff Sergeant McNair, and now, this new contact, the so-called Julian. But Donniger had to keep up with the work and information coming in from more than a hundred agents around the country. Factor in Homeland Security, NSA, CIA, several other security agencies that came under Homeland Security, along with the police forces of several major cities, and no wonder he was looking tired.

They were listening—for the fifth or sixth time—to a recording of the phone call from Julian. Ben found it interesting that the FBI agent had a copy ready even before he arrived, less than an hour after he received the call. Interesting, but not surprising. If the FBI hadn't been eavesdropping on his calls before his little covert operation to meet up with McNair, they sure were now.

"Who else is going over this?" Ben asked.

"Our own audio forensics people are analyzing it right now. I sent a copy to Emily Olstadt at NSA also. They're going to compare it to their library of voice prints, have their linguistics team listen to it as well."

Donniger looked at Ben. "Alright, he's educated, he's got good information, and he's organized. He sounds rational. But no demands. So what was the purpose of his call? And why you?"

Ben gave it some thought before answering.

"Why me? I'm not sure. The only thing I can think of is my connection to McNair, or to Lieutenant Colonel Girelli at Tupelo. I would guess the common thread is McNair, though. Somehow this guy knows about the threat and he knows me. So we have to assume he's part of it."

"Well, that brings us to the other question. What was the purpose of the call? No warning, no demands, no threats. Nothing."

Ben had been mulling that over. *Why did this guy call me?* That was the more important question. An apparent terrorist calls him, gives him some key information that only someone close to the threat would know. Most of the FBI investigators didn't even have all the information.

"I think he called to establish his credibility with me. That means he wants to talk to me and he wants me to pay attention to him. I can't think of any other reason for the call, unless it's a red herring and he's trying to throw us off the trail."

"Which means he'll be calling again, and my guess is pretty soon," Donniger answered.

A phone buzzed. The FBI assistant director looked at his cell phone and pressed the "talk" button.

"Donniger." He listened for several moments. "OK, and you're still working it?" He listened again. "Great, thanks."

Ben looked across the table. "Anything new?"

"Yeah, that was someone in the audio lab. They're still going over the tape, but they're pretty sure the guy who called you is Iranian."

"Why do they think that?" Ben asked.

"The accent. The linguistics people are pretty sure the guy speaks Farsi, but is obviously very fluent in English. American English. They think either he's spent a lot of time here, or he's a fan of American television."

Ben sat quietly, wondering to himself what was going on. "So some Iranian agent or sleeper who's involved with this plot calls me. Maybe some guy who's been living in this country for a few years. He lets me know he's for real. But why call me? Why did he call the FBI yesterday, but today he calls me? Sounds like they're playing around with us."

"You mean your red herring idea," Donniger said.

"That's right."

"Maybe. But our audio tech says this isn't the same guy who called us yesterday. So we have two different guys, making two different calls. One call is to us, making demands and threats, the other call is to you—no demands, no real information. I get the feeling we're sitting here waiting for another shoe to drop."

"And no hits on the picture of the woman," Ben said, thinking out loud. The FBI had gone over Jennifer's computer from Seville and found a file of photos, including several of the young mystery woman Jennifer knew as Elena. They had accessed Jennifer's online photo account at Shutterfly, where they recovered nearly a dozen shots of the woman who had befriended Jennifer and then helped kidnap her.

"We've sent those photos of Elena to all our FBI offices and as a "Be On the Look Out for" notice to local police departments. And you'll see her picture this evening on a lot of news programs under a missing person alert."

Ben noticed again that Donniger was looking tired and a little older than his 45 or so years. "How long since you've been home?" he asked Donniger.

"Home? You must be kidding. I haven't been home in five days and I don't expect to get there soon."

"How long will that go on?"

Donniger looked out the window. The office faced west and he looked at the afternoon sun. "Until this incident is over. A couple of agents are still going over each of the handlers' financials and phone records again. Another couple of agents are revisiting neighbors, gas station people, bars. We're interviewing anyone who knows Specialist Hartman and what he was up to before he went out on leave."

Ben asked, "You think McNair had help?"

"No, but we might have overlooked something. Not that I think we'll get anything. We're going over his home computer again, and we're still looking through his daughter's laptop and cell phone. But we haven't found anything that he didn't tell us about already."

"So you've got your hands full."

Donniger gave a little laugh. "Keeping track of the FBI activities is the easy part. It's working with everyone else. We've got NSA, CIA, D.C. police, Army CID, of course."

"I get the picture."

Up until now, Ben had worked in a relatively small world. Strictly an Army world, with occasional contact with the local police, who were only too happy to co-operate.

"But no real progress," he continued.

Donniger looked pretty grim. "No, nothing more than what we knew before yesterday's call, no leads, no nothing, except now we're thinking this may be the work of some Iranian terrorists. And now we've got a picture of one of them. The CIA is working on a possible Iranian connection, seeing what they can find out through their Iranian assets. And NSA says there's some chatter going on in the Iranian government circles."

"You sound pretty pessimistic."

"Yeah, I guess I am. We're doing all this gruntwork here stateside, but we haven't made any real progress. Maybe NSA or CIA, or even Interpol, will find out something. But I'm beginning to believe this is gonna fall on the emergency response teams. I know the contingency planners have been plenty busy." The FBI agent didn't mention that he had sent his wife and two daughters to stay with his wife's sister in Pennsylvania.

Donniger had painted a pretty dismal picture and Ben couldn't disagree with him. The two of them tossed ideas back and forth for another half hour, but it was clear they weren't making any progress. It was after six when Ben called it a day and headed back to Belmont Bay. He sent Sara a text message a few minutes before leaving the FBI Building:

Ben: *Finishing up here soon.*
Sara: *Take your time. I'm still at the gym. How about dinner at home tonight?*
Ben: *Your place?*
Sara: *Unless you're going shopping.*
Ben: *Got it. OK, your place, call you on the way home.*

He planned to call her once he cleared the Route 1 Bridge, heading south for Belmont Bay. As he crossed the Potomac, he could see Ronald Reagan National Airport on his right and the Pentagon a little further off in the distance. He wondered if the airport was one of the targets.

Crazy, Ben thought to himself as a plane flew overhead on its final approach to National. *We can design almost accident-proof airplanes, create an incredible system that keeps track of a few thousand aircraft all over the world, and then we have to spend almost as much money and effort trying to make sure someone doesn't blow one up just to see how many people they can murder.*

Over to the west, he saw the Pentagon, the huge facility looking like a shopping mall on steroids. How many people there were going sleepless trying to get intel on the people behind the stolen VX-212? Not only to prevent a few thousand civilian deaths, but also to avoid the extreme embarrassment of having thousands of Americans murdered using America's own weapons—which was probably the terrorists' point.

Ben knew that Arlington National Cemetery lay just beyond the Pentagon, although he couldn't actually see it. He thought, *At least most of them died because they chose to serve their country, not because some man, woman or child happened to choose the wrong train or flight or was just in the wrong place at the wrong time.*

He pressed *Voice Dial* on his GPS unit and waited for the woman with the Australian accent to politely ask him to "Say a command," which strangely sounded like a command to issue a command.

"*Call Sara,*" he commanded, which he voiced politely but firmly. His GPS lady did better with a firm, or at least a loud, voice.

Sara picked up on the first ring. "Hi, Ben. Are you on the road?"

"Yes, I just crossed the Route 1 bridge. Traffic isn't too bad. Maybe because it's Saturday night and I'm heading out of town, instead of into town."

"OK, take your time, honey. I'll have cocktails ready when you get here and dinner is in the oven."

Ben and Sara tried to take good care of each other, but he hadn't expected her to take care of their Friday night plans. He smiled to himself. He had been so involved with the Tupelo incident, with the FBI, with McNair and his daughter, he hadn't given a thought to how Sara's project with the Washington couple was going. And thinking about it, he didn't really care, and he knew that was alright.

That evening
Belmont Bay

Forty minutes later, Ben was at his place in Belmont Bay. He dropped off his briefcase and washed up. He would make it to Sara's by seven.

Sara's place was not too close, not too far. He usually enjoyed the 10-minute drive, but tonight he was anxious to see her. He realized he couldn't keep up the façade of not filling her in on the details—she was his best sounding board and always helpful. He had to admit, though, in the past few days, Donniger had been pretty helpful, too. On the other hand, Ben had been pretty helpful to Donniger.

Sara opened the door as soon as he rang her doorbell.

"There you are," was her warm greeting, along with a long hug and a kiss.

They had drinks on the deck, facing toward the southeast—a beer for him and a vodka tonic for Sara. Just past the garden and the parking area were some boat docks, and then Belmont Bay itself, which opened into the much larger Chesapeake Bay in a few miles. During the boating season they usually motored down the smaller bay until they reached the Chesapeake. Then they would raise the mainsail, unfurl the jib and sail into the bay.

But they weren't on *Blue Lady* and this wasn't the boating season. This was a brief respite from working with a task force of a few hundred people who were trying to prevent a major terrorist attack on American soil using an American-made weapon.

The last time we didn't have any warning, Ben thought to himself as he looked over the boat docks. *This time we do—but will it make any difference?* The fact that this whole episode was an Army affair, an Army responsibility, grated at him. An Army facility with a breach of security. An Army WMD loose on American soil. And maybe worst of all, an Army non-com who had stolen the material and turned it over to a couple of terrorists.

Ben looked over at Sara, thankful that she knew it was helpful just to be there. He had already told her about the call from the man who called himself Julian. Now she was worried that it was becoming personal.

"Does the FBI have any idea why this man called you?" she asked.

"No, and neither do I. I'm guessing he got my number from McNair. I'll have to ask him about that when I get back to Belvoir. Maybe the FBI has already."

"And is this guy a part of the terrorist group?" was Sara's next question.

Ben stared at his beer for a few moments.

"That's the funny thing about the call," he finally answered. "He didn't demand anything. He didn't even make any threats. But he made it clear that he knows what's going on."

Sara looked at Ben. "These people don't phone an Army CID investigator just for fun. He wants something, so maybe you should think about what he might want from you."

Ben already knew that. He and Donniger had just spent the better part of a few hours trying to figure out what the phone caller—Iranian or otherwise—was up to.

Sara had grilled two steaks for their Saturday night dinner. Ben had brought a bottle of zinfandel that he saved for special occasions. Dinner at home, big greeting, lots of understanding. He could get used to this. They were just sitting down to dinner when his personal cell phone rang. His screen showed "private number," and he thought he knew who it was.

He pushed the talk button. "Captain Hawkins."

A voice answered. "A pleasure to speak with you again, Captain."

"Good evening, sir. Do you still want me to call you Julian?"

"Julian is just fine. Sorry to interrupt your evening, Captain, but we do have some important business to discuss."

"Yes, we certainly do, Julian, and I'm wondering how I can help you," Ben replied. The call sounded far away. Was Julian overseas with a satellite connection? But then why would he worry about someone tracing the call? No, he had to be in the U.S., and close enough to be concerned about the FBI or police locating him.

"And how is our friend Sergeant McNair?" the Iranian agent asked.

"Well, first of all, he's not our friend. He's your co-conspirator and he's our prisoner, but he's not our 'friend.' But I take your point. You know him and you know what he did."

"Indeed I do. And now it's time just to listen, as I'm sure I only have about another 30 seconds. You already know what your Sergeant McNair did. But I am not the one who made him do it. And I believe his daughter has arrived back in the United States safely."

Ben laughed. "Yes, she has. Did you have anything to do with that?"

"An interesting question, Captain."

Kashani hoped he had gained some credibility with the Army investigator, but he knew he was walking a fine line.

"And what do you plan on doing with what you stole from us?" Ben asked, not wanting to describe any details.

"I am not the one who stole the material, Captain. Nor am I the one who stockpiled illegal chemical weapons. But perhaps there is a way out of this. I don't really care what you do in Iraq or anyplace else, be assured of that. Look to Louisiana and Texas, Captain. And oil refineries. That's all I can tell you at this point."

"All you can tell me? Why can't you tell me more?"

"If I could, Captain, believe me, I would. You Americans are not the only ones who think that crazy people have taken over the world. I believe this is the work of Al Qaeda. I will be in touch again. Good night."

Colonel Kashani hung up. If the business weren't so serious he would actually be enjoying this. But the business *was* serious. His mission was to prevent a major disaster for his country, to stop an event that would arouse the most powerful nation in the world and direct their fury at his own nation. Baiting the Americans was one thing. Incurring their wrath was another, and even the hardliners in Tehran knew it was the last thing they could afford. It would set his country back at least 25 years and probably mark the end of the Islamic Republic of Iran.

He only hoped to get out of it alive.

Ben heard the disconnect. He reached for his other mobile phone and pressed the speed dial, the one designated "F." A special agent in FBI headquarters picked up on the first ring.

"Did you get it?" Hawkins asked.

"Yes, Captain, we got it—just barely. The call came from a motel in Alexandria, just outside D.C., and the phone's still pinging the GPS location—it's not moving."

"Are you headed there?"

"Yeah, I've alerted Assistant Director Donniger and a team will be leaving in two minutes. He's staying at HQ. The team should get there in 10 to 12 minutes."

"What's the signal doing now?"

"Still stationary," the communications technician answered. He was working the FBI's very new and rarely used Stingray phone tracker, which could track mobile phones even when not in use.

"OK, would you have the team contact me as soon as they secure the location? I'm calling Donniger right now." Ben hung up and pressed another speed dial. Donniger picked up on the second ring.

"You heard about my contact."

"Yes. Team's on the way. Ten minutes out."

"He interrupted my Friday night dinner."

"Life's tough."

"I don't get a homecooked meal that often."

"I'll cook for you when this is all over."

Ben laughed. They were just killing minutes until the five agents reached the motel in Alexandria. Ben realized he could be there himself in less than 30 minutes.

Just one break, Donniger was thinking. *How often these cases are solved thanks to just one break. But then, this wasn't exactly 'one of those cases.'*

Ben was thinking, *30 seconds. Julian knew he had only about 30 seconds. Why was he sitting there, stationary, pinging away, just waiting to be taken?* Ben thought he knew the answer.

"I'll call you as soon as I know anything," Donniger said, and hung up.

Ben looked across the table at Sara. She looked beautiful, and dinner looked lovely, but he had to admit that he hoped their dinner was about to be interrupted. He took a sip of wine and waited. It wasn't long before Donniger called.

"That son of a bitch wasn't there. His phone was there—it was still turned on, in fact. But he wasn't there, goddammit."

"What did you find?" Ben asked, trying to figure out what Julian was up to.

"We found a piggy-back phone. One cell phone rigged up to another. Who knows where the call actually originated. Could have been across the street, could have been China, for all we know."

"You'll check the phone for prints, call log, where it came from…" Ben said, more to himself than to Donniger. Of course they would.

"Yeah, of course, but I'm pretty sure we're not going to find anything. These look like a couple of prepaid throwaway phones. We'll canvas all the phone shops in the Washington area and try to find where they came from, but I'm not hopeful."

"No other clues? Nothing in the room?" Ben asked.

"No. Looks like no one was even staying there. One of my agents is interviewing the people at the registration desk and the housecleaning staff, but it's one of those places where people just come and go. So far, all we have is a vague description of a white male, average height, average build."

"What about a credit card?" Ben interrupted.

"Oh sure, we have a name and a credit card number. Mr. Peter Johnson, with a post office address in Delaware. We're running it down, but I'll give you odds that it comes up empty. We're pulling all the motel videotapes, but that will take a little while. I'll give you odds on those, too.

"So," Ben said, mostly to himself, "He's smart enough to set us up here, screw around with us. He knows what we're after. He calls with some specific information that may or may not be useful. The question I keep asking is, *'why the call'?*"

"I haven't had time to think any more about that yet. Meanwhile we're running through the call itself—accent, his tone, his attitude. We sent a digital copy to NSA. But mostly I want to get a team of guys on what he said—oil refineries, Louisiana and Texas."

"I know you have to do that. But as we said after the first call, he could be just blowing smoke, trying to get us to run around. Like mentioning Al Qaeda."

"True enough. I think that's exactly what he's doing. He could be trying to misdirect us, get us to use our resources looking at the wrong leads. But we don't have much else to look at right now, do we?"

"But Tom, it brings us back to the first question: Why did he call and why the little game with the phones?"

"I'll give it some thought. Why do *you* think?"

Ben had already given it some thought during the conversation with Donniger. "I think he's trying to show us how smart he is. He wants us to pay attention to him."

"Well, it worked. We're paying attention to him."

"And I don't think he's connected to the earlier call from Joseph."

"Why do you say that?" Donniger asked. Ben knew what the FBI agent was doing. He was an investigator too. Donniger wanted to know what Ben's thoughts were before he offered his own. It was a good technique for brainstorming, especially if you didn't have any ideas of your own.

"Joseph threatened us, told he has the VX. He demanded something. This guy never threatened us, never demanded anything. He was calm, almost friendly. And now that I think about it, he never said he had the VX."

"Alright, fair enough. I'll have to think about that. I want you to post that thought on the website, let our ideas people look at it. And the next question is, if he's not with Joseph, and he doesn't have the VX, we're back to the same question: why is he calling us?"

Ben had no idea. But he was pretty sure that Julian would have some more information for them. He only hoped it would be very soon.

"I'll be at my office in Belvoir early tomorrow. Talk to you then," Ben said.

"OK, we'll be busy tonight. Get some sleep. Who knows what's gonna hit the fan tomorrow."

"Right. Good night," Ben answered and hung up. Sara was sitting quietly, listening to Ben's side of the conversation.

"No luck?" she asked him.

"I don't know. No, we didn't find him. But he did find us—or at least me—and I think he may be our best lead to ending this thing."

"And I take it you're working tomorrow."

"Absolutely. Doesn't mean we can't enjoy tonight though."

Which is exactly what they did, knowing the evening was likely to be the most time they would have together for the next several days.

Saturday

B en was in his office at Ft. Belvoir early when the call came in from Donniger. He had been going over the task force website, seeing what had turned up since the night before.

"Captain, stop what you're doing and listen up," Donniger started.

Ben still didn't care for Donniger, and there was some lingering distrust on both sides after the incident of the FBI agents tailing Hawkins and Hawkins losing them. But Ben didn't doubt Donniger's dedication to the job and he didn't doubt his instincts. He listened up.

"We were able to find out a little more about where that call came from last night."

"I thought he relayed it through another cell phone," Ben answered.

"Yes, but one of our cell phone specialists—do you believe that, we've got technicians who specialize in cell phone stuff—he was able to trace the call to a general area. And it wasn't overseas."

"How come I get the feeling you're gonna tell me it came from my parking lot?"

"Not quite. But it was within two miles of the motel where we found the piggy-back phones, and maybe a lot closer. He could have been across the street. The point is, he's here and he's close by."

"I get it," Ben answered. "How did your guy trace it to the general area?"

"We matched the time and length of the call to the nearest tower and the source of the signal to that tower. The signal came in directly from another phone, which our guy says has to be within five miles. But that area has very good coverage, so it was probably within two miles."

"Like you said, maybe across the street. I'll bet he was watching you enter the motel room. Maybe testing how good we are."

"Maybe so. There's more. We followed up on that tip the guy gave you. We put out an alert to every oil refinery in Texas and Louisiana. Then we had our IT security team review everything they had on cyber attacks on oil refineries in that area in the past six months to a year."

Ben knew a little about the FBI's capabilities to investigate the cyber attacks that occurred in the U.S. at the rate of more than 1,000 a week. It was unclear how many of these were merely malicious events, how many were attempts to steal information, and how many were efforts to disable a network. The theft of classified information about military capabilities or military operations or plans was a serious concern. The greatest concern, though, was a foreign government or organization actually shutting down a military or vital civilian computer network—a computer "missile attack."

Just a year ago, a carefully coordinated attack had shut down several U.S. and South Korean government sites for several hours. The FBI also knew that every day, millions of scans were made of U.S. government, business and private computers, searching for unsecured ports. They had traced cyber attacks from virtually every country in the world, but the vast majority were from Russia and China.

Like the 4th of July incident, some of these were denial-of-service attacks that shut down a network. Other intrusions were attempts to download data that should have been well-protected. Unfortunately, it was difficult and often impossible to detect when data had been stolen.

Ben had worked with Army IT specialists on several of his previous assignments, so he had some idea of their capabilities to detect and to defend against cyberwarfare. But those projects had been nothing like this, and he was learning how little he actually understood.

Homeland Security and the FBI work with other federal agencies, as well as with state and local governments, to defend against cyber attacks and to investigate suspected attacks. After 9/11, the FBI had directed particular attention to networks such as air traffic control, electrical grids, and financial systems. Much of the work was done by the FBI's Cyber Crime Task Force.

Homeland Security had the U.S. Computer Emergency Readiness Team—US-CERT—to help other federal agencies, but neither Homeland Security nor the FBI had the legal authority to force them to protect their systems, and progress had been slow and inconsistent. At least most of the agencies had slowly begun to adopt Einstein, a cyber security program that could both defend against cyber attacks and identify possible intrusions into computer systems.

Non-government facilities were a whole other story. Many private facilities—power plants, water treatment facilities—were actually better protected than most government facilities, but many others still used outdated technology to protect their networks. And 20th century technology wasn't very effective against a dedicated and committed attack by hackers using 21st century technology.

Based on the tip Hawkins had passed on to Donniger, the FBI Cyber Crime Task Force had concentrated on the networks of dozens of oil refineries. Coupled with the theft of the VX-212, they assumed any attack would try to control or shut down a refinery, not simply shut down a computer network. What wasn't clear was the connection between a lethal nerve toxin and intrusions into an oil refinery's computer network.

"What did they come up with?" Ben asked Donniger.

"None of the refineries had the Einstein program in place, so we uploaded the program and used it to scan their networks. The program found a series of intrusions about eight months ago at the networks of several oil refineries in Louisiana and Texas. That's the best they could do so far."

"What were the intruders looking for? And what did they get?"

"That's a little trickier. They found a pattern of repeated visits, probably from foreign sites. We can see the pattern. We just can't see exactly what they wanted or what they found."

"Can't you track what pages they visited or what information they took?"

"We wouldn't even know they were ever there if we didn't get that tip and go over their entire networks with Einstein. These guys were clever. They didn't interrupt service or shut down the network. They didn't try to take control of any part of the site. They didn't even plant any viruses or worms, at least not that we could find. You know what a 'worm' is?"

"I have a general idea. So these were strictly information searches?"

"That's right. Once they got what they wanted, most of their traces disappeared. It's only the pattern of several visits that we picked up, and we probably wouldn't have gotten that if we weren't looking very carefully."

"So the tip was good. This guy wasn't trying to misdirect us."

"I'll withhold judgment on that," was Donniger's answer. "I'm not convinced this isn't part of their plan. But we have to act on it."

"How can someone get into a network, especially a supposedly secure one at that, look around, and then we don't even know what they looked at?" Ben asked.

"The best I can tell you is what they explained to me. They had to explain the difference between a virus and a worm to me. Hey, my 16-year old understands this stuff better than I do. But they told me an intruder— if they know what they're doing and they have a powerful enough system of their own—can create something called a temporary peer-to-peer network. They initiate a temporary connection to get the data they want. The network thinks the intruder is one of them, in other words. Once the intruder has the data, he closes his end of the network and disappears."

Ben got the gist of it. Someone got into a network and looked around. The intruder learned a lot about the oil refinery, or about several oil refineries. They didn't block access or plant any viruses, at least none that they knew of. Now the challenge was to figure out the connections between the intrusions and several pounds of stolen VX-212, and to someone steering them in what Ben hoped was the right direction.

"If they leave almost no trace, how do we know about these intrusions? Maybe this is all a wild goose chase."

"We're gonna follow this lead, even if it may be a wild goose chase. But to answer your question about how we know someone was looking around these networks, we found a pattern of many brief intrusions and then disappearances. A legitimate peer-to-peer contact doesn't make itself disappear. And these contacts were extremely brief—a matter of seconds, just enough to download some data."

"And this happened at several oil refineries."

"Yeah, six of them, all in Louisiana and Texas. Once we found the first intrusion, and we understood the pattern, it was easier to identify the others."

"OK, so maybe it's a wild goose chase, and maybe the call I got was meant to send us on our way. What's next?"

"We've contacted every refinery in Texas and Louisiana and issued a security alert. I've got the FBI field offices in Houston and New Orleans doing some footwork, but it's a real big area, so I'm not holding my breath."

Ben didn't think searching for someone doing something unusual in Texas or Louisiana was much of a lead, and he knew Donniger had to be thinking the same thing. He asked him, "Is that the best we can do?"

"IT is looking more closely at the hits on all the refineries. They think they may narrow the list. But even if we knew which refinery—or maybe there's more than one—what then? That's just the 'where.' We still don't know the 'what'."

"Something connected to a few pounds of nerve toxin. What would you do with it at an oil refinery?" Ben thought out loud. "And my caller, Julian. Does he know which one? Or like we said, maybe he's just running us around."

Donniger was silent as he thought about his CID counterpart. Well, not exactly his counterpart. Captain Ben Hawkins was only an investigator, and a military one at that. Not FBI. Not a senior agent. Not a field office assistant director. He had done well bringing in Sergeant McNair, but he had been a loose cannon about it, deliberately keeping Donniger and his team out of the contact. Hawkins wasn't a team player, and if there was anything Donniger wanted, it was a team player. But for whatever reason, team player or not, he was the only contact with their only real lead, Julian. *Why was that?* Donniger wondered.

"Well, Captain, let's look at what we've got. Someone's got four pounds of some very nasty stuff—enough to kill a lot more people than 9/11 did. Someone's calling you and giving you some hints and has convinced us to pay attention to him. And you're sure you're telling us everything you know about this guy, right?"

"What's that supposed to mean?" Ben asked, surprised by the question. He knew Donniger was still angry about the McNair phone call and the secret meeting, especially after two of his agents were left in a parked car for a few hours. But this was different.

"After that stunt the other day, I have to wonder if you're holding anything back."

"You mean that stunt when you put a tail on me without telling me about it? Come on, Donniger, let's move on here and concentrate on the threat in front of us." Ben wasn't going to let the FBI agent push him around, but he didn't want to get into a pointless argument about it.

"OK, as long as we're clear about it: this is a team operation. No heroics, no working on your own. Are we on the same page, Captain? Because I can always get you removed from the team completely."

Ben didn't understand why Donniger still had this bug up his ass, and he was pretty sure Donniger couldn't risk having him off the team, but he wasn't going to rise to the bait.

"Yes, we're clear about it. Now can we get back to the issue here?"

Donniger looked at some notes in front of him. "Alright, maybe—and let's remember that we have no second source on this—maybe someone wants to use that nerve agent at an oil refinery. What would you do with it?"

Ben had been considering that question most of the morning. Nerve toxin. VX-212 nerve agent. Very potent, enough to kill 20,000 people even if the terrorists were sloppy, but maybe 100,000 people if the agent were dispersed "efficiently." Oil. More precisely, oil refinery, which meant gas, diesel, heating oil. Gas. What was the connection?

Ben began thinking out loud. "What if the goal is not to kill a lot of people? Could you use a nerve agent to shut down an oil refinery? What would shutting down an oil refinery do to this country?"

"Hell if I know how you would do it, or what it would mean. But I can ask someone at Homeland Security to work on it." Donniger's cell phone rang. "Hold on, Captain." He listened for a few moments, said "OK, thanks. Keep me posted," and ended the call.

Donniger got back on his call to Hawkins. "That was IT. They found traces of repeated hacks into the networks of two refineries—one in Baton Rouge and one in Baytown, Texas, about 30 miles east of Houston. They have something in common"

"Which is?"

"They're big—very big. They each process something like half a million barrels of oil a day. They're both owned by ExxonMobil. And between them they process something like 10 percent of the oil we use every day."

Ben thought for a few moments as an idea began to form. Could it be they weren't planning to use the nerve agent to kill *people*, but in effect, to kill an oil refinery? They could use the VX-212—an American WMD—to do serious damage to the American economy and to change the daily life of every one of its citizens. Take away 10 percent of a supply that was already tight, at least at the refinery level, and it would make the 1974 gas shortage look like a mild inconvenience. The immediate effects would be long lines at gas stations and some kind of rationing. The effects on businesses and the American economy would be a lot worse. It could be brilliant—and very, very damaging.

Ben was about to say something when he saw another incoming call. He looked at the screen and saw "private number."

"Tom, I've got a call coming in and it's labeled 'private number.' You know what that probably means. I'll call you back. I'm pretty sure it will be a short call." Ben pressed disconnect and picked up the new call. It was indeed his new friend, the one he knew as Julian.

Just outside Washington, D.C.

Colonel Kashani had arrived in the D.C. area late Thursday afternoon and checked into three different motels outside the Beltway, using the three different credit cards he had picked up in Paris. And he had been busy. Two calls to Mahmoud. Two calls to a Captain Ben Hawkins of Army CID. Both were very important and he believed both had been successful.

The calls to Mahmoud were to establish himself as his new contact, ostensibly because of some recently developed high level interest in Mahmoud's plans. Kashani had gotten all the contact information he needed during his conversation with Major Heidari and Captain Ashkani at Qazvin. He didn't need any information from Mahmoud—yet—and he didn't ask for any, except for Hawkins' name and cell phone number, which Mahmoud had gotten from McNair.

The two calls to the American Army investigator had also been productive. His purpose had been to establish his credibility, to let this Captain Hawkins and his superiors know that he was someone to listen to. After all, Kashani couldn't do what he had come to the U.S. to do by himself. He would need Captain Hawkins and the FBI to co-operate.

Kashani had been impressed by how quickly the FBI showed up at the first of his hotel rooms. Of course, he wanted them to discover the phone-to-phone contact he had used. In fact, he was exiting the hotel lobby as he began his conversation with Hawkins and was sitting almost across the street when the FBI agents arrived. He was pretty sure they would take him seriously now.

Now he was making his third call to the Army investigator. He punched in the number and heard someone pick up on the second ring.

"Hello, Captain. This is Julian."

"Hello, Julian. Nice trick with the two phones," Ben answered politely. No point in being rude just because someone kidnapped an American student, stole a weapon of mass destruction, and was now threatening the lives of thousands of Americans.

"I thought that would get your attention."

"Oh, you had my attention from the get-go. You have it now. Do you have something for us?" Ben asked, still polite.

"How about my suggestion about the oil refineries down in the south part of your country? Was it helpful?" The Iranian intelligence officer was hoping the Americans' post-9/11 Homeland Security was as good as he believed it to be.

"Hard to say. But yes, we did find that someone has been breaking into the computer networks of several oil refineries."

"I hope I can continue to be helpful. In fact I expect to have more specific information for you shortly," Kashani added.

"So what is this all about, Julian? Why are you so interested in helping us?" Ben asked his caller.

"As I said on my first call, Captain, you are not the only ones worried about the crazy people threatening our world. What good would it do anyone to kill a few thousand innocent souls—American or otherwise?"

"So you want to stop it."

"I want to stop it."

"And we should listen to you."

"I think I've demonstrated that my information is worth listening to."

"But you haven't helped us stop anything yet. You've just given us a few possibilities."

"That's true, Captain, but I hope to do more soon. And why would I have given you *any* information if I didn't want to help you?"

"That's what I've been wondering, my friend. But my colleagues at the FBI think you're just playing with us, that you're trying to direct us elsewhere."

"Perhaps they are just upset that they didn't find me at the hotel room."

"Ah, you saw that. Perhaps they are," Ben answered, realizing that Julian must have been very close by when the FBI showed up the night before.

"I don't ask you to trust me, Captain. That is not possible in this situation. I understand that. I just ask you to listen to my information. It's really in your own best interest. As well as mine, I admit. It's time for me to go, but I will call you again later today." Kashani disconnected and Ben heard only silence.

"Did you get anything?" Hawkins asked Donniger as soon as the assistant director answered his phone.

"No, the call wasn't long enough. Somewhere in the D.C. area is all we could get. But I heard the part about the hotel room—so he *was* nearby, the little prick."

Ben gave a short laugh. "Sounds like he's getting under your skin."

"He got under my skin as soon as he made the first call, but that's OK. I'm *glad* to hear he was near that hotel. We're running something called Skyhawk and we may get some kind of picture of him."

"Alright, I'll bite. What's Skyhawk?" Ben asked.

"Skyhawk is a program that can download and store all the video camera data from a specified geographic location—security cameras, traffic cams, ATM cameras. It synchronizes their time clocks and then organizes all the data to create something pretty close to a three-dimensional model of that site over time. Then we can look around the location, manipulate the views, zoom in and out, move back and forth in time. It's like re-creating whatever happened in that location—at least, whatever the cameras caught. If we're lucky, we can actually track someone as he moves through the location."

"Ah, Big Brother at work. But what good does that do us? We don't have a photo to compare with, so how do we know who to look for or where he was?"

"Right now it probably won't be a help, unless we get a shot of him going into or out of the motel where the phones were. But if we get another series of shots, Skyhawk can cross-reference them and pull out any matching images using a facial recognition program. It's not exactly a high probability, but it's not a long shot either, especially if we get an idea where he is next time."

"I'll keep that in mind. But for now, what did we learn from this call? Obviously he wants us to take him seriously. And he wants us to believe he's here to help us."

"That's what he *wants* us to believe. And he said he would have more specific information for us. But we need that info *now*, not later," Donniger said, his voice rising. *And I need to get some rest*, he thought to himself. He hadn't seen his family in five days and hadn't slept more than four or five hours a night during the past week.

"I'm going to see McNair in a little bit," Ben said. "I'm going to play him my recording of the call, see if he recognizes the voice. Is this guy McNair's Joseph? I don't think so, but we have to rule it out. I'll keep you posted." Ben hung up.

Sergeant McNair had been returned to the stockade at Ft. Belvoir and Ben planned on seeing him later that day. He decided to get a quick bite and visit the sergeant as soon as he finished lunch. This guy Julian was getting to him, too. What did he want? Who was he working for? How did he know the details of this operation? And how had he gotten his name and phone number? Maybe Sergeant McNair had a few more answers for him.

Around noon
Outside the Beltway, Washington, D.C.

It was around noon when Colonel Kashani made his next call. This would be his third call to Mahmoud Najidad. Kashani had used his first two calls to establish his credibility. He let Najidad know that he had been briefed by Major Heidari in Qazvin and told him the eyes of the Revolutionary Supreme Council were upon him.

Kashani failed to mention that Major Heidari was under house arrest, or that the senior leadership in Tehran was in a virtual panic about a state-sponsored act of terrorism against the United States. Najidad also didn't know that Colonel Kashani was actually in the United States, not Iran. Kashani would keep him in the dark about that as well.

On the second call he praised Najidad's planning and sacrifice, practically promising him the 72 virgins himself. He hoped he hadn't overdone it.

"Mahmoud, our faithful soldier," he started out. "I expect your preparations are almost complete."

Now Kashani would play the role of the stern leader. He had found in his line of work that making demands often worked better than actually asking for information. He would encourage Najidad, he would push him and he would make demands—and then wait for the information to come.

"Yes sir, they are," Mahmoud answered.

Mahmoud was pleased to hear that the Supreme Council itself was aware of his plan. But he wasn't stupid. He had recruited and trained the agents himself, he had developed this plan almost singlehandedly—and he was concerned. Where was Major Heidari, the Qods Force officer who had supported him and the plan for the past two years? That was a question he had asked on the first call and the answer—Major Heidari was still in charge, but the Supreme Council wanted a more senior officer to oversee the operation—didn't sound right.

"And you have assured me that this event can't be traced back here to any of us at Qazvin," Kashani continued, not mentioning that he had left Qazvin nearly a week before after spending just a few hours there.

"Absolutely not, sir. Only my assistant and I know the details of where and how we will disperse the material."

"It's important that we know when this will happen so we can be prepared to deal with the foreign pressures that will come to bear on us. The Americans and their western allies will be looking for someone to blame for this great defeat. Don't make us wait too long, Mahmoud. Are you sure you're close?"

"Yes, yes, don't worry. I have planned and prepared for many months, you can depend on me," Mahmoud answered with exasperation. Did these political bureaucrats think they could pressure him or make him change his plan? He was not about to be rushed. He had worked too long and given up too much to change his plans now. The Americans would pay a heavy price and Mahmoud would make this apparatchik understand how carefully he had prepared for this day. And who did this bureaucrat think he was talking to? He was Mahmoud, the mastermind of a brilliant attack on the Great Satan, an attack that would use their own weapons to kill thousands of the infidel hypocrites.

And in the next few minutes Colonel Kashani learned a great deal more about when and where Mahmoud would strike. But would the young American investigator, Captain Hawkins, and his colleagues believe him?

A few minutes later

Ben was just getting ready to head over to the post stockade where Harry McNair was being held when another call came through from the man he knew as Julian.

"Captain, I have more information for you," Kashani began.

I'm listening," Ben answered. Everything was being recorded, of course, and a trace was working, but this call might be the most important to date. Would Julian's information be enough to allow them to end this thing? He knew the FBI and NSA were working hard on identifying the shadowy stranger, but there just wasn't enough to go on.

"I already told you to look at oil refineries in Texas and Louisiana. Now I will be more specific. The target is the refinery at Baytown, Texas. I don't believe anything will happen for two more days, maybe three. That's all I can tell you now."

Mahmoud had been quite clear that he wouldn't be ready for at least another two days.

"All you can tell me?" Ben said, his voice rising. "How will this attack occur? Why are you holding out on me, with just a little more information on each call?" he demanded.

"Captain, please, I am telling you all I know as soon as I know it. No one wants a tragic incident, except some crazy idiots who are operating with absolutely no authority. No one controls Al Qaeda terrorists. They are not even from my country, but that is not the point," Kashani answered, trying to distance himself in case he—and his new associate, Captain Ben Hawkins of Army CID—were not successful.

Kashani was well aware that his presence in the U.S. and his calls to Hawkins created a whole new risk, but it was a risk that he and General Gulab knew they had to accept. He also knew this wasn't an Al Qaeda operation, but he hoped to send the Americans looking elsewhere.

"OK, Julian, Baytown, Texas. In two days, maybe later. How many people? What are they planning to do?" Ben asked, trying to will more information out of his caller.

"If I learn more, I will call you." Kashani said. Then he hung up and Ben was left listening to silence.

"Goddammit, did you get anything new?" Ben yelled at whoever was listening in and recording the call. He knew he wouldn't hear anything for a few minutes, and that would be through Donniger. He was also more anxious than ever to talk to McNair again.

After ending the call, Kashani looked in his rearview mirror. He knew he wouldn't see anything even if there were anything to see, so it was more out of his own nervousness, and he realized that, too.

He was driving south on Route 29 through Arlington. As long as he kept moving, any attempted phone trace would keep chasing the signal as it moved from cell tower to cell tower. As soon as he completed the call, he turned off his phone and removed the battery. Then he left Route 29 and headed west on the smaller side roads.

The last call to Najidad had thrown a monkey wrench into Kashani's plans. He had hoped to contain the situation himself, making direct contact with the man who had the VX-212 and who was the key to the planned release of the chemical WMD. He would have cleaned up the mess and made sure that no ties to his own country were left behind. Whatever you thought about them, no one wanted to incur the wrath of the United States. Iraq had proved that. Afghanistan had confirmed it.

Instead, Colonel Kashani had just learned that Najidad was far cleverer than he had anticipated and he was kicking himself for making the classic error of underestimating his opponent. By dividing the four pounds of VX-212 and planning two separate attacks, Najidad had made Kashani's job considerably more difficult.

Kashani couldn't be in two places at once, particularly if one of those places was Texas and the other was Washington, D.C. He wasn't even sure about the Washington location, but something Najidad had said about the "heart of America" gave him that impression. Kashani would concentrate on the Washington attack and hope the FBI could handle the one in Texas.

That meant he would have to share more information with the Americans, but he would also have to withhold some information if he didn't want the Americans too close while he searched for the second agent, the woman Najidad called Saman. Withholding information could be risky, since he needed to earn the Americans' trust, or at least their confidence in him and his information.

He would continue to use his contact, this Captain Ben Hawkins. After several calls to Hawkins—and some information he had picked up by googling his name—Kashani had come to like his American contact. The CID officer seemed to understand that Julian was trying to help the Americans. But could he count on the young investigator and his FBI colleagues to do the job that needed doing? And to do it without discovering Najidad's connection to his native Iran?

That afternoon
Ft. Belvoir

Ben posted the details of the latest Julian call on the team website before heading for the stockade at Ft. Belvoir. This was the first time a specific target had been identified, and that would certainly stir up a hornet's nest. It also meant a meeting at the Washington FBI offices later today.

Then he called the MP station at Ft. Belvoir and gave them a headsup that he would be there soon to see their most important prisoner. On his way to the post, Ben stopped off at Bozzelli's Deli to pick up sandwiches for McNair and himself, since he wouldn't have time to stop for lunch.

A few minutes later, Ben was sitting in a small interrogation room in Belvoir's prisoner holding area with staff sergeant Harry McNair. They each had a sandwich in front of them. Ben knew that he still needed McNair's full cooperation. Assistant Director Donniger wanted McNair in FBI custody, but he hadn't won that battle—yet.

"Alright, Sergeant, listen up. Is this the guy who called you down at Tupelo?" Ben asked McNair, and pressed the "play" button on the recording of the call he had just received.

McNair only had to listen for a few moments. "No, that's not the guy. Who is he?"

Hawkins had considered how much information he should share with the guy who had put his country at risk. Daughter or no daughter, Ben still couldn't reconcile what McNair had done. But trying to prevent the attack was a lot more important than what happened to McNair or what Hawkins felt about McNair's crime.

"He's someone who claims he wants to help us stop the attack. Probably Iranian, if you believe the NSA guy. And he knows a lot about what's going on."

"Like what?"

"Like your name. And my cell phone number. And the fact that your daughter was let go. He asked how she was." Ben didn't mention Julian's information about oil refineries in Texas or anyplace else.

"I hope you let him know she's just fine. Maybe I could tell him myself."

"Right. So this is not the guy who contacted you and you don't know who it is. You've never heard this voice."

"That's right."

"And you never heard from anyone but this Joseph."

No. No, wait. I already told you it was a woman who made the first call. She's the one who told me they had Jennifer. I never heard from *her* again—just Joseph."

"Yeah, well the woman is probably the one who entered the country using your daughter's passport. Jennifer already identified her as someone she knew in Seville, someone going by the name of Elena. You don't remember anything about a second man or anything more on the woman?" Ben asked.

"No. I told you, after the first call, the only one I heard from was Joseph. And he never talked about anyone else or what they were going to do, other than to say they were going to ship this stuff back to their own country. Joseph kept saying how they were going to restore freedom in their country."

"Yeah, and you believed him. Right. And you want *me* to think that you actually believed that they came to the U.S. with a very sophisticated plan to steal closely guarded material from the United States Army—and then smuggle it *out* of the country.

"Did I believe him? I don't know....I guess I didn't want to think too much about it."

"Was there ever any talk about what country?"

"No. I asked him a couple of times, but he said that was not my concern."

"Alright, hold on." Ben took out his cell phone, logged onto the team website and put in a note that McNair had not made a voice match. He guessed that Donniger and the audio forensics guys would pick that up in a few minutes.

So Ben's caller was not McNair's caller. Ben wasn't surprised. *But who was he? More to the point, who was he working for?* Ben thought about it for a few moments and then remembered where he was.

"How's Jennifer holding up?" Ben asked McNair. *What a mess,* he thought to himself. His daughter kidnapped, and McNair caught in the middle. Now she's safe, but he knows he could be responsible for the deaths of thousands of people. Plus he's facing God knows how many years at Leavenworth.

"She's worried about me. I told her not to. She's back in the United States and that's all I care about. They let her visit me yesterday. I don't know if I ever thanked you for holding up your end of the deal. I got no problem with what happens to me. That's the least of our worries, isn't it?" The impact of what he had done and the thousands of lives he had put at risk had hit home once Jennifer had been released.

"Well, Sergeant, you're right about that. You're the least of our problems right now."

Ben called the MPs to escort McNair back to his cell and headed back to his office on the other side of the post. He wanted to follow up on some information he had just seen on the team website.

Half an hour later

Ben called Donniger from his desk at CID headquarters. "Did you see my posting about no voice ID on my caller?" he asked the assistant director. "McNair did not recognize the voice."

"No, Captain, I didn't see it yet. Thanks for the heads-up."

"I figure that's good news. Or at least it's not bad news."

"What do you mean?" Donniger asked, not making the connection.

"Well, it would have been bad news if the guy calling me was the same guy who blackmailed McNair into stealing the stuff in the first place. It's good news that Julian is not Joseph."

"I see your point. By the way, our own linguistics people studied those three calls you got from this Julian. They're pretty sure he lived in the U.S. for at least a couple of years."

"I saw that on the website. So at least he wasn't lying about that, either. In fact, everything he's told us so far has checked out. I also saw something about trying to match a license plate. What's that all about?"

"I don't have time to go over all that right now. We're going over your last call and the telecommunications people are having some success tracing it back to where it originated. It was from just outside the Beltway. We're also putting together a team to follow-up on the Baytown lead. I want you to come into town so we can go over what we've got. There's nothing more you can do down at Belvoir." Donniger sounded tired. It also sounded as if the pressure was getting to him, but that was not surprising.

An hour later Ben entered the Hoover Building through the Pennsylvania Avenue entrance and was escorted to the eighth floor. He had a sense that events were coming to a head, but they were still heavily dependent on information from a single source. That source was unidentified and the information he provided couldn't be corroborated, and that made him very uncomfortable.

He swiped his team ID card on the door security keypad and entered his code. The door unlatched and he walked into the Game Room, where half a dozen agents were at work. Tom Donniger was at the head of the conference table.

"Captain, have a seat. Special Agent Myers is just finishing up going over the plans for Baytown. Then I'll bring you up to speed on what he got on that last call to you from Julian."

Ben sat and listened while Myers highlighted how the FBI WMD team would deal with the information about Baytown. They obviously thought the information was high quality.

"Gentlemen, one team of agents will work with the refinery's security force to prepare the facility to deal with a possible attack. A second team will be working with state and local police resources to try to prevent an attack. Based on the tip from your mysterious source, the second team will concentrate on the Baytown facility, but other FBI resources will also prepare the Baton Rouge facility, where several computer breaches have also been detected."

"The good news is we've got a lot of resources in the area," Myers continued. "Our Houston field office is only about 25 miles from Baytown.

The Houston office WMD coordinator has already been alerted. The field offices in Dallas and San Antonio are each sending in about a dozen agents they've assigned to us, including their WMD coordinators. We can also call in agents from the New Orleans office if we need to, but they'll be handling the Baton Rouge refinery."

"Thank you, Craig. All the local coordination will be out of Houston, right?"

"Yes sir, with Special Agent in Charge Mike Stanton, the Houston WMD coordinator, in charge at the local level. He's worked with the Texas state police in the past on contingency drills, so they have a good working relationship. He's contacting the Baytown local police and the Baytown Oil Refinery security chief as we speak. All information and actions are to be relayed directly to here. I put Special Agent in Charge Stanton on the website access list and issued him a personal ID and password."

"OK, good work, Craig. You see, Captain, we can move fast when we have to. It's been what, 90 minutes since your phone call warning about Baytown?"

"Yes, about that. Impressive. Let's hope the information is good. We don't have any other source or any confirmation, do we?" Ben said, voicing his concern about putting all their eggs in one basket.

"No, we don't, and that concerns all of us. I don't want us to target-fixate on Baytown just because we *want* the information to be good—or because we don't have any other target information. On the other hand, this target makes a lot of sense."

"Why is that?" Ben asked.

Donniger opened a folder that was lying on the conference table.

"Baytown is about 30 miles southeast of Houston and just off Galveston Bay. Not much of a town, except that ExxonMobil is there. Population is about 80,000. A lot of them work for Exxon."

"So why Baytown? Because it's got the largest oil refinery in the U.S., that's why. They handle just over 500,000 barrels of oil a day, which is about 5 percent of our refinery capacity. So what happens to this country if you take out 5 percent of our gas, our diesel, our home heating oil and whatever else a refinery produces? Nothing good, obviously."

"I've passed that question up to Homeland Security and they'll put a team on it—worst case, best case, contingency plans. We have to assume these people may pull it off."

"Yeah, well, pull what off?" Ben asked. "How do they use a couple of pounds of a nerve agent to shut down an oil refinery? Anyone working on that?"

"We *are* working on that, Captain. In fact, we've worked on that scenario for a couple of years now, so we're not starting from scratch. We've looked at hundreds of possible threats, including oil refineries."

"Look, Tom, I'm not trying to say we're not prepared or you haven't done your homework. I'm just saying, even if it *is* Baytown or maybe Baton Rouge, we don't know *what* they're trying to pull off."

"I understand. Right now, the security people at Baytown are involved in a crash refresher course in counterterrorism. But I happen to know the WMD coordinator out of Houston—special agent by the name of Mike Stanton. He's got a special interest in oil refinery security. Not surprising, since half of our oil refineries are within a few hundred miles of his office. I also know the Baytown facility has run simulated terrorist attacks at least every year for the past several years."

"So you're taking this information as high-grade," Ben noted.

"That's for sure, Captain. We're gonna go over the Baytown plans for another half hour, but then I've got to work with another team that's working another lead. Completely unrelated."

"And you were going to tell me about a possible license match."

"Yeah, well, not a match, but a lead on getting one. I already told you about Skyhawk."

"Yeah, traffic cameras, private security cameras, ATMs. You have access to all of them, right?" Ben asked.

"Yes, but it's more than that. Like I said, we can pull a lot of the private and government video feeds together and integrate them by time and location. If we find a particular target, we put a digital mark on it and Skyhawk can follow the target as it appears throughout any other videos. It creates a three-dimensional view that you can move around in, re-orient, change the perspective."

"Alright, you already explained that. It sounds like a science fiction movie, but I think I get it. Have you used it before?"

"Sure we've used it, for about a year now. It's almost like visiting the scene again, whenever you want. As you said, it's something out of a science fiction movie, you know, where you can re-create reality."

"And has it been useful?" Ben asked.

"Occasionally. It's incredible the way it can re-create an accident scene. Actually, we don't use it that often—it's kind of overkill and it uses a lot of computing power. But you also wanted to know about that license plate investigation."

"Yes. Whose license plate? Julian's?"

"That's the one we're trying to identify, though we haven't had any success yet. But one of our technicians had the idea of using Skyhawk to ID as many license plates as we can in the half hour before and after we got to the motel room where Julian had those cell phones rigged up. Which, by the way, had been wiped clean of prints, of course."

"Sounds like a lot of license plates," Ben commented.

"We limited it to vehicles that came within four blocks of the motel. We still came up with more than 600 we could ID."

"OK, so we can ID 600 plates. Maybe one is Julian, maybe not. Maybe he got there by Metro, or on a bus. Even a taxi," Ben suggested.

"Fair enough. Although I don't see our Julian waiting for a bus or risking being identified by a taxi driver. Take the Metro—maybe. And maybe we should run the Metro videos through the program, see if we can track someone from the nearest Metro station to the motel." Donniger said.

"Just a thought. But how are these license plates going to identify our man?" Ben still didn't see the point and it seemed as if resources were being used just because they were available. But then, maybe that was the FBI way.

"I don't know yet. We have to get another set of license plates to run our sample against. That could happen if he calls and pulls the same stunt again. We try to match the plates from the two scenes, see if any plate shows up in both places. In the meantime, you're through with this McNair, right?" Donniger asked, switching topics.

"Why?"

"I don't think he's got anything more that's useful to us and I don't want to be distracted. I'm just saying, don't spend a lot more time with him. Concentrate on Julian, forget McNair. McNair doesn't know anything about these guys' plans, but Julian may."

"Funny you should mention that. First of all, I agree with you. While I was driving in, I got to thinking about these calls. There have been three of them so far."

"Yeah. And?"

"Well, I'm going to go on the website again. Or maybe you could have someone at your audio lab tie all the Julian calls together, remove my voice, then play through them all at once. It seems to me, each time Julian called, he had a little more information for us. And he seemed to be giving it to us as soon as he learned it."

Donniger looked at Hawkins. "OK, that sounds right. What's your point? He seems to be doling out the info bit by bit."

"Like I said, I want to listen to him again. But what if he was giving us the info as he got it himself? On his last call he said something like, 'I'm telling you as soon as I know it myself'."

Donniger looked thoughtful. He thought he got the point.

"You mean, he's got his own source, and he's feeding us the information from that source as soon as he gets it?"

"Exactly," Ben answered. "And remember, McNair had not heard his voice before. Julian was not McNair's contact."

"OK," Donniger said, waiting to hear what Ben was driving at.

"And Julian is in the area," Ben said, now thinking out loud.

"Sure, he has to be. He planted the two phones in Arlington, his second call was from that area."

"So where has he been? We just heard from him. He's giving us specific information, maybe very good information. He isn't Joseph, but based on what he could tell us about the operation, he must be in touch with him. He knows McNair, he knows me. He even knows McNair's daughter's name."

"OK, Captain but we've been over that. Where are you going with this?" Donniger sounded irritated at Hawkins' rambling.

"And what was it he said about Jennifer? 'And I believe she is safe,' or something like that. How would he know that?"

"OK, so he knows a lot. And he seems to want to tell us a lot. He also says he wants to help stop this." Donniger replied, trying to be patient.

"So like I said, where has he been? And why now?" Ben paused. "When did Joseph first contact us?"

He looked at the event timeline posted behind him. *"Late Thursday afternoon."*

"And Julian's first call to me was Sunday. Why did he wait almost three days before getting into the game?" He wondered out loud again.

148

"What if Julian didn't contact us earlier because he couldn't. Or there was no point to it. Maybe he wasn't in the country, maybe he hadn't met up with Joseph yet, maybe he didn't have my number yet."

Donniger pressed him again. "What difference does any of that make?"

"Maybe no difference. But I'm thinking that our friend Julian has not been living in the Washington suburbs waiting for the chance to help us if something bad should go down. I'm thinking he came here just for that purpose."

"That's assuming *your* friend Julian is not just trying to throw us off the trail and is not actually part of the whole operation," Donniger offered, returning to his earlier theme.

"I understand we have to accept the possibility that he's part of the operation. We also have to accept the possibility that he's not. My point is, if he wasn't here already, then he came here recently..." Ben paused again, which was starting to annoy Donniger.

"Yeah, and...?"

"And wouldn't he be driving a rental car?" Ben said, finally saying what he had been trying to think through.

Donniger stopped fidgeting. "A rental car. He might be driving a rental car. And you're thinking maybe he rented it in the past few days."

"Right."

Donniger continued. "Let's say he rented sometime in the past week. We run the 600 license plates we've got against the registration of every car rented in the past week. Say out of any rental agency from metropolitan New York down to Richmond. See if we come up with any matches. And if...."

"Hold on,'" Ben interrupted. "You say you can get a list of all the cars that were rented in the past week between New York and here...and ID all the cars that were travelling within four blocks of that motel for the half hour before and after the call to me."

"That's right. Although we didn't get every car, just most of them," Donniger explained.

Ben looked thoughtful. "I like it. Might work, might not, but at least we have a list to try to match against. And we don't have to wait for his next step."

Special Agent Myers spoke up. "I'll get on that list of rental cars."

"Alright. Give me an update in an hour. Interesting idea, Captain. Maybe a long shot, but if it pans out we may find out what car he's driving and what name he's using. I'm guessing it's not Julian," Donniger said. "Everyone else, carry on. Captain, let me talk to you for a minute."

The other agents left, leaving only Assistant Director Tom Donniger and CID Captain Ben Hawkins in the Game Room.

"Like I said, Ben, nice idea. Thanks for coming in."

"Sure. I'm gonna run through the tapes of those phone calls again. Anything else?" Ben assumed there *was* something else.

"We're working on a couple of leads, we've got about three dozen agents heading for Baytown, NSA is monitoring international calls and internet chatter—we are, too. But your Julian is still our strongest lead."

"Yeah, I agree. But we don't like it, do we? Waiting for *him* to call *us*."

"No, we don't. I would like to have him in custody. And I need to know that you won't pull the kind of stunt you pulled the other day with McNair, Captain," Donniger said, looking at the CID investigator.

"You mean losing the two agents who were tailing me?" Ben retorted, just to rub it in a little.

"That's exactly what I mean. Your boss stood up for you, but he had no business giving you a pass on that one."

"That was strictly Army business at the time, Tom. Army noncom went AWOL, I picked him up. But I understand we're way beyond that now," Ben answered. "I don't see a problem." Ben couldn't see himself trying to handle someone on his own in the middle of a possible WMD attack. The man was probably a foreign agent anyway.

"Good. Glad we cleared the air. Just so you know, we've almost finished re-interviewing everyone at Tupelo, including Lieutenant Colonel Girelli and Jack Roehm. We also pulled their financial records. Nothing came up. Looks like Sergeant McNair was operating on his own, just as he said."

"OK, got it. No surprise. I'll be here for another hour, then I'm heading home. I'll log in later tonight. You might want to do the same, get some rest." Ben suggested.

Donniger looked at his watch. "I'll be right here. I set up some living quarters on the 4th floor. Are you working out of Belvoir tomorrow or up here?"

"I'll be at Belvoir unless I get a call from you," Ben answered. He wasn't sure how much he could do other than wait for a call from Julian—and Donniger and his team would know about the call as soon as he did. He headed to his work area down the hall.

At about the same time, and just a few miles away, Colonel Kashani was thinking again about the renegade Iranian agent Mahmoud Najidad. The clever little bastard had made his job a lot tougher by planning two separate attacks more than a thousand miles apart. Would he be able to direct the FBI to one attack while he concentrated on the second?

What Kashani didn't know was that Najidad had lied to him about the two attacks, and his job was about to get even tougher.

Sunday

It was a cool and cloudy day as Haydar turned into the entrance to the shopping mall parking area and drove around to the northeast side of the mall. The huge parking area surrounded the stores on all sides, but the quickest entrance for the road back to Stony Point Parkway was on the northeast side, which is where Omid told Haydar to park. They were about 100 yards from an entrance into the indoor shopping area—close enough to leave quickly, but not close enough for the security cameras to get a good picture of their vehicle.

It's cool today, so the ventilation system will be running full-time, Omid thought to himself. That was a good thing.

Mahmoud's instructions were quite clear, and both Omid and Haydar had visited the shopping mall previously. Haydar carried a small household appliance in a department store shopping bag, and he looked like any other shopper returning a purchase. He even had a receipt for the purchase, made about two weeks before. His English wasn't good enough to be understood very easily, but Haydar wouldn't be talking to any sales clerks.

Haydar had practiced in their motel room the night before, unpacking a second, identical appliance, turning it on, and then casually walking away. Omid's job was to watch him, make sure he followed the instructions. Moral support, really. Haydar wasn't known for his brains, but he *was* known for following directions, and that would be enough.

Mahmoud and Saeed had prepared the instrument several days before and it was ready when the men arrived in Knoxville from North Carolina. It wasn't really much of an instrument. Just a small, portable, battery-operated household humidifier. It was cute, too, bright blue and in the shape of a hippopotamus. Not too large, but big enough to hold two quarts of water, which in this case was two quarts of water mixed with two ounces of VX-212. The men weren't exactly sure what VX-212 was, but Mahmoud had been very clear about how they were to handle it and what it would do to them if they weren't careful.

The two men got out of the car. Each of them put on a baseball cap and then they separated in the parking lot. Two youngish, middle Eastern-looking men doing their shopping in the middle of the afternoon might attract attention.

Haydar entered the shopping mall, with Omid about 20 yards behind. He took an escalator to the second level and strolled toward the food court area, casually looking in store windows along the way. When he reached the food court, he chose a table next to several large indoor plants, and settled into a chair just in front of one of them. A few moments later, Omid stopped at the table and sat down with a tray carrying two hot dogs and a soda. He pushed the tray in front of Haydar and then left the food court.

Haydar took a drink of the soda. Then he turned to the shopping bag behind him, reached down, and turned a household timer to "five minutes." A moment later he stood up and left.

Five minutes later, just as Haydar reached the car where Omid was waiting for him, the timer clicked once more, and the humidifier began pumping out a fine water mist, a mist laced with the American-made nerve toxin. By the time the two men were driving north on Stony Point Parkway, several shoppers had already inhaled some of the toxin-laced air. Muscle paralysis set in quickly and they started to choke as their respiratory systems began to shut down.

In moments, another 15 or so people were having difficulty breathing. Omid's hope that the HVAC system would spread the poisonous mixture didn't come to pass—the small humidifier just didn't have the power to drive the mist into the circulating air. Still, more than two dozen people started to die before someone hit an emergency alarm and shoppers began fleeing the mall.

Mahmoud will be very pleased, Omid thought, as he and Haydar left the parking lot. They heard sirens in the distance as they merged onto the parkway for the 45 minute drive north.

Good luck, Omid thought, as emergency vehicles with flashing blue lights and wailing sirens rushed by them, heading south to the mall. He didn't know the rest of Mahmoud's plans, but he knew that this was just the start of the attack against America and he was pleased that he was a part of it.

A half hour later, the two men were more than 20 miles from the shopping center. As instructed by Mahmoud, they used smaller side roads as they drove north to an address given to them by Mahmoud, an apartment neither had been to previously. There they would be met by a young woman who would give them further instructions from Mahmoud.

In another half hour, Hadar pulled into the parking lot of a small complex of garden apartments. He parked the car and a moment later he and Omid knocked on the door to one of the ground level apartments, apartment 3J.

"Who's there?" he heard a woman ask. They could hear a television news report in the background.

"We have some fine perfumes," he answered.

The door opened and an attractive, dark-haired woman looked out. The men would never learn that her name was Saman. Another one of Mahmoud's precautions.

"Do you have jasmine?" she asked.

Then she stepped aside and Omid and Haydar entered the one bedroom garden apartment. The two men saw the television images of emergency vehicles and ambulances at the shopping center they had left an hour before.

"There is a terrible incident on all the news stations. What do you have to report?" she asked immediately.

Omid spoke for the two of them.

"We did exactly as instructed and we left with no difficulty. There was no one following us. I checked several times. What has happened since we left? How successful was the attack? " Omid asked eagerly.

"All the news stations are talking about it," Saman replied. "You can see all the emergency vehicles and ambulances at the shopping center. They're not reporting how many people have died, but they say dozens have been taken to hospitals."

"Excellent, excellent!" Omid said excitedly. He was proud that he and Haydar had done so well, and he began to think about the welcome they would receive from their fellow Revolutionary Guards back in Qazvin. He and Haydar each pulled up a chair to watch the televised images.

"You must be tense after that mission," Saman said. "I prepared some lunch for you. It's better that you don't go out."

Saman went into the kitchen and soon brought back plates filled with chunks of lamb and rice. She poured tea for the two men and the three of them watched several news programs, switching from channel to channel. The CNN station showed a news crawler on the bottom of the screen: *"A Virginia state police spokesman says at least 16 people have died in an incident at the Stony Point Shopping Mall."*

Omid grinned. "All our work and practice paid off, Haydar. The Americans will remember this day forever."

Neither of the men knew of Mahmoud's other plans, the plans for the real attack. Neither knew their job had been to mislead the Americans, while Mahmoud prepared for the real attack.

"Would you like more tea?" Saman asked, as the men finished their lunch.

"Thank you, sister, but I think I'll lie down for a while." Omid replied.

"Yes, you've been very busy. You can rest here tonight. Mahmoud has plans for you for tomorrow."

Omid left the living room. A few minutes later he was asleep in the apartment's single bedroom. Haydar started to doze off as well, falling asleep on the living room couch to the sound of the televisions news reports on the terrorist attack in Richmond.

Saman went into the small bathroom and placed a phone call.

"You have seen the news?" she asked as soon as the call was picked up.

"Yes, I've been watching," Mahmoud answered. "I hope the damage is much greater than what has been reported, but they tell lies to protect themselves. This was a great setback for their so-called Homeland Security. Let's see how they like having their own citizens poisoned!"

Mahmoud tried to calm down, but he was feeling the power of hurting the great Satan. *I wonder what that bureaucrat back in Iran has to say now,* he thought with satisfaction.

"The men are here and sleeping now."

"Good. You prepared the tea properly?"

"Yes, of course. I prepared it just as you told me to."

"And you are ready to continue as we discussed."

"Yes, if I must. You said there is no other way."

"That is correct. We must leave the Americans hurt and confused and we must not leave any connections to us. We have more work to do. Much bigger targets. You understand that."

"Yes, Mahmoud, I do. Do not worry. I will be leaving soon." Saman had her own plans.

"Saman?"

"Yes, Mahmoud?"

"Haydar and Omid would understand also."

An hour later, the young woman, now with blond hair, put a small suitcase into the trunk of her SUV. In a few hours, after receiving a phone tip from Mahmoud, the police would find two bodies in apartment 3J, along with gloves and faint traces of VX-212. A toxicology blood test of the deceased men would show traces of VX-212 from the mask Saman had held over each man's face while he slept.

Mahmoud had explained to her patiently that it was important, very important, to throw the police off their trail, and that Haydar and Omid still had that important role to play. They couldn't be left behind alive anyway. He didn't actually use the word "expendable," but Saman had learned that human life didn't count for much to Mahmoud.

Saman would be long gone, of course. This was just the start of their attack on America.

Monday

Mahmoud Najidad looked across the work area. He and Saeed had arrived back in the area the day before. This morning they were working in a hangar on the edge of a small airfield. Ironically, they had chosen a little town called Liberty, about 30 miles north of Baytown, Texas. Najidad knew about Camp Liberty, the huge American base in Iraq. Perhaps that's what attracted him to this airfield several months ago—the chance to strike at the Americans from their own country and from a place called Liberty.

Mahmoud was tired after the long drive, but he was also relieved—and elated. All the news stations were reporting on the attack on the shopping mall in Richmond and the media coverage was nonstop.

Excellent, Mahmoud thought. *That will keep you busy!*

Of course, all the news reports were claiming that only 28 people had died in the attack, but Mahmoud was sure they were lying. The American authorities would do anything to maintain their false sense of security, but he would change that, too!

Najidad had been away for several weeks and he had been busy. As Joseph, he had threatened and finally gotten the cooperation of the American soldier, McNair. Of course, Major Heidari had been indispensable. He had the resources in Spain to arrange the kidnapping of the sergeant's daughter, and his support and oversight had been crucial.

The trick had been to convince the American sergeant that their goal was to take the material out of the country. Mahmoud wasn't sure McNair truly believed him, but it was plausible enough for McNair to convince himself that it might be true. In return for his cooperation, McNair's daughter would be released unharmed, and some dangerous material that was slated for destruction anyway would be spirited out of the country to who knows where. McNair agreed pretty quickly once he heard his daughter's voice and realized they were deadly serious.

It had taken McNair close to two weeks to collect four pounds of VX-212 nerve agent. Najidad would have preferred more, but McNair said his commanding officer had gotten suspicious. Then Najidad gave McNair instructions for delivering the stolen nerve agent. Afterwards, Mahmoud added the extra touch of wiring money into McNair's account, just to muddy the waters.

Mahmoud was still pleased with his plan, nearly two years after he first started putting it together. The three attacks would damage both the enemy's economy and their arrogant sense of security.

The beauty of 9/11, Mahmoud thought, was not the 3,000 or so lives that were lost—his country had lost that many loyal fighters every month in its eight-year war with Iraq, when their enemy was supported and supplied by the Americans he had come to hate. No, it was the aftermath, the damage to the American psyche. Planes had been grounded, a whole new security system created, government agencies blamed each other, and people looked suspiciously at each other. The Americans went all over the globe, looking for enemies in its so-called "war on terror." Najidad took particular pleasure that, incredibly, some Americans even blamed their own government, claiming it was a conspiracy deep within the power circles of Washington, D.C.

Supposed terrorists had been locked up in various countries and in American military prisons, and the Muslim world had seen a new kind of America. No, the Americans didn't talk about their human rights quite so confidently anymore. And the greater the divide between the United States and the billion or so Muslims around the world, the better it was for his own country of Iran.

Mahmoud had developed the outlines of his plan almost two years before and he convinced Major Heidari, his commanding officer at the Revolutionary Guards' Quds Force, that the plan would work. Heidari and Najidad spent nearly a year refining the plan, recruiting agents and putting them in place.

So far, every part of the plan had worked perfectly. Saman had befriended the sergeant's daughter, and a month later lured her to the rented villa outside Seville. The sergeant had refused to co-operate at first, until the threat from Mahmoud and the sound of his daughter's voice convinced him otherwise. It helped when Mahmoud explained to Sergeant McNair that his plan was to smuggle the nerve toxin out of the country to help his fellow freedom fighters in their battle for their own homeland.

There had been a few wrinkles in the past few days, though. He hadn't seen anything posted on their website from the two agents who were holding the sergeant's daughter in Seville. Mahmoud had a high regard for the Americans' National Security Agency and its ability to monitor international phone calls. He didn't want to risk placing a phone call to Seville or to Major Heidari in Qazvin. He was especially concerned about the lack of contact from Major Heidari, but this Colonel Kashani had an explanation.

On the other hand, they had successfully accomplished their first mission, the attack at the shopping center. Mahmoud had hoped for more deaths than the 28 now being reported, but he still considered it a success, a small strike at the enemies of his country who looked the other way when thousands of his countrymen—including his own father—were killed by the Iraqi gas attacks.

The shopping center attack would also mislead the Americans, Mahmoud reasoned. And while they were reacting to the first attack, he would launch the second.

Najidad was a true believer—a believer that the Islamic Republic of Iran had its own destiny, a destiny it had strived to achieve for more than two thousand years. Najidad didn't think of himself as a revolutionary or Islamic fundamentalist at all. No, he was a patriot, fighting for the future of his people. Or was that just what he told himself to justify his war against America?

Even Najidad wasn't sure where his Persian nationalism ended and his personal hatred of America began. It was the Americans who had supported the Iraqis during their eight-year war with his nation. The Americans didn't object when Saddam gassed thousands of Iranian troops, his own father one of them. But Najidad also believed that his nation was destined to be the dominant power in the region, as it had been for centuries. And now the United States was in Iran's way, with its powerful military presence in the Gulf and throughout the region.

Ironically, in the aftermath of 9/11, many of the smaller and not so small kingdoms and countries were cooperating more than ever with the Americans. Not always openly, perhaps, but cooperating nonetheless.

Jordan, the house of Saud, Egypt, Kuwait—they couldn't seem to do enough to help the Americans Mahmoud had come to hate.

Najidad understood the fear that had spread throughout the royal families and governments of the Middle East, as Bin Laden and his supporters called for the destruction of the ruling families and the imposition of Sharia, the true Islamic rule of law. What place did megayachts and private jets and western customs have in the world of Sharia and the rule of the mullahs? Even Saddam Hussein, with an ego befitting a king, had frightened Arab leaders throughout the region far more than he irritated the Westerners.

But 9/11 and the fulminations of that idiot Sadam Hussein had given the Americans virtual free rein throughout the world. Mahmoud's attack would punish them for that, and make them look within their own borders again.

Yes, the first strike had been a success. It had proved the nerve toxin was as lethal as expected, and now America was frightened again. And he, Mahmoud, had done it with just a few people. True, only two dozen or so people had died, not as many as he had hoped for. But just wait until tomorrow.

The next strike would be in Texas. With the help of a computer specialist in Qazvin, Mahmoud had surveyed several oil refineries in America's own Gulf states—Mississippi, Louisiana and Texas. They had chosen the refinery in Baytown because it was the largest, and there were a dozen small airfields within a 25-mile radius. Capable of processing more than 550,000 barrels of oil a day, the Baytown Refinery satisfied just over 5 percent of America's daily appetite for gas, diesel and heating oil.

The attack would put Baytown out of production for several months, perhaps even a year or more. What would a 10 percent cut in gasoline supplies do to the American people and the American economy? Major Heidari had run an economic model on that scenario, and the predicted damage was serious.

The oil embargo put into place by the Arab oil-producing states after the Yom Kippur War, and the subsequent gas crisis of 1973-74, led to higher prices, gas rationing, inflation and even a mild recession throughout the Western world. It also led to an influx of huge amounts of cash to the oil exporters of the Middle East. Perhaps most of all, it made the Americans and their allies realize—at least for a little while—just how vulnerable they were.

The beauty of my plan, Mahmoud believed, was that it would accomplish all that again, except for generating dollars for the moneygrubbing sheikhs. Heidari's model actually predicted a small drop in worldwide prices for oil as refining capacity decreased. But the damage to the American economy and the American people would be done. Mahmoud considered it a "surgical strike," since only the Americans would be affected.

Then, as the Americans were reacting to the attack on their largest oil refinery, and realizing—again—that their American soil was not safe, there would be the third and final attack, this one by Saman. In order to achieve maximum psychological damage, her attack would take place within 48 hours of the attack on the oil refinery, while the Americans were still trying to figure out how to cope with the disabling of a major oil facility. It would strike at a very different kind of target. Saman's attack would be aimed at people, not oil tanks.

Meanwhile, Mahmoud and Saeed had more work to do. It would take them the rest of the day to transfer the nerve agent from the canisters to the tanks that would be used to disperse the toxin at the Baytown Refinery. The material had to be handled very carefully, of course, but Saeed had already proved he had the skills and equipment to do the job.

This job was a little trickier than preparing the aerosol canisters. Saeed was mixing the VX-212 with a fine, slightly adhesive liquid. The resulting compound would be heavier than air, and it would leave an invisible toxic residue. It would be both lethal and very difficult to clean up.

After two years of planning and several months of putting that plan in action, they were very close. Another day, perhaps two. He just hoped that the colonel, the one with all the questions, didn't interfere anymore.

Our attack on the shopping center must have been quite a surprise, Mahmoud thought to himself. *And why couldn't Major Heidari deal with him and leave Najidad to his work?*

That same morning
Baytown, Texas

Special Agent in Charge Mike Stanton and three FBI agents had arrived in Baytown late the night before. The emergency call from Tom Donniger, director of the FBI's national counter-WMD team, had come in on Saturday afternoon. Stanton was at Minute Maid Park, enjoying an afternoon game the Astros were winning in their home ballpark, when his cell phone vibrated. He spent several minutes on the phone with Donniger. After finishing the call with the assistant director, he immediately placed calls to the WMD field coordinators at the FBI offices in San Antonio and Dallas, who put their own teams on short-notice call. Nearly two dozen agents would be in the Baytown area by Sunday afternoon, with another two dozen available on four hours notice.

As coordinator of the Houston WMD unit, Stanton's mission was to "investigate, disrupt and prevent" an attack such as the one now being threatened. He had to plan and prepare for the arrival of more than 20 agents who would need oversight and direction. It had become obvious in earlier drills that it does no good to have a lot of manpower if most of them have nothing to do.

Stanton's first steps were to set up shop for the Baytown team he was putting together and to notify local authorities. His first call was to the head of security for the Baytown refinery, who had offered them office space and telecommunications. That location would have to do until an FBI operations specialist located another site and set up a fully secure communications and IT facility.

They weren't starting from scratch. Donniger had briefed him about the potential threat. He had also sent him an encrypted signal on the secure FBI internet service assigning him an address and password to access the team website. Stanton and his fellow agents had already reviewed everything the team members had posted, along with the threaded conversations that had taken place to date.

The good news was that Stanton's WMD team had conducted their most recent training drill only three months before, and the drill had been at the Baytown facility. True, that simulation was based on an armed attack on the facility, but at least they already knew the security and operations people and were familiar with the physical plant. The bad news was that they weren't even sure that Baytown was the target, and they had no idea of the specifics—just that it involved the use of a highly toxic nerve agent.

Stanton assigned Frank Beckman, his second-in-command, to brief the chief of security for the refinery, a man named Tyler, and the local authorities. Tyler was a former police chief from the San Antonio area, and Stanton had been impressed by him at the last exercise.

It would be up to the local authorities, primarily Baytown's mayor and chief of police, to mobilize the emergency responders. Stanton had stressed to the mayor that the local people would have to prepare quietly. There was nothing to be gained by alerting the local civilians. That was likely to panic the community and alert the potential attackers at the same time.

The WMD response team had carefully evaluated the pros and cons of mass evacuation following the last drill. Evacuation sounded like a good idea—except they had no way of knowing if Baytown was even the target. Organizing a mass evacuation would require a major public communications effort, and that would certainly get the attackers' attention. The suspected terrorists would just adapt and move on to a secondary target.

Stanton's cell phone rang. He looked at the screen and saw it was Donniger, the national coordinator. He pressed the "talk" button.

"Special Agent in Charge Stanton."

"Mike, this is Tom Donniger here. I'm at headquarters in D.C. How's your operation going there?"

"Good morning, Tom. We've got a temporary operations center setup in the refinery. I've also got someone setting up a secure facility in town and we'll move there within two hours, three at the latest. We've briefed the mayor and chief of police. They're alerting their first responders and the local hospital personnel. No evacuation, right, like we talked about?"

"That's right. We won't make any public announcements, and no one but the mayor and the refinery people know about the threat. Everyone else has been told this is a repeat drill."

"Good. With what happened in Richmond yesterday, the last thing we need is to create panic. What about your own people and their gear? Do you have all the hazmat equipment in place?"

"Yes. Every agent has his own hazmat gear and we've got extra units here at the refinery. The coordinators from San Antonio and Dallas are sending in some additional gear with their liaison agent. That should be here within an hour."

"OK, any equipment or assistance you need from here, just let me know. You're ready to co-ordinate with the San Antonio and Dallas guys?"

"We're reviewing our action plan right now. Beckman and I pulled up the current WMD attack action plan after you called yesterday. It looks pretty good, but we revised it for this scenario. It's posted on the website, and I asked Millhauser and Goodman to go over it, see how they like it."

"OK, I don't want to get in your way. I'll look at the plan online. I know we talked about it after your last drill. But there is something I'm particularly concerned about. Actually, a lot of things."

"Well, there's a lot to be concerned about. This is something we've dreaded since 9/11. Is there something specific, Tom?"

"Yeah, Mike. I know it's your operation, but I recommend against pulling in any more agents from San Antonio or Dallas based on a tip from someone we don't know, someone who could be a foreign agent or terrorist himself. I think he was feeding us disinformation as part of the Richmond attack. An Army CID investigator we're working with thinks it's good intel, but this is way out of his league. What if Dallas or San Antonio is the target? Or Houston? I don't want us putting all our eggs in one basket."

"Got it, Tom. I'll keep it in mind. And I'll keep you in the loop."

"Yeah, make sure you do. My director was already looking over my shoulder. After what happened yesterday, now the President wants hourly updates too."

Ft. Belvoir

Ben was in Major Corliss' office, going over the Tupelo case and the previous day's attack in Richmond. Now that the FBI was in a full court press, with their National Security Branch alerted and involved, and the Army sergeant who had stolen government property in custody, Ben's job was pretty much done. He had offered to continue working on the case, but Donniger's answer was, "We'll call you. Your only job now is to be ready to talk to this guy Julian if he calls again."

Ben wanted to make sure that he and his boss were alright after Ben had evaded the FBI surveillance on him and left two agents sitting in a parking lot for several hours. After all, he had briefed his boss about the call from McNair. How was he to know the FBI would follow him?

"Don't worry about it, Ben," Major Corliss told him. "You were on Army business and you were contacting your suspect. Technically, it was none of their business."

"That's how I see it, so I'm not concerned. Besides, there's no way Donniger or his agents were going to bring McNair in. And now the guy *is* in custody and he's telling us everything he knows."

"Well, it's tough to argue with success, so let me worry about Donniger. You handled it fine, and you did the right thing to give me a heads-up. It might have been touchy otherwise."

"Well, you usually give me a lot of leeway, but this is a special case."

"Just so you know, that's why I kept Donniger in the loop. He knew McNair contacted you."

"You told him?" Ben asked, surprised that his boss had gone behind his back.

"Yeah, I told him. I didn't think he would put a tail on you—or maybe they were already there. But I also told him not to worry, that you could handle it."

Ben didn't know whether to be pleased at his boss' confidence in him or annoyed that he had alerted Donniger.

"On the other hand," Corliss continued, "Your losing the FBI team sure pissed them all off. I guess they'll just have to get over it."

Ben returned to his office. He still had access to the team website and he had looked through the entries covering the past 24 hours before meeting with Major Corliss. He was up-to-date with the activities around Baytown. Could the FBI team prevent the attack? How could they if they didn't even know if Baytown was the real target?

That's what's nagging at me, Ben thought. *Why has Julian been calling? He said he was trying to prevent an incident. So why didn't he warn us about Richmond? How did he know about the cyber attacks against the oil refineries, or about McNair and his daughter, for that matter? Who was he? More importantly, who did he work for?*

Ben thought back to his talk with McNair the day before. He had been very clear—he had never heard the voice before. Julian was not Joseph. Clearly, he was a new player. *Who was he working for?* Ben reached for the phone. He wondered how the efforts to match a license plate were going.

166

It was almost noon and Special Agent in Charge Stanton and his team had been busy. They were still working out of a small outbuilding at the refinery. Their own operations center in Baytown itself, away from the refinery, was taking longer to set up than he expected, but the operations people had assured him it would be ready in another two hours.

Stanton and his team had developed and refined their counter-WMD plan over a period of several years. The plan was designed around what had become the classic FBI action plan for domestic terror threats, an approach known as PDC: *Prevent, Disrupt, Cope.*

The *Prevent* tactics use intelligence and investigative work to achieve the ideal outcome: prevent an attack. The public rarely heard about these successes, most of them relatively low-level or localized threats that the FBI had thwarted. Occasionally, the media picked up on a failed attempt when the FBI moved in and arrested suspects.

In this case, the intelligence had come from national sources, primarily Army CID and NSA. But all the intelligence boiled down to nothing more than the possibility that the Baytown ExxonMobil oil refinery was the next likely target of a terrorist attack using a lethal nerve agent.

The challenge to the Baytown FBI Unit was to localize that intelligence, to uncover specific information that would enable them to prevent the local attack. That would take an intensive field investigation effort— and perhaps a few lucky breaks. And time was not on their side.

The *Disrupt* component involves security—the security provided at airport terminals, sensitive government facilities or, as in this case, at the Baytown Oil Refinery. Theoretically, good security can stop an attack in those cases when *Prevent* has failed. Theoretically.

The problem with the *Disrupt* tactic is that it is primarily defensive. It gives the initiative to the attacker, who chooses the time, the place and the tactics. And it's not good enough for a security operation such as TSA to be successful 99.99 percent of the time. The defender has to bat 1.000.

At Baytown, *Disrupt* would be provided by Tyler and the rest of the security team at the refinery, under FBI supervision.

Cope comes into play when *Prevent* and *Disrupt* fail. *Cope* is what the emergency responders and hundreds of others did in Manhattan when the

World Trade Center twin towers came down. The first responses are *rescue, evacuate, treat*, and *communicate*. Eventually all levels of local, state and federal government become involved.

Cope is also why the CDC in Atlanta, the local first responders, and the local medical facilities, including Baytown Hospital, were quietly implementing their emergency response plans. These were the people who would have to deal with the outcome of a successful attack.

Meanwhile, Stanton had already talked with Millhauser and Goodman, the WMD coordinators from San Antonio and Dallas. The three of them had gone over the action plan put together by Stanton and his second-in-command. Agents from all three field offices were onsite and had started their assignments. Tyler, the head of security for the refinery, had beefed up the refinery's internal security and instituted Code Red precautions, as called for in the WMD action plan they had designed with the FBI nearly two years before.

The goal, of course, was to prevent an attack. That would take manpower, legwork, and a lot of investigation work. He hated to admit it, but a little luck might be the most important ingredient.

What experience teaches any investigator is that no one lives in a vacuum. Unless these suspects had never been to the Baytown area, someone had seen them, talked to them, sold them gas, food, clothes, equipment or *something*. If these agents were operating in the Baytown area, someone must have had contact with them.

Stanton had more than a dozen agents available for field investigation, and more agents on standby if needed. The coordinators would question civilians—grocery store clerks, fast food workers, gas station attendants, bank tellers, hardware store clerks, motel workers, real estate agents. In-house data analysts would comb through security and traffic cameras. The WMD coordinator began to worry about the scope of the work and the manpower he had available. He also began to wonder about Assistant Director Donniger's advice not to call in more agents from San Antonio and Dallas.

Ft. Belvoir

Ben was on the phone with an analyst at FBI headquarters in Washington. He was checking on the FBI's attempt to identify Julian's car by matching a license plates from a traffic cam shot with recent car rentals.

"So no match with any rental car plates?" he said to the analyst.

"No, no luck so far, and we've checked most of the ones we've got. But we did get something—a shot of a guy in the right time sequence who looks interesting."

"Interesting how?" Ben asked.

"Well, the security cams picked up a guy who was in the area, could be Middle Eastern. We found him in a couple of shots, but none during the time when the call was taking place."

"Anything more specific?"

"Not yet. We're running a facial recognition program against all the INS photos of non-citizens coming into an East Coast port of entry in the past month. Nothing yet, but the photo isn't too good. Want me to send you our best shot of the guy?" the analyst asked Ben.

"Yeah, that would be great. How come this isn't up on the team website yet?" Ben had checked the site before calling the analyst and hadn't seen anything about the Skyhawk search.

"I ran it by Assistant Director Donniger, but he didn't want it up there yet. He doesn't think the intel is good enough."

"Uh huh," Ben muttered. "Alright, I'll look for the photo. Thanks for the info."

"No problem, Captain. I just sent it to your cell phone—you should have it any second."

Ben hung up and heard a ping from his phone. There was the e-mail and the attachment. He opened it and saw a medium resolution photo of a dark-haired man, maybe in his late 40s, who was looking away from the camera. The shot might not be good enough to get a match even if INS has a photo on file, he thought. *Hello, is that you, Julian?* Ben wondered.

He also began to wonder about how Donniger was handling this operation.

Early afternoon
Baytown

Stanton was looking over the gridwork and assignments when his cell phone rang. He didn't recognize the number, but all the team members had this number. He pressed the *Talk* button.

"Special Agent in Charge Stanton."

"Special Agent Stanton, this is Captain Ben Hawkins of Army CID."

Stanton recognized the name. This was the guy who had investigated the shortage in the nerve agent at the Army chemical facility. His boss had then called in the FBI and Homeland Security.

"Yes, Captain. What can I do for you? We're kind of busy down here."

"I know, Agent Stanton, I know. I'm the guy who got the tip about looking at Baytown." Ben wanted to make sure the FBI agent would take him seriously.

"Oh, that's right. You were the contact for one of the terrorists, weren't you?" There was a lot of information on the site by now, which was one of the downsides of the new "share everything" approach put into place after Sept. 11. Stanton had forgotten about the connection between the Army investigator and the mysterious caller who might—or might not—be part of the terrorist cell.

"I picked up the guy, an Army non-com, who stole the nerve agent and handed it over to our suspect, and yes, I also got the phone calls from someone who knows a lot about what's going on. He's using the name Julian."

"Got it. And he's the source of the intel on Baytown."

"That's right. But as you know, he didn't give me anything more specific than that Baytown is the probable target, and he never warned us about Richmond. So you've got your hands full trying to pin it down."

"Yes, and there's a lot going on right now. But hold on...you said, 'probable target.' I was told there were several other possibilities, like Galveston or Baton Rouge."

"Told by whom? Donniger?"

"As a matter of fact, yes. He cautioned me that there were several other possible targets for a chemical attack."

"I can't disagree with that, Mr. Stanton. There *are* other possible targets. But this contact, Julian, whoever he is, knows a lot about what's going on. And he says the target is Baytown."

"But you've got no confirmation, right? This is single source information, isn't it?"

"True enough. But think about it. Why would this guy contact us and give us *any* information? Why point us within a thousand miles if its misinformation?"

"Yeah, I've been wondering about that. Maybe he was doing a 'smoke and mirrors' act, diverting your attention, make you spend your resources elsewhere, which is why he didn't tell you about Richmond. So what are you suggesting?"

"I'm not sure I'm suggesting anything, other than I think this informant is giving us good intel. Not *all* the information we need, but the information he *has* given us has been accurate. How are you doing with your search?"

"I've got a dozen agents out in the field, but we've got hundreds of people to interview and about a thousand square miles. It's a pretty big haystack."

"A dozen? I thought there would be more than two dozen agents there by now."

"I was advised not to call in San Antonio or Houston since they might be targets themselves."

Ben was shocked. He thought Donniger had agreed to send as much manpower as possible to Baytown. Galveston or Baton Rouge *might* be targets? So what were those agents doing?

"Listen, you're the Special Agent in Charge, I'm not FBI and Tom Donniger isn't my boss. But I'm telling you that the only intel we have says that Baytown is the target, and it doesn't make sense to me to conduct a search half-assed. If you can get another dozen agents, I say you should do it. What have you got to lose?"

Stanton paused. What he heard made sense. Donniger's comments were suggestions, not a direct order, Stanton told himself. As the on-site agent in charge, he had a lot of leeway. On the other hand, it was his ass on the line, not this guy on the phone.

"Thanks for the heads-up, Captain. I'll take it under advisement."

"Thanks for hearing me out. Like I said—we don't have much, but what we do have says it's Baytown."

"Thank you again. I've got to go." Stanton hung up. This guy wasn't FBI and Stanton wasn't ready to tell him his intentions, but he was getting more and more concerned about his lack of manpower.

Late afternoon

Stanton was in the FBI office that was now operational in Baytown, about five miles from the refinery. He had a direct line to Tyler, the security chief at the refinery. Tyler had implemented the Code Red plan and reported the refinery as secured from both physical and electronic intrusion. Extra guards had been posted and all vehicles entering the refinery had been cordoned off to a separate area for inspection. The refinery IT people had instituted a new, level three encryption program.

It was just over 24 hours ago that Stanton had taken the call from Assistant Director Donniger. By now, a dozen FBI agents had questioned more than 200 individuals in the Baytown area and had come up with nothing. They each carried a copy of a digitally manipulated photograph of Joseph that Sergeant McNair and an FBI technician had developed. So far, no one had identified the man. They needed to expand the search area, but the question of manpower kept coming up. He needed more intelligence and more men—and preferably, both.

Ft. Belvoir

Ben was still in his office, looking over the team website. As far as he could tell, they were at a dead end, almost as if they were just waiting for another attack to occur. In a way, it was worse than 9/11. This time they had been warned, and Homeland Security, the FBI and NSA were all working on it, but bottom line, they weren't any closer to recovering the VX-212 than they were a few days ago.

The deputy director of the CIA had already reported that several of their assets within Iran had reported increased activity in senior security circles and several government offices. The FBI searches in the Baytown area were updated every 15 minutes, but each the same thing: "Investigation ongoing. No results to report."

Ben's phone rang.

"Captain Hawkins, this is Assistant Director Donniger."

"Yes, Assistant Director?" Ben noted the formal tone and the careful name identification, and he assumed the call was being recorded. *OK fair enough*, he thought.

"I understand you put in a call to the special agent-in-charge at Bay-town," Donniger said, in voice just a little more formal and louder than necessary.

"That's right, Tom, I did," Ben answered, trying to keep the conversation friendly. "And I was surprised to hear that you don't have more men on the ground there." *Might as well stake out my position up front and let him criticize it, rather than let him put me on the defensive.*

"And you recommended that Special Agent in Charge Stanton bring in more manpower."

"Yes, I did. Unless you have some other leads they're working on, it seems to me this one should get a lot more the attention."

"Let's make a deal. You're still on the team because of your work with McNair and because you're the only one this guy Julian has contacted. But you do your work. Leave the running of this operation to the FBI."

"I'll do just that, Assistant Director. But if I have an opinion, I'm gonna voice it—unless, of course, you want to put it in writing that I shouldn't offer any ideas or comments." Like any organization, the FBI had its own bureaucratic rules and games. But Ben had been in the Army for more than 10 years and the Army was a pretty good training ground for learning how to work the chain of command, insist on written orders, and do whatever else it takes to get a job done.

"Fine. You have an opinion, put it on the forum. Or call me. Just don't bother my operations people."

"I'll take it under advisement, Tom. But if I were you—I'd send in some more agents. And I *will* put that on the website."

Ben hung up. He was surprised, not so much that Donniger was pissed off, but that he had bothered to call him at all. *Maybe that's what happens when you're used to getting your way,* he thought. His mind wandered back to the threat facing them and the calls he had received from Julian when his phone beeped.

Ben looked at his cell phone screen as Sara's number popped up. He pressed the connect button.

"Hi, honey," he said. "How's everything?"

"Everything is great, here, Ben. Did you forget?"

Apparently he had. "Forget what?" he answered, trying to pay attention, but his mind kept wandering back to the irritating call from Donniger.

"You were going to try to get out early, maybe meet me down at the Officers' Club." They had reached an unspoken understanding not to spend time in Washington unless absolutely necessary.

Ben's involvement with the threat team had become minimal since McNair had been picked up. Mostly Donniger wanted him available in case Julian called again, but otherwise he seemed to want Hawkins and Army CID on the sidelines. That was fine with Ben and his boss, Major Corliss, since they had no experience or training in anti-terrorism. Even Julian's calls had not panned out yet and maybe his "red herring" idea had been right all along. Maybe Julian *was* trying to make them look in the other direction.

"Sorry, Sara. I was just going over the case with some FBI people and time kind of slipped away."

"I thought you were out of the loop now that this is an FBI operation."

"Yeah, I know, and I am—sort of. But I can't put it away, particularly when we're all waiting for something terrible to happen. I feel like I should be doing more. Could I have done something different to prevent the shopping mall attack? What did I miss?"

"First of all, you're only one person, one investigator, and a damn good one too. The FBI couldn't stop the attack, the whole Homeland Security Department couldn't stop it, so stop beating yourself up."

"Sure, that's what I keep telling myself. But maybe I let that guy Julian lead me on. Anyway, the Assistant Director, Donniger, just made it very clear that he wants me to stay out of the way."

"Well, that sounds foolish to me. You're the one who's gotten phone calls from that Army guy, and now this mystery man, this Julian."

"That's one of the things bothering me. If this guy knows a lot about this operation, why is he sharing the info with me? Did he know about the Richmond attack? But there's something else...."

"Which is...," Sara prompted him.

"How is it that he knows a lot about what's going on, but he doesn't know the specifics?" Ben asked, as much to himself as to Sara.

"I'm not sure what you mean."

"I'm not sure exactly either. I guess I'm wondering how this guy Julian knows a lot of details, but he doesn't know when and where. I don't

174

think he *did* know about the Richmond attack. It's almost as if he's finding out as he goes along. So who is he? Here's a guy who's picking up information, feeds it to us, but he doesn't have all the specifics. So he's not on the inside, he wasn't in on the planning...." Ben said slowly, trying to get a hold on the thoughts circulating through his mind, thoughts that wouldn't quite surface.

"It's almost as if he came across this operation, and now he's trying to help us stop it. But he can't just pick up the phone and call it off." Ben's shoulders sagged. There was nothing hard here, nothing to put in front of the FBI team—but there *was* something.

Ben considered putting the thought up on the forum website, but he was beginning to think his comments weren't carrying much weight anymore. Maybe they never did. Maybe he was just the local investigator, the foot soldier who uncovered the crime and brought in the perpetrator. National security and terrorist sleeper cells and foreign agents were out of his league. They were certainly outside his experience.

"Ben, it sounds as if you have a lot more thinking to do. If you don't want to leave your office, I can pick something up at the Officer's Club and bring it over there. Say, 45 minutes."

"Sure, honey, great." He wasn't listening very closely. Sara had seen him like this before.

"OK, see you in a little bit." Sara hung up. The best thing she could do right now was to serve as Ben's sounding board. Making sure he had dinner couldn't hurt either.

Ben was still holding onto his cell phone, lost in thought. *How is it that Julian knows a lot...but not enough?* He discarded the idea that Julian was holding back information. Why would Julian have contacted them in the first place if he were going to withhold information? Then Ben began to think about Jennifer McNair waking up one morning and finding everyone gone.

He was still lost in thought when his cell phone beeped again. This time it wasn't Sara.

"Hello, Captain. This is Julian"

"Julian. I was just thinking about you."

"And I have been working on the problem facing you. I have more information for you."

"Why don't you just give me your phone number so I can contact you?" Ben asked him.

"I will consider it. I must consider that perhaps you could locate the phone even with the GPS locator disabled. That would not be good for either one of us, Captain, I assure you, and I do not have time to play phone games as I did on the first call. Are you ready for the information?"

"Yes, of course."

"A few moments ago I sent a photo to your cell phone. This is a photo of the man you are looking for. One more thing. This man has a background in aviation. At least, a background of sorts. He knows how to fly small planes. I will call again within 24 hours, sooner if I have new information. But I should caution you, I may not have any additional information for you or your FBI."

"Julian?"

"Yes, Captain?"

"Why didn't you tell us about yesterday's attack? Twenty eight people died. I thought you were trying to stop them. You know, the ones you called 'crazy people'."

"I am very sorry for what happened yesterday, Captain. But you must believe me. I knew nothing about it until I saw it on the news."

He paused, waiting for Ben to respond.

"I will call you again within 24 hours, but I cannot promise any more information." Then he hung up.

Colonel Kashani looked at the screen on his laptop computer. He was now in the third of the three rooms he had rented, this one in the JW Marriott on Pennsylvania Avenue, right in the capital itself, only a few blocks from the White House. He had returned his rental car, but he had another one reserved in a different name.

Yes, you must believe me, my young friend, he thought to himself again.

Kashani was becoming increasingly worried that the next attack would not be stopped and all his efforts would have accomplished nothing. The last thing the Revolutionary Council needed was for the Americans looking to lash out again. Iraq and Afghanistan had already seen what that could lead to. And General Gulab was convinced that their Arab neighbors wouldn't stand in the way if the United States took action to stop their nuclear program. The Arabs were even more opposed to Iran's nuclear ambitions than the West was. They were just a lot quieter about it.

There were also many voices in their own government already opposed to Iran's nuclear ambitions. An outraged United States would give them the perfect pretext to stop their nuclear program. Kashani could already hear the arguments from the more moderate forces within the Council: "We must stop this madness or the Americans will stop it for us."

Ft. Belvoir

Ben downloaded the photo as soon as Kashani hung up. It showed a pleasant looking man in his late 20's, with straight dark hair and a medium dark complexion. The photo looked remarkably like the image created by Harry McNair and the FBI technician. Ben forwarded it to the team website with a red flag alert, along with the information about their suspect's ability to pilot an airplane.

Ben had barely been able to contain himself during the call from Julian, but he had forced himself to calm down when Julian said he had a photo of their suspect. *Better to gain intelligence than to lose his temper and maybe lose his contact*, he told himself. *But is he trying to help us, or is he sending us on false leads?*

He decided to make another call to Baytown. He would deal with Donniger later.

Mike Stanton saw the caller ID and picked up the call on the second ring. "What can I do for you, Captain?"

"Mr. Stanton, I just received another phone call from my contact, Julian. He's the unknown informant who's been feeding me information."

"Yeah, Captain, I recognize the name. He's the one who put us on to Baytown, right?"

"That's right. His first intel was to look at cyber intrusions at oil refineries in your area, which we found. He also knows the specifics about what was stolen, so he has good sources. Five minutes ago I got two more things from him."

"What is it?"

"The first item is a photo of our suspect. And it agrees very closely with the facial rendition Sergeant McNair put together with an FBI tech. I put it up on the website and red-flagged it, but I'll send it to you directly if you give me your e-mail address."

Stanton gave Ben his address. Then he said, "I just got pinged, so maybe that's your photo on the website. By the way, I spoke to Assistant Director Donniger about your suggestion that we get some more manpower down here."

"Oh, I know. He called me about an hour ago and told me to stop interfering."

"But here you are."

"Yes, here I am, Mr. Stanton. You ready for the second item?"

"Yes, go ahead."

"Julian said our suspect, this guy Joseph, has a background in aviation. Specifically, small planes. He knows how to fly them."

"You're still paying attention to that informant."

"Yes sir, I am. I don't think he knew about the first operation, but he seems to know about this one."

"OK, so maybe he's useful, maybe not. He says our suspect can fly a small plane. I'll give that some thought and update the people here. Anything else?"

"Yes. He only learned how to fly about two years ago."

Special Agent in Charge Stanton was quiet for a moment. "That *is* interesting. Interesting—makes you wonder if he's planning on flying a plane loaded with nerve agent into the oil refinery. By the way, I called my counterparts in San Antonio and Dallas about an hour ago. I should have another dozen agents here later this evening."

"Donniger agreed?"

"I didn't ask him. Captain, this is my operation. He can make suggestions and he can replace me, but he can't overrule me. I gotta go now and put together a plan to canvas any aviation-related sites in the area. Thanks for the heads up. Just so you know, we don't have any local information yet. Either these guys have never been here or they are very, very careful."

"Good luck, Mr. Stanton. I'll call you as soon as I hear anything new."

Ben hung up and sat back. OK, they were making a little progress—maybe. Now the Baytown team could focus their search, they had an actual photo of the suspect and in a few hours they would have another dozen agents who could expand the search area. That *was* progress—providing Julian's information was good.

He was still thinking about Julian's motivation when Sara stuck her head in his office.

"Soup's on," she called out.

Ben looked up, startled.

"How'd you get here so fast?" he asked her.

"Fast? I called you almost an hour ago. They were a little slow at the Officers' Club, but here's dinner."

She took out two sandwiches and put them on Ben's desk. "Why don't we have these in the conference room?" Sara figured that would be one way to get away Ben from his desk for a few minutes. She was pretty sure he would be spending a few more hours on the post before coming home.

Tuesday

Baytown, Texas
Just before dawn

Mike Stanton heard a knock on his door. He had fallen asleep just a few hours before on a cot in the back area of the large office space his team had activated the day before.

Before trying to get some sleep, Stanton had worked with Beckman, his second-in-command, about the latest information on their suspect. The two men decided to develop an operational plan that used most of the additional agents from San Antonio and Dallas to handle the investigation of all local aviation facilities and personnel.

The bad news was that there were more than a half dozen small airfields located within 50 miles of the Baytown Oil Refinery, and more than 20 airfields within 100 miles. Since no local civilians reported seeing the suspects, the plan called for a physical search and questioning of aviation personnel, starting with the airport facilities 50 miles out, and working in. Investigation of facilities outside the 50 mile range would start with phone calls to the airfield managers, followed up by on-site visits after all sites within 50 miles were investigated.

"Yeah, what is it?" Stanton called out. His watch read a few minutes before 5 a.m.

The door opened and Beckman stop his head in. "Boss, we have a contact that could be significant. I think you'll want to check it out."

About the same time

Mahmoud looked at his watch. The sun would be coming up soon. He got up and looked out the hangar window. He could see the first streaks of dawn off to the east.

A good day for flying, he thought. He had been checking the weather forecast every day. The day's forecast called for warm temperatures, with hazy skies and only a slight breeze out of the east. Yes, a perfect day for flying. Maybe a perfect day for dying, too, which Mahmoud had accepted as a possibility. He wasn't interested in martyrdom, unlike those zealots who seemed almost anxious to die. On the other hand, as his father used to tell him as he struggled with his war injuries, death is certain. It's only the timing we're not sure about.

Saeed had finished his work late last night as promised. Together they had tested the pressurized containers with an oil and water mix one more time. The system worked flawlessly. Then Saeed, with Mahmoud acting as his assistant, replaced the oil and water test mixture with the oil/VX-212 mix. The oil would be the carrier for the VX-212. The deadly mix, dispersed in a fine mist, would literally rain down on the entire oil refinery complex as Najidad flew just a few hundred feet above the complex.

"You've done well, Saeed. Very well. I will be sure to say so in my report to Qazvin," Najidad had promised his assistant.

"Thank you, Mahmoud. I am only doing my duty," Saeed answered. Mahmoud Najidad made him very nervous, and he was anxious to finish this assignment and be rid of him. Then perhaps he and his family would be safe again.

Now Saeed was sleeping on a cot at the back of the hangar. He had fallen asleep hoping if he would see his wife and daughter soon. Mahmoud had told him he had one more task for him, though. After the attack, he was to pick up Mahmoud at a location they had already scouted, a deserted field about 30 miles northeast of Liberty. After that, they would split up and Saeed would be allowed to return to his pre-Najidad life in Raleigh, North Carolina. That's what Najidad had promised him.

Najidad tried to rest also, but he found he was awake most of the night. After more than two years of planning and preparation, after all the risks he had taken, in just a few more hours he would take the final steps to punish and humiliate the Great Satan. He also had one more task to finish before his preparations were complete. A necessary, if unpleasant, task. He didn't expect Saeed to understand, the way Haydar and Omid would have.

A few restless hours later he saw the first streaks of the Texas sunrise.

He would be flying a 1940 Stearman biplane. The plane was a classic old barnstormer still used sometimes for crop dusting, but mostly for tourist rides and at air shows. Najidad had purchased it a year ago, and he occasionally flew it in the area, both to keep his flying skills sharp and to let the local people get used to seeing the classic old silver-painted plane.

The Stearman had plenty of power and was equipped with an aerial smoke system and an up-to-date Garmin 250XL GPS navigation system. Najidad would use the smoke system to disperse the nerve agent from about 200 feet above the sprawling Baytown oil refinery. It would look like one of the aerial displays the previous owner had put on at several air shows around the Midwest. This time, however, it wouldn't be pretty colored smoke coming out of the Stearman, but a lethal mixture of oil and a paralyzing nerve agent.

Najidad had made several practice flights over a deserted wooded area in the Big Thicket National Preserve, about 25 miles northeast of Liberty. After locating a section roughly the same size as the huge Bayfield refinery, he practiced flying a circling pattern over the trees at 300 feet, flying a south-north leg for two minutes, making a tight 240° turn to fly a northwest-southeast leg, then turning 240° again to fly a final southwest-northeast leg. After several trials, he was able to complete the pattern in about nine minutes.

He planned to complete the pattern and then exit the airspace over the refinery and head east. He hoped any observers on the ground would simply wonder about the classic old bi-plane flying lazily over the area, at least until the nerve agent began doing its dirty work. He would then head east toward the town of Bayfield itself and disperse any of the remaining oil/toxin mix, just to add to the death toll and to keep emergency responders busy.

After completing the mission, Najidad's plan called for him to turn to the north, climb to 2,500 feet, put the Stearman on auto-pilot and head back in the direction of Liberty. The old cropduster, with its modern auto-pilot and navigational system, would continue to fly for at least another hour after he parachuted out. If everything went according to plan, he would be driving east to Beaumont while the air traffic controllers tracked the Stearman in the opposite direction. He wouldn't be meeting Saeed at a field north of Liberty. But then, Saeed wouldn't be there either.

Najidad had already programmed the refinery location into the navigation system and had made several practice flights to within five miles of the site. It would take about 30 minutes to fly from the small, uncontrolled airfield at Liberty, heading southwest to Baytown. He wouldn't be filing a flight plan, of course, but his mental time of departure was just about an hour away. Najidad wasn't experienced enough to risk flying at night, and an unregistered night flight might get the attention of an air traffic controller around Baytown and Houston anyway.

He had chosen the Liberty field for its location. At just over 30 miles from Baytown, he wouldn't be seen by the Baytown locals, but the airfield was close enough so that his final flight wouldn't take very long. It was also a small field with no control tower, which meant no radio contact.

He also took a certain satisfaction in the name. *Liberty Airfield.* Just like Camp Liberty in Baghdad, Lady Liberty, the Liberty Bell, and who knows how else the Americans had laid claim to the name. *We'll see what liberty does for you this day*, he thought with a smirk.

How many people would die from the aerial attack? Najidad and Saeed had talked about it again last night.

Most of the personnel at the refinery would die, of course. Even if they remained indoors, most would die when the air handling system pulled the killing mixture into the air conditioning system. Some of the mixture was likely to drift downwind toward the west and kill some of the locals who lived or worked around the oil refinery. Saeed guessed that about four or five hundred people would die within the first hour. Najidad guessed the number would be more than a thousand, especially when he flew over the town of Bayfield as the coup de grace of the aerial attack.

Actually, neither of them were particularly interested in how many American civilians would die at their hands. Najidad had not gone through two years of planning and preparation, with some risk to his own life, just for the deaths of a few thousand Americans. No, this was not a mere terror attack that killed a few dozen or a few hundred people. This was a grand strategic move against the Great Satan.

Najidad took great pride in the history and the accomplishments of his land. Wasn't his Republic of Iran the modern day successor of ancient Persia, one of the oldest nations in history? His birthplace was an ancient nation even before Muhammed the Prophet appeared to spread the word of Allah across the Middle East and beyond. They had fought the Greeks, the Romans and the Turks, recovered from the onslaughts of Alexander the Great, and survived as a Persian Shiite nation surrounded by Arab Sunnis.

But they had done more than survive. Mahmoud believed with all his heart they were destined to once again be the leader of the Middle

East. What other nation had shaken off the tentacles of the Great Satan, humiliated them, and threatened them throughout the region? Not the oil rich kings and princes, who sold their ancient lands for western gold. Not the rulers throughout the Middle East who quietly co-operated with the Americans, and even with the Jews, just to stay in power.

No, Najidad thought, it is *we* who stood up to the Americans, and stood up successfully. We humiliated them in their own embassy, threatened them in the Persian Gulf, and even today taunt them with our nuclear program.

And the day had finally arrived. Two years of planning and preparation, from Qazvin to Seville, from Washington, D.C. to Baytown, Texas. Now even the Supreme Revolutionary Council knew about his operation. In just a few more hours, the entire world would know that the attack on Sunday was just the beginning. And as the Americans struggled to deal with the first attacks on their own soil since 9/11, Saman would strike in their nation's capitol.

He, Mahmoud Najidad, would do all this. The Americans' economy would be seriously damaged, there would be fuel shortages again, and fear would spread throughout the people, just as it had after the last attack. *All this we will do using the chemical weapons you yourself created,* Najidad thought. *The world will see your hypocrisy when you preached about chemical weapons even as you had thousands of tons of these weapons yourselves. And perhaps this will repay you for the sacrifices of my father and all the other fighters who suffered because you looked the other way as Saddam and his henchmen gassed our people.*

He began his final preparations.

Baytown, Texas

"Alright, everyone ready to go?" Stanton asked the agents gathered around him.

Eight agents were in the FBI now-operational Baytown office. Beckman, Stanton's second-in-command, had briefed Stanton while he was getting dressed. Two agents had located the operator of a small airfield about 30 miles north of Baytown who recognized their suspect. The agents had rung his doorbell at 4:20 a.m. The airport manager opened the door a few moments later:

"FBI, Mr. Bennet. We need to ask you a few questions," one of the agents said, as they both showed their IDs.

"About what?" the manager asked, not quite fully awake.

"About who's using your facility, sir. May we come in?"

The two agents entered the airfield manager's home and the three of them sat at a table in the kitchen.

"What's this all about?" he asked.

"Just a few questions, sir. Do you recognize this man?" The agent showed him his mobile phone screen, which showed the photograph Ben had forwarded to Stanton.

"Yeah, sure, that's Joe."

The agents looked at each other. The younger of the two men stepped outside the kitchen to call it in.

"Do you know his last name?"

"Yeah, Joe Adams. What's this all about?"

"We need to ask him a few questions as part of an investigation we're conducting," the agent answered. "How long have you known him?"

"At 4 o'clock in the morning?" Bennet asked.

"If you could just answer the question, sir."

"Sure. About six months. He came to my place and wanted to rent a tie-down for a small plane. A beauty, too, a 1940 Stearman. Has he done something wrong?"

"We'd just like to ask him a few questions. Sorry about the hour, but we do need to locate him as soon as possible. Do you know where he is now?"

"I know he's back in the area. He rented some hangar space from me about a month ago, said he wanted to do some work on the plane inside the hangar. I saw his car by the place yesterday, although I didn't actually see him."

"You said 'back in the area,' sir," the agent prompted.

"Yeah, I didn't see him for a coupla weeks, but I saw his car by the hangar yesterday."

"Do you know where he lives?"

"Now that you mention it, I don't. But I'm sure I have a record of it on the rental agreement. I can dig it up on my computer here at home."

A few minutes later the two agents had a local address and a description of Joe Adams' car. By then, Beckman had put a phone tap on Bennet's home phone and was organizing a team of agents to head to the Liberty area.

The two agents waited in their car until the local police cruiser pulled up. One of the men approached the vehicle and showed his ID.

"OK, officer, you'll maintain watch on the house, right?"

"Yeah, got it. My chief called me and said whatever you want."

"Just so you know, this guy's not a suspect, but he might have contact with someone we're very interested in. We should be able to get another agent out to relieve you in a few hours." The agents would have preferred to keep the surveillance in-house, but they just didn't have the manpower this far out yet and they had another visit to make. The address the airport manager had given them was about 10 miles away.

Fifteen minutes later the senior of the two agents called the operations center in Baytown.

"The suspect's house is dark. No sign of any activity. We don't see a car matching the description the airport manager gave us. Nothing in the driveway, nothing in the neighborhood."

"OK, the boss says 'do not approach.' Maintain surveillance of the house. We'll have a team heading for Liberty Airfield within 10 minutes."

A few minutes later

Special Agent in Charge Mike Stanton and seven other agents were about to head for Liberty Airfield, 30 miles north of their operations center. Each agent had been issued field hazmat clothing and gear. A specialized hazmat team would be minutes behind them in a fully equipped hazmat van.

"Frank, when is that overhead visual gonna be online?" Stanton asked his second-in-command.

"The colonel in charge says the drone will be over the Liberty Air-field area in 20 minutes. The video feed is live now."

During the last simulated WMD attack, Stanton had introduced the use of an Air Force drone to monitor activities on the ground. Far quieter and less visible than a helicopter, the MQ-1B Predator could loiter overhead for more than 24 hours if they were flying it without a weapons load. The technical people referred to it as a UAV—an unmanned aerial vehicle. With a wingspan of 27 feet and a take-off weight of just over 2,000 pounds fully loaded, the Predator wasn't exactly small, but once it reached an altitude of 5,000 feet it was almost undetectable. The UAV had scored a lot of successes tracking—and killing—high value Taliban targets in Afghanistan.

This Predator was assigned to the Texas Air National Guard. The pilot was sitting in an office at Ellington Field, just south of Houston, controlling the unmanned vehicle through a satellite uplink.

Prior to the simulated attack six months earlier, Stanton had spent several hours setting up the coordination with Ellington. It had paid off during the simulation, as Stanton and his team learned how to take advantage of the real-time video feeds, which could be both optical and thermal, using the infrared camera. The use of overhead drones was becoming standard FBI practice, due in part to Stanton's report and recommendations following the Baytown drill.

Perhaps it would pay off today. The FBI team would have a birdseye view of everything that went on around Liberty Airfield, courtesy of the Texas Air National Guard. They also carried a handheld FLIR—forward looking infrared radar—that might prove useful as they approached the hangar.

"And we're receiving the signal?"

"Yes, sir. Klein is handling it and he's already receiving the video stream from the drone."

Stanton looked at the agents standing in front of him. They had already run through the plans for approaching the airfield and the hangar. They knew the drill. He still wanted to take two minutes to go over the mission one more time.

"OK, our number one priority is to locate and isolate the nerve agent. The suspect is secondary. Once located, whatever happens, the nerve agent doesn't leave that location. Everyone clear on that?"

Seven agents nodded. All but one of them had participated in the drill six months earlier. Locate and isolate. Locate and isolate. It had been drilled into them six months before, and again in the past 24 hours.

"And you know the danger. You've got your personal hazmat gear, but that's no guarantee." Each agent carried a hazmat suit and breathing apparatus, but the gear was bulky and made it impossible to move quickly or quietly. They carried the gear, but they only donned the hazmat suits or breathing apparatus when there was a specific threat.

The team was anxious to go.

"And everyone has an injector?" Stanton asked. The auto-injector would push atropine, pralidoxime and diazepene into the recipient's bloodstream. The pharmaceutical cocktail would counteract, or at least mitigate, the effects of the nerve agent. Theoretically. If given immediately.

"Secondary target is the suspect. We think there are two, a man and a woman. One way or another, they don't leave the scene."

The agents understood what that meant.

Stanton knew most of the agents had families. He knew some of their families personally. But each had volunteered for this duty. They had trained and prepared for a day such as this. They didn't need a pep talk.

"Alright, I'm not going to give you a song and dance. But this may be a chance to prevent another 9/11. And that's what we're going to do. And we're gonna do it now. Let's move out."

The team moved to their vehicles.

Two minutes later a convoy of two dark Ford Expeditions and a dark green sedan was heading north on Route 146. Liberty Airfield was 30 miles away and Stanton was pretty sure the clock was ticking.

Fifteen minutes later, the three vehicles were more than halfway to Liberty, speeding up the highway as faint streaks of light began to appear off to the east. They had alerted the local police and the emergency lights on the lead vehicle were flashing as they sped up the four-lane road.

Stanton was in the second vehicle with Klein, the agent who was monitoring the video feed from the Predator. The three FBI vehicles showed up as light-colored images on the dark background of the screen as the Predator passed overhead at just over 100 miles per hour. A few minutes later the drone was over Liberty Airfield, cruising at about 60 miles an hour at 4,000 feet. The UAV was virtually invisible at that altitude, at least to a human observer on the ground.

"What are we getting now?" Stanton asked Klein a few moments later. The agent was holding the video screen in front of him and was in full-time voice contact with the pilot, who was sitting about 40 miles away in a comfortable van at Ellington Field. He passed the small video monitor forward to Stanton.

"You can see the runway running east to west there. There's the main hangar on the south side of the runway. Most of the planes are at a tie-down area between the road and the hangar."

"The airport manager said this guy took some hangar space about a month ago and started keeping his plane inside. Make sure the pilot keeps the hangar in sight. What about warm bodies?"

Klein switched the receiver to thermal view. The Predator had the capability to scan using both optical and infrared cameras simultaneously. The infrared camera could detect thermal images from an altitude of 10,000 feet, and even higher for strong heat signatures.

"I'm picking up one image, probably a body image, moving a little bit. Another image, much lighter, stationary, not sure what it is." Klein was glad he had spent several days working with the pilots and Air National Guard people at Ellington.

"So two individuals inside the hangar," Stanton replied, feeling hopeful for the first time since the call from Donniger.

"I'd say one individual for sure, and possibly two. The second image is lighter, not moving. Maybe well-insulated, like someone's inside a sleeping bag or under a metal table. Much smaller heat signature. The stronger image is starting to move around now, definitely a person."

"And the plane—an old bi-plane, looks like a crop duster, silver. Any sign of it outside the hangar?"

Klein knew what the plane looked like. He had gone online and downloaded a photo of a 1940 Stearman, and was holding the photo in his right hand. He talked into his mouthpiece, asking the pilot to move the optical camera over the tie-down area.

"The light's not great, chief, but I don't see anything like that." Klein wasn't an expert on old single-engine planes, but there were no more than a dozen planes parked outside and none was a biplane as far as he could tell.

The three-car caravan crossed Trinity River, which put the airfield about a mile away. Stanton ordered the lead vehicle to reduce speed and shut down the emergency lights. In a few moments they would turn off all lights. There were a few more streaks of light in the dawn sky to the east.

The team had taken 10 minutes to plan and rehearse the approach and assault before leaving Baytown. Stanton and the lead driver would drive their two cars right up to the hangar door. The third car would hold back near the single runway, driver in place and engine running.

The hazmat van should be a half hour behind. Stanton actually hoped they would need the hazmat specialists—that would mean they had found the chemical weapon—but he hoped they wouldn't have much to do other than secure the material. There were a lot of *ifs*, though. *If* this was their target. *If* the nerve agent was still here. *If* they were in time.

Stanton ordered the three drivers to stop just before the turn into the airfield. The cars were darkened now, but daylight was creeping up over the horizon, and visibility was improving. It was improving for their suspect as well, so time was running out.

"OK, Klein, what've you got?"

"No movement outside. One thermal image inside the hangar, moving around a fair amount, second image still hasn't moved. But Captain Beale just gave me a sideways look from 2,000 feet and the hangar doors are open. Hold on. Hold on. Mike, I'm getting another thermal image. Increasing. Increasing. Still getting hotter. No movement. Jesus, I'd say someone just started an engine."

At about the same time
Belmont Bay

Ben looked over at the bedside clock. It was just before 7 a.m. in Virginia. Usually by now he would be up and getting ready to head into Ft. Belvoir. He'd had a restless night, with thoughts of VX-212 and Harry McNair and Julian running through his head. He couldn't accept that an American citizen, military or otherwise, had let several pounds of weaponized nerve toxin get into the hands of a foreign agent. What would he have done if he had a daughter being held hostage?

Where were the two suspected terrorists, Joseph and Elena? Why hadn't the FBI been able to make any progress locating and apprehending them?

And what was Julian up to? His information seemed to be good, but there was no way to know for sure—yet. Was Julian feeding them bad intel? Maybe the whole oil refinery attack was a red herring after all. Maybe the target was something else entirely. He wondered how the WMD team in Baytown was doing.

Dawn
Liberty Airfield

Mike Stanton was thinking it was looking more and more like this was it. The airport manager, Bennet, had identified Joseph. The agents who had questioned the airport manager just over an hour ago had forwarded information about his airplane, an old crop-duster bi-plane with a powerful new smoke system. Bennet had seen the man he knew as Joseph Adams test it a month ago. And now someone, presumably Joseph, was messing around inside a hangar at dawn, and it looked as if he could be getting a small plane ready for flight.

"Where is the target now?" he asked Klein, who was concentrating on the only image that had moved. Air Force Captain Beale, the pilot at Ellington, had brought the Predator down to 2,000 feet, and was focusing on the hangar and the surrounding 50 yards. The images were remarkably clear.

"Target of interest is at the back southwest corner of the hangar. Some movement, not a lot. New hot image still getting hotter, no movement. One last thermal image, not much of a body signature, still no movement."

"Are you getting this on the handheld?" Stanton asked another agent.

"Yes sir, I had the same two images and then a third image lit up. Very concentrated, very hot, no movement."

The convoy of three vehicles stopped just before the service road into the airfield. Stanton looked over and took a quick glance at the display of thermal images transmitted by the Predator. "Make sure you stay close to me, Taylor," he instructed the agent with the handheld unit. Then he issued the command into his radio: "Everybody, Go, Go, Go!"

The lead Expedition turned into the airfield road and accelerated. The driver moved quickly down the first 200 yards, then tapped the brakes as he moved slightly left and headed across the runway. The second SUV followed the lead while the third vehicle, with two agents inside, pulled alongside the runway and stopped. Their assignment was clear and specific: no aircraft was to use the runway.

The two SUVs approached from the side of the hangar and pulled up just before the open hangar doors. Six agents exited the cars quietly. They could hear the steady *thump-thump* of an engine at idle. Two agents, dressed in full field hazmat gear, with "FBI" stenciled in large yellow letters on the front and back, remained just outside the hangar on one side of the hangar doors. Four agents crouched on the other side of the hangar opening, each resting a hand on the shoulder of the man in front of him. Stanton was the first man in the group. He peered around the open hangar door and saw the silver bi-plane toward the rear of the hangar space.

Stanton raised his fist for a moment, signaled by pumping his fist up and down, and then started to move forward. The four agents moved inside quickly, fanning out to the sides of the hangar. One of them carried a wireless Taser XREP, which used a 12-gauge shotgun to extend the range of the stun gun device to nearly 100 feet. Between the impact of the projectile and nearly 20,000 volts of shock, the target would be disabled for at least 60 seconds. If they could stun the suspect, fine. If not....

The sound of the Stearman's engine had masked their approach. The four agents were halfway to the back corner before Najidad saw them. His jaw dropped and he froze in place.

"FBI, FBI, don't move!" Stanton yelled.

Najidad stared at the agents in shock for a moment. Then he dropped the aerial map he was carrying and ran toward the tail end of the bi-plane just a few feet away. The four men were more than 40 feet away and he could still make it to the plane.

Two of the agents ran toward Najidad with their 9mm semi-automatics trained on him. Another agent was armed with a conventional 12-gauge shotgun and he moved to the front of the plane and began pumping rounds into the engine block, just as they had rehearsed in Baytown. His job was to make sure the Stearman never left the hangar.

Najidad almost made it to the tail of the plane when he was hit in the leg by a 9mm slug. Now the bi-plane wings partially blocked the agents' field of fire and Najidad was able to climb into the cockpit before a second bullet hit him in the left side and entered his lung. He fell inside the cockpit and ducked down as bullets peppered the fabric covering and he could hear the slapping sounds as the rounds struck around him.

The 12-gauge heavy load was taking its toll on the six-cylinder engine and it began to cough and sputter. Oily grey and black smoke began pouring out of the engine cowling and the uneven prop wash was swirling the smoke around the hangar. The engine sputtered and slowed down, raced for a second or two, then sputtered again, slowed down and finally stopped. The hangar became eerily quiet. The Stearman wasn't going anyplace soon.

It had been only 30 seconds since the agents had entered the hangar, and now two of them climbed onto the wing and looked down at Joseph, their 9mm weapons fixed on him. He lay against the far side of the cockpit with his right hand on the smoke system activator. And he wasn't dead.

"Don't move. It's all over Joseph—or whatever your name is." Stanton kept his gun on the wounded man, but he eyed Najidad's hand on the toggle switch. Najidad smiled grimly and tried to raise his left arm. Then he flipped the switch.

Stanton fired at Najidad twice and then leaned into the cockpit, stretching his arm out to reach the toggle switch. Najidad's hand had fallen off, but white smoke was already pouring out underneath the old cropduster, just a small stream at first and then more as pressure built up. It took only two or three seconds for Stanton to reach the switch and flip it off, but everything seemed to be happening in slow motion to the senior agent.

"Target is dead! Countermeasures, countermeasures!" Stanton yelled, as the white smoke began to mix with the grayish smoke already swirling around the hangar.

The four agents assigned to enter the hangar had decided not to wear full chemical field gear, but each one carried a mask. Two agents had their masks on even before Stanton called out. A few seconds later all four had their masks on and were outside the hangar entrance as the two waiting agents rolled the doors closed.

"Seal it up, all hands, seal it up!" Stanton shouted and three more agents helped close the hangar doors. Then, just as they had rehearsed at Baytown, each agent used an autoinjector to shoot a pharmaceutical cocktail into his upper arm. The atropine, combined with several other inhibitors, was supposed to counteract the effects of the VX-212.

An hour later

The eight-man team was still at Liberty Airfield. The hazmat response team had arrived a half hour before and was still busy securing the VX-212 in the Stearman's smoke tank and decontaminating the hangar area. Four specialists in bright yellow hazmat suits were moving around inside the hangar. It would be several days before the area would be declared completely clean.

A medical technician worked with the FBI agents in a closed-off decontamination area, helping them wash down and change into uncontaminated jumpsuits. She continued to monitor each of the four agents who had been inside the hangar. Two of them were beginning to have trouble breathing.

"Chief, I want to get you and Reynolds to the hospital. The sooner the better. Medevac chopper is ready to go." Stanton and Bruce Reynolds, a ten-year veteran, had been closest to the smoke cloud.

"Not until Beckman gets here." Stanton was ready to step down as soon as his second-in-command arrived. The hazmat team had positively identified Joseph and had just confirmed that the substance in the hangar was in fact VX-212. The way he was feeling, Stanton thought, he could have told them that. They also found the Baytown Oil Refinery listed on the airplane's GPS list of waypoints.

Stanton's handheld radio buzzed. "Got another body in here," one of the hazmat specialists inside the hangar said "In the back corner. Male, fairly young, could be Middle Eastern. Looks like a bullet to the back of the head."

That explained the second image on the video screen. Apparently Joseph didn't want to leave anyone behind.

"Be sure to get good pictures for facial recognition before you seal up the body bags. Prints, too. E-mail them to D.C. ASAP," he instructed.

Stanton knew they still had a lot of work to do, most of it at the FBI labs at Quantico. They would take a fine-tooth comb to Joseph's car, cell phone, personal effects, and everything they found in the hangar, the aircraft, and the apartment the two men had lived in. That might help them re-create Joseph's movements over the past month and fill in some of the blanks. They would also try to identify the second body.

194

His breathing was becoming more labored. *Strange*, the FBI agent thought to himself. *I feel like shit, but I feel pretty good.* He decided to make some phone calls and then let them take him to the hospital regardless of Beckman.

Stanton had already reported to Tom Donniger back at FBI headquarters in D.C., who had been following the raid since their departure from Baytown. His next call was to his wife, who was relieved, upset and worried. She insisted on driving down from Houston so she could see him at Baytown Community Hospital.

His final call before leaving the scene was to the Army CID investigator, Captain Ben Hawkins. He was beginning to perspire and began using the oxygen mask more. There was full morning light by now and it looked like it was going to be a clear and warm day in South Texas.

Ft. Belvoir
About 9 a.m.

Ben was at his desk looking at the team collaboration website when his team phone chirped. He saw it was the FBI agent in charge of the Baytown operation, Mike Stanton.

"Hello Mr. Stanton. What's happening down there?"

"It was good information, Captain. We got the stuff and the site is secured. Joseph is dead, along with somebody who was apparently working with him. Male, probably Middle Eastern. The guy was dead before we got there, so we think Joseph killed him once he was no longer useful."

"Are you OK? You sound different."

"Joseph was able to release a small amount of the nerve agent before he died. Four of us were exposed to it for a few seconds, but we're doing OK." Stanton paused to use the oxygen mask. "We have a medical team here and we should be fine."

"Do you know what was he planning to do?"

"Looks like your information was on the mark, Captain. He had plans and overhead photos of Baytown Oil Refinery, he had a small airplane and it looked like he was about to fly down there and disperse the chemical agent. Early this morning, in fact. The engine was running when we showed up and the hazmat people said it was definitely VX-212. It was closer than I want to think about. But at least we got the son of a bitch."

Stanton coughed. He put the oxygen mask over his mouth and took several breaths.

Ben thought about what the FBI coordinator had just said. Everything Julian had told him was accurate.

"No sign of a woman?" he asked.

"No. One other accomplice, male. As I said, dead when we got there."

"Well, congratulations. You and your team did some job."

"Thanks, Captain. But the reason I called was to thank you for that call yesterday. It was a good heads-up."

Stanton coughed again. "I gotta go, Captain. The medical people are bugging me and they want me to get on the chopper. I'll try to call you later today."

Both men signed off and Ben gave a heavy sigh of relief. Julian's information *was* good. In fact, it was clear they wouldn't have stopped the attack without his help. Ben was relieved that his confidence in Julian and his information had been justified.

Maybe Sara could start going into Washington again. *One accomplice, male,* he thought to himself. *So where was Elena? The one who was Jennifer's friend, at least until she kidnapped her.*

He sent a text message to Sara telling her about the success in Texas. He didn't suggest they celebrate in Washington though. Not just yet.

So the FBI did it. They stopped the attack, Ben thought to himself. *But where was Elena?*

Noon
Hoover Building
Washington, D.C.

Tom Donniger looked around the conference room on the fifth floor of the FBI headquarters building. Several dozen photos from the operation at Liberty Airfield scrolled across the video monitors around the room. The room was quiet in spite of the success of the early morning raid.

About a dozen agents and specialists were sitting in, including Emily Olstadt from NSA and the president's advisor. Army CID investigator Captain Ben Hawkins sat at the far end of the table next to his boss, Major Corliss. It had been 10 days since the first team meeting.

"I assume everyone's heard the news by now. Two of our people didn't make it."

Everyone *had* heard the news. Special Agent in Charge Mike Stanton and Special Agent Bruce Reynolds were closest to the plane's cockpit when the terrorist hit the smoke release switch. The two men received the greatest exposure and their autoinjectors hadn't been enough.

"Mike Stanton and Bruce Reynolds never made it to the hospital. Both died on the medevac chopper on the way in. Respiratory distress. Their breathing shut down and there was nothing more the EMTs could do."

"Did you talk to Mike after the raid?" one of the agents asked Donniger.

"Yeah, he called me just after 6 a.m., as soon as the place was secure. His second-in-charge is e-mailing me an after-action report in an hour or two."

"What about their families?"

"I called Betty Stanton, Mike's wife, and Mrs. Reynolds early this morning. They both took it pretty hard. No surprise. Neither of them knew exactly what their husbands were working on. Betty Stanton thought it was another drill."

Phillips, the president's advisor spoke up. "The President will want to call them sometime later today."

"I'm sure they would appreciate that, Mr. Tyler. Look, everyone, I know it's terrible that we lost two people today. But let's not lose sight of what they accomplished. Special Agent in Charge Stanton, Special Agent Reynolds and the whole WMD team did an outstanding job preventing what could have been the largest terrorist event in this country *ever*. And that's including 9/11. This could have turned out a lot worse. A *lot* worse."

Everyone in the room already knew that. It helped, but only a little. Several of them knew one or both men.

"I also want to acknowledge Major Bill Corliss and Captain Ben Hawkins of Army CID in the back there," Donniger continued, and Ben nodded. "As you know, CID first brought this case to us. Captain Hawkins brought in one of the perpetrators, Army Sergeant Harry McNair." It sounded as if Donniger had forgiven Ben for handling McNair on his own.

"We'll continue the debriefing in various stages. This is just to make sure everyone is up to date. The Liberty site was secured early this morning. The hazmat team will take another day or so to decontaminate. They've secured the stolen material and they're preparing it for return to the Tupelo facility."

Ben figured it was as good a time as any to test his new friendship with the assistant director.

"How much of it do you have?" he asked.

"What do you mean?"

"How much VX-212 was recovered?"

"The material was loaded into the cropduster's smoke dispersal tank, mixed with some kind of oil. We believe all four pounds of the nerve agent are there."

"But you haven't been able to actually measure it," Ben continued.

"No, we haven't. The plane carried a 24-gallon tank and it was about half full. It will take awhile to determine how much of the mixture was oil dispersant and how much was nerve agent, but we think we have all of it and we have two terrorists accounted for. What are you getting at, Captain?"

"What I'm getting as is that we don't *know* we have all of it. And we *know* we don't have all the terrorists," Ben persisted.

"You're talking about the woman?"

"Yes, I'm talking about the woman. Elena Santana. Where is she? Why did she come into the country? And what about Julian? What was he up to?"

"Good point, Captain. There are still a number of loose ends. We're trying to find out where the two terrorists in Richmond and the other two guys came from and we've got some leads. We had to wait until their personal effects were decontaminated. We've got two cell phones and we're looking through the phone logs as we speak. We're still looking for the woman and we've sent her picture to local authorities, along with an alert. The search for your friend Julian hasn't yielded any results to date either. That photo from Alexandria didn't get any hits at INS. What else would you suggest?"

Donniger seemed annoyed, but he was also too experienced to ignore the observations of a seasoned investigator. He also didn't want to be the one who overlooked a piece of intel or an investigator's suggestion, no matter how offbase he thought it was. This case would be studied and analyzed for years to come.

"I suggest that we assume there's more VX-212 out there until we can prove there isn't. And that we find this Elena Santana."

"Alright, Captain, until the hazmat team makes a final determination, we'll assume there may be some VX-212 still unaccounted for. And we're continuing the search for Elena Santana. And Julian. Now, do you have any *specific* suggestions for that search?"

"What about the phone calls to or from Joseph's phone?"

"As I said, we've just started looking through them. The hazmat team had to decontaminate the phones, but they did pick up several numbers, incoming and outgoing. Two of the numbers are cell phones here in the Capital area, but apparently neither of those phones is on. We weren't able to ping them."

"Yeah, and I doubt they ever will be," Ben suggested. "They're probably burn phones, used once or twice, then thrown away."

"Yes, Captain, that occurred to us," Donniger said sarcastically. "We posted the two numbers on the team site. Any other suggestions?"

Ben didn't have any.

The meeting broke up a few minutes later. Most of the team members were feeling more upbeat in spite of the loss of two of their agents. The two men had been in the forefront of counterterrorism work and had done their job exceedingly well. They were more successful than they could have hoped for. And they died. A thousand lives saved? Ten thousand?

Knowing how bad the attack could have been—and how close it had come to succeeding—gave the loss of two colleagues a certain perspective. As their team leader, Assistant Director Donniger, had put it, "Even if Mike Stanton and Bruce Reynolds knew the outcome, they would have gone ahead anyway." Knowing that Donniger was probably right helped. Stanton and Reynolds hadn't died in vain.

Donniger pulled the two Army officers aside as people began exiting the room. "I'd like to talk to both of you before you head back across the river."

"Sure, Assistant Director," Major Corliss answered. "What is it?"

"We still have a lot of work to do on this operation. I'd like to think it's mostly debriefing, but I'm not going to argue the point. We still have three people of interest here: your Sergeant Harry McNair, that woman Elena Santana, and your mysterious friend Julian."

"And?" Corliss responded.

"What's the status on McNair? You think we got everything we could from him?"

Corliss understood the pressure Tom Donniger had been under, but they had covered this ground just a few days before.

"Tom, you want to question him again, fine. Come to Belvoir and have at it. But he remains in Army custody and his prosecution will be an Army affair—unless I hear otherwise from my superiors. I doubt very much anyone's going to push for a civil case on this."

"Alright, alright. I may take you up on your offer. His daughter gave us some information on Elena Santana, but I don't know how much it will help. She had a couple of good photos and she told us Santana's fluent in both English and Spanish, but other than that...."

Ben was waiting to find out why Donniger had pulled them aside.

"And you haven't heard from Julian again?" Donniger was looking at Hawkins now.

Ah, that was it. Julian. Ben looked at the FBI agent. "Tom, when I hear from him, you hear from me. *If* I hear from him. And I assume you're listening in on my calls anyway, aren't you?" Ben had already seen how quickly the FBI was aware of his calls from Julian, which was fine with him. He had told Sara more than a week ago to assume that all *their* phone calls were being monitored as well.

"Well, you managed to make some special arrangements with McNair. I want to make sure you don't try the same thing with Julian." Ben noticed that Donniger hadn't answered his question.

Now Ben was annoyed, but he was not about to play this game, or be pushed around by the senior agent.

"Jesus, Tom, do you really think Julian is going to call me and ask to turn himself in? Besides, maybe what we *should* do is buy him a first class ticket to wherever he wants. We never would have stopped the second attack without his help."

"True enough. But we still want to know who he is, where he's from, and what he's up to. And that's not just me asking, it's someone a few pay grades above me. I'm getting a lot of pressure from very high up to find this guy and pick him up. For all we know, he was behind the Richmond attack, and you can't prove otherwise."

"I understand that, Tom. But I still say this guy, whoever he is, helped stopped that attack in Baytown—that's a fact I *can* prove. And he may be the best way to stop any other attack. Anyway, I don't think he's going to call and tell me where he is, but if he does, I'll let you know. I'm guessing you'll do better getting those answers from your friends at NSA or CIA."

"Oh, they're working on it, 24/7. Since this thing started. There are some people in very high places asking if these people were operating on their own, or was this a state-sponsored operation. In other words, was this a terrorist attack, or was this an undeclared act of war? Because if it's Iran...."

Major Corliss spoke up. "I'm guessing, Tom, that the people trying to figure that out are at NSA and CIA, too. Anything we can do to help, let us know. But we're heading back to Belvoir and we're going ahead with the case against McNair. I figure our involvement is winding down, unless you have other information, or you have something else for us."

"No, Major, I don't have anything else. We were very lucky today, in spite of our losses. Thanks for all your help. I mean that. If anyone from another agency wants to ask you some questions, I'll give you a call.'"

Then Ben said, "Oh, Tom, one more thing. That attempt to ID Julian by picking up his license plate, running it against rentals. Anything ever pan out?"

"No. We got a couple of photos of a guy who seemed to be hanging around the area, but none of them are good enough for facial recognition. Could be he knew how to stay in the shadows. And none of the license plates we could identify matched the plates of any car rented in the Washington-Baltimore area within the past month."

"Too bad. Let us know if anything comes up. And I'm sorry about Mike Stanton and Reynolds. I never talked with Reynolds, but Stanton seemed like a good man."

"He was."

The two Army men walked down the hallway and took the elevator to the parking garage. It was a quiet ride across the Potomac River. They were just approaching the Route 95/495 intersection at Springfield when Ben's cell phone buzzed. The screen read, "Private." He put it on speaker.

"Captain Hawkins."

"Good afternoon, Captain. This is Julian."

Tuesday Afternoon

South of Washington D.C.

"Good afternoon, Julian. I was hoping to hear from you."

"I hope my calls have been helpful, Captain." Julian knew time was running out. Najidad had said three to four days. Today was day number two.

"I have good news for you," Ben answered. "Your information *was* helpful. The terrorists *had* targeted an oil refinery, just as you said. We were able to stop them."

Julian almost cheered through the phone, but he contained himself. "Excellent!" But he also heard the words "terrorists." Could they have captured the woman as well?

"So there were more than one?" he asked, his voice hopeful.

"Yes, there were two people involved." Ben was not about to tell Julian that both terrorists were dead. "If you will meet with me, I can give you all the details."

"A very attractive offer, Captain, but you will understand if I do not accept. Did you did capture a woman?"

"No, there wasn't a woman there, but...," Ben answered, trying to prolong the conversation.

Julian interrupted him. "Then, Captain, I believe we still have a problem and I believe you may not have recovered all of your chemical weapon—unless you can tell me otherwise. Do you have all of it?"

"That hasn't been determined yet, but we think so." *At least the FBI thinks so. I'm not convinced,* Ben thought.

Colonel Kashani slowed down as he approached the North Springfield exit. He was travelling counterclockwise around the D.C. Beltway, letting his phone signal bounce off different cell towers. Of course, anyone tracking his phone signal would see the pattern fairly quickly and figure out his route. Neither he nor Ben Hawkins knew they were within two miles of each other.

"Captain, my congratulations on stopping that attack. But I'm afraid there is another operative out there. A woman going by the name of Elena Santana. And she has some of your nerve agent." He pressed "disconnect" and exited the Beltway. He had a lot to do, starting with a call to Qazvin, Iran.

"Julian...Julian!" Ben yelled into the phone, but there was no response.

Ben looked over at his boss, who had been following the conversation. "Did you hear that, Boss? Julian says there's another terrorist out there—and he's pretty sure we only stopped *part* of the attack. And did you notice that he knows her name?"

Major Corliss was on the phone to Tom Donniger a few moments later. The FBI agent hadn't heard about the Julian call yet.

"Julian just called, Tom. And it's not good news."

"How long was the call?" was Donniger's first question.

"I'd say just under a minute."

"OK, probably not enough for more than a general location. They'll let me know in a few minutes. What's not 'good news'?"

Corliss repeated the conversation almost word for word to Donniger, who probably would hear an actual recording of it within a few minutes. Donniger was quiet for a few moments before responding.

"Major, are we on speakerphone?"

"Yes, we are. Ben Hawkins is here with me."

"Good. As I see it, we need to find this Julian. He knew about the operation and he helped us stop it—at least the Texas attack. Now he says there's another one and it's imminent. We need to know how he knows so much and who his sources are. And how come he didn't tell us about this other terrorist before, or about the two guys in Richmond?"

Ben interrupted. "But so far he's been helping us. We don't want to spook this guy." As far as Ben was concerned, the invisible stranger, whoever he was and whomever he worked for, had been the source of valuable information. Information that had already stopped one deadly attack. But apparently Donniger had other thoughts.

"We may be past that, Captain. Obviously Julian has some connection to Elena Santana and, as you said, he knows her by name. It's pretty clear that he knows a lot more about her and about these attacks, and he's been holding out on us. If another attack *is* coming, right now he's our only lead. So we're going to work harder on getting a fix on him the next time he calls. And you're gonna help us do it."

A half hour later, Ben and his boss were back at the CID offices in Ft. Belvoir. They had listened to Donniger's plan for locating Julian, but Ben was skeptical. Donniger thought capturing Julian would help stop the attack. Ben believed Julian had proved his usefulness and the last thing he wanted was to take him out of the picture. Only one of them could be right.

Later that afternoon
Ben and Corliss had picked up sandwiches to bring into the office. They had a late lunch in Corliss' office, going over the new information and Donniger's thoughts about nabbing Julian. Ben was not happy with Donniger's determination or with his plan to try to pick up Julian.

"Unfortunately, Ben, it all hinges on Julian calling you again. We don't know when that will be, or even *if* he's gonna call again."

"Oh no, Boss, he'll call again. No question. He seems as determined as we are, which is the part we haven't figured out. I'm just wondering how much Donniger is holding back from us, or how much the CIA is holding back from *him.*"

"Well, I'm sure they know a lot more than they're telling us, but that's OK. I guess their job is to find out where these people came from and who they're working for. Our job is to help the FBI stop this, and we're not out of the woods yet."

"I agree. And I'm not sure how much stopping the Baytown attack will matter if another target is hit. But we wouldn't have stopped the Baytown attack if it hadn't been for Julian and his information. It doesn't make sense to me to try to take him out of the game."

"Look, Ben, this whole thing is out of your hands—and that's *good* news. We have McNair in custody and we helped stop a major domestic terrorist attack. Let Donniger and the FBI handle the rest of it. Just do what they say, got it? We don't need you or anyone else trying to be a hero."

"OK, Boss, I got it."

204

Ben finished lunch and returned to his own desk. He called Sara as soon as he sat down. He wanted to make sure she wasn't making any plans to go into D.C.

About an hour later
Ben spent much of the afternoon thinking over Tom Donniger's plan. It wasn't much of a plan, and they hadn't made any progress locating Elena Santana, even with the good photograph they had circulated nationwide and the facial recognition profiles they had run.

He could think of a number of reasons why they hadn't located her. She probably had altered her appearance by now. She would be staying out of sight until she was ready to strike. She could have left the area, maybe gone to New York or Baltimore, or anywhere else in the country, for that matter.

As for Julian, from what Ben had seen of how he operated, Donniger's plan to pick him up was a long shot. On the other hand, Hawkins didn't have anything better to offer. Yet.

It was mid-afternoon when the call came in to Ben's cell phone. *Okay, step one*, Ben thought.

"Julian, don't hang up. We want to work with you and I know you want to work with us. I need a way to contact you."

"That is an interesting proposal, Captain."

Kashani paused. He, too, had been thinking that it be might wise to have a way for the young Army officer to contact him. The fact that the Americans had a plan for just that capability could make it more risky.

"Captain, I will call you within an hour with a phone number you can use. Until then, a reliable source tells me the woman's target is in Washington. The Metro system, perhaps. Or possibly Reagan National Airport." Kashani's call to Qazvin hadn't yielded specific information, but Major Heidari had offered several possibilities based on his work with Mahmoud Najidad.

"When?"

"My source said within 48 hours of the second attack. Now that the attack has been stopped, it could be any time."

"But this Elena doesn't know the attack in Texas has been stopped, does she?"

"No, Captain, I don't believe so. But I assume she knows something about when that attack was supposed to occur."

"Are you able to contact this person?" Ben asked.

"No, I am not."

"What if you could?"

"What if I could what? Contact her?"

"Yes. We have her cell number. And we have the cell phone number of her handler, the one we knew as Joseph. We can configure any phone to look as if the incoming call is from Joseph's number."

"Very interesting, Captain. And you want me to make the call."

He's a quick study, Ben thought.

"That's the only way, Julian. She can't know yet that Joseph's attack failed. She's probably waiting for a call from him. And you're the one who has some knowledge of these people and what they're planning."

That's the problem, Kashani thought. *The more I give you, the more likely you will figure out who I am.* He couldn't risk being found out. His country's future depended on it. But he couldn't ignore several thousand lives either, and he was still trying to prevent stirring up the hornet's nest the United States would become.

"I will call you again within the hour, Captain Hawkins," he promised, and hung up.

Ben dialed Donniger. "I just got a call from Julian. I think he'll try to make it work."

"Yeah, I just heard he called. Did you outline the plan?"

"Very briefly. He said he would call back within the hour and give me a number to reach him."

"That would make things simpler. By the way, you know that call you got from him earlier this afternoon?"

"Yes."

"Nearest we could pinpoint was south of D.C., in the Springfield area. That's not too far from Belvoir, is it?"

"No, it isn't. And I was just outside of Springfield when I took the call."

"Alright, let me give you another bit of intel. This is from NSA, not five minutes ago. Moments after you got that call, NSA picked up a call from that same Springfield area to Iran. They're processing it right now."

"So this is an Iranian operation?"

"NSA isn't ready to say. But they did say there's been an increase in communications activity at a number of government locations in Iran, including a few military sites. So somebody over there has been staying up late."

Ben was quiet. This whole operation was outside his experience, which was fine with him.

"Iran. So Tom, it seems pretty clear this guy is here to stop this thing. The question is, is he working for a government—Iranian or otherwise? Or against it?"

A half hour later

Ben was still waiting for Julian's follow-up call when his office phone rang. He picked it up on the third ring.

"Captain Hawkins, CID."

"Hello Captain. You know who this is. I'm assuming the FBI isn't listening in on this line. Don't work late. There's something waiting for you at home. And it would be better if you didn't share this call with anyone else—at least not yet. That would only complicate matters." The line went dead.

Ben hung up and leaned back in his chair. So Julian had tracked him down to his office phone. That wasn't so hard. But clearly Julian didn't want the FBI listening in, and he wasn't falling for Donniger's plan. That was no surprise. Ben was more certain than ever that Julian worked in Intelligence. Maybe for the Republic of Iran. Maybe for someone else. But he knew his business, he was smart, and he was very, very careful.

Don't work late. There's something waiting for you at home. Ben thought about the message. And he thought he knew what was waiting.

Fifteen minutes later, Ben was in his car and leaving the post. He could be in Belmont Bay in another 15 minutes. He was just pulling into his parking space when his team cell phone rang. The caller number wasn't displayed.

"Captain, this is Tom Donniger. No word yet?"

Now why would he call me to ask a question he knows the answer to? Ben thought. "No, Tom, nothing yet. But you already know that, don't you?"

"That's true. We just noticed that you're on the move. Just remember to keep him on the line for more than 30 seconds. We'll keep monitoring." The FBI agent hung up.

Ben saw the FedEx package as he got out of his car and walked toward the front door of his townhouse. There was no address label on it. No return address either. *Well, I guess I won't be able to send a thank-you note,* Ben thought wryly.

He went inside and opened the package. He saw the cell phone inside. He knew saving it for fingerprints would be pointless. The phone was on and the address book file was open. Only one number was listed. Julian.

I should call Donniger, he said to himself. *Why should I go out on a limb?* He remembered Major Corliss' orders to him: *"Let Donniger and the FBI handle the rest of it."*

He hesitated. *I should call Donniger.* But he knew Donniger's plan would send Julian to cover, and their best chance to stop the second attack would be gone. *We wouldn't have stopped the first attack without his information. Why would we want that source to dry up?*

Ben believed his mysterious caller was telling the truth and had always been telling the truth. And there were just too many lives at stake. He dialed the number.

"Hello, Captain. Obviously, you received the package, and now you have a way to contact me."

"Yes, Julian. Thank you. And obviously, you don't want the FBI involved."

"Your FBI can be very heavy-handed, Captain. My guess is *their* chief interest is to have me in custody. *My* interest, and I believe *your* interest, is in stopping the attack that is supposed to follow the one in Texas—the attack that will occur in Washington if it isn't stopped."

He was certainly right about the FBI, Ben thought.

"How do you know all this?" Ben asked the man he was beginning to think of as his co-worker. *Incredible. And NSA thinks he might be Iranian?* Ben hadn't had time to think that one through. *Why would Iran send a team to commit a terrorist act against the United States and another team—or agent—to stop it?*

"That really doesn't matter, Captain. But I think I've demonstrated that my purpose is to help you prevent a terrible incident. And has it occurred to you that some in your own country might want the attack to succeed?"

"What are you talking about?"

Kashani smiled to himself, not surprised that such a thought had not occurred to the young Army officer. Well, after all, he was an investigator, not an intelligence or political officer, and certainly not a strategic planner.

"Think about it, Captain. If a terrible incident occurs, and, fairly or not, that incident could be blamed on a foreign nation, what would be the consequences to that nation?"

Ben saw Julian's point. And he knew there were voices from both within and outside the current administration calling for military action against Iran before that country had its own nuclear arsenal.

But to actually allow a chemical attack against the United States to succeed? *No way*, Ben thought. *No way.*

"Now, Captain, do you have Elena Santana's phone number for me?" Kashani asked, interrupting Ben's thoughts.

And then Ben gave Julian, a possible Iranian agent, the phone number the FBI had found on the dead Najidad's cell phone. They spoke for several more minutes. Before hanging up, Julian reminded Ben about the phone call that was overdue. The one the FBI was waiting for.

"I will call you on your cell phone in a few minutes. You will offer me the phone number and then ask me to meet with you. I will say 'No' to the meeting, of course." And so the die was cast.

Ten minutes later, Ben received the call from Julian. The call lasted just over a minute as they talked through their rehearsed script. The call from Donniger came in just a few minutes after Julian hung up.

"Well, at least he's got Santana's phone number now. But you couldn't get him to meet with you."

"No, Tom, and I'm not surprised. He was interested in the cell number, but he wasn't interested in configuring his phone to look like Joseph's. How good is your fix on his location?"

"He was only on for about 60 seconds. We have him in the Alexandria area, but it's about a one-mile radius. He's very careful, isn't he?"

"Yes, he is. I think he's a trained agent. So what does it matter if his phone isn't configured?"

"That would have done two things. One, we figure Santana would be more likely to pick up the call if she saw Joseph's number. Two, we could have backtraced him on the call much more quickly, and located him as well."

"What about when he calls the Santana number now?"

"Since we're monitoring that number, we can still backtrace him, but it takes longer. At least one to two minutes, sometimes a little more."

Ben thought that one over. It sounded as if Donniger was more interested in capturing Julian than in securing the last of the missing VX-212. He thought about what Julian had asked: *Has it occurred to you that some in your own country might want the attack to succeed?* This was becoming a very complicated game and he was right in the middle of it.

Wednesday

It had been a long night, and it started out as a gray, overcast day.

The second call from Julian had gone as planned. Ben was surprised at how cool he had been, not only carrying on a conversation with a foreign agent while the FBI listened in, but doing so in collusion with the agent and the FBI at the same time.

Julian had been just as cool. Whoever was listening in had no reason to suspect that he and Hawkins had just been talking on a cell phone the FBI didn't know about. The call had lasted just over a minute as Ben and Julian talked through the conversation they had outlined.

Now all Ben could do was wait. This was the best chance they had to reach Elena Santana. Julian seemed sure she had the rest of the VX-212 McNair had stolen, and the specialists at Tupelo Chemical Research Center hadn't been able to say otherwise yet.

There were still questions that nagged at Ben. *How does Julian know about Elena Santana? And that she might have some of the nerve agent?* Julian hadn't shared *that* information before yesterday afternoon. *Why was that?*

It had been a long night for the FBI counterterrorism team as well. Teams of agents were questioning hundreds of motel and hotel workers throughout the capitol area, trying to find someone who recognized Elena Santana's photograph. Based on the tip from Julian, Donniger had also stepped up surveillance of the entire Washington subway system, including an increased police presence at the Metro stations. He also ordered both police and plainclothes FBI agents to Reagan National Airport, just across the Potomac River from the Capital.

Ben went online to check the team website before leaving home, but there was nothing new. He checked a local station for the weather forecast, which called for a 50 percent chance of showers later in the day. *50 percent chance*, Ben thought. *Can't go wrong there. Wonder what our odds are?*

He was in his office at Ft. Belvoir by 8 a.m. He checked the website again. Nothing new.

It was hard to believe the events in Texas had happened only 24 hours before. Maybe they *had* gotten all the VX-212 when they caught up with Joseph. Maybe Julian was wrong. Maybe the people at Tupelo who were analyzing the chemical mixture recovered at the Liberty Airfield would have good news soon. Maybe Santana was gone and they would never hear from her again. Yeah, and maybe he would win the Power Ball lottery this week.

He was scanning the office copy of the *Washington Post* when he noticed the news item on the Republic of Iran: *CIA Reports Iran May Be Close to Nuclear Weapon.* According to the article, the CIA now believed Iran had the capability to enrich enough uranium to weapons grade level to have one, and possibly two, atomic weapons within two to three years.

Ben put in a call to Tom Donniger. He knew that whatever happened, he was going to have trouble with the FBI, with his boss, and maybe even with his Army career. He had really gone out on a limb on this one.

"Tom, this is Ben Hawkins. How are you and your people doing?"

"Most of them are out in the field looking for Santana. I talked with Stanton's and Reynolds' wives last night. They're not doing too well. And I see Julian hasn't called you since yesterday. Other than that, things are going well."

He sounds tired, Ben thought. *He's barely left the FBI Building in the past week, and there's no end in sight. No good end.*

"I see you're taking Julian's tip seriously. All the increased security personnel in the Metro system...."

"Yeah, we are, but it's not enough. I hope you're wrong about there being more of that VX-212 out there, but I'm beginning to think you may be right. Anyway, we're going on the assumption there's more out there."

"Keep me posted," Ben said, and hung up. Tom Donniger sounded pessimistic and discouraged. *Time is running out*, he thought. *Maybe the increased security and surveillance could stop an attack, but how do you pick out one person from a crowd of commuters and tourists? And who knows what she looks like now? No, Julian was still their best chance. At least, I hope so.*

He went into Corliss' office to review the plans for proceeding with the case against Staff Sergeant Harry McNair, wondering if he might soon be on the wrong side of a military court martial himself. Now that his daughter was safe, McNair had made it clear he would plead guilty to whatever charges the Army was prepared to bring forward. Ben was still in his boss' office when his cell phone rang.

"Captain, Tom Donniger. I thought you deserved a follow-up call. Tupelo just called. They say the VX-212 from Baytown is a pound short."

Later that morning

Ben briefed his boss as soon as he finished his call with Donniger. He was back at his desk when his office landline phone rang.

"Hawkins."

"Good morning, Captain. This line still isn't monitored, I hope."

"No, it's not, Julian. Any luck making contact?" he asked. They both knew who they were talking about.

"Yes, Captain. I told you I would try last night. She didn't pick up the call, but I left a very convincing message. She called me back late last night. We spoke for several minutes. I didn't risk a call to you because I had no new information."

That first contact with the woman was for credibility, Kashani thought. *Just* as *with Najidad. I informed her that Najidad's mission had failed. And that the Supreme Revolutionary Council needed to know when a successful attack would occur. But of course, Hawkins didn't need to know these details.*

"This morning I called her again and asked for specific information. I insisted. She told me the target is the Metro system. This evening's rush hour. I believe her."

"The Metro. Rush hour. Like 5 to 6 o'clock, right?"

"Yes."

"Where in the Metro system? There must be a hundred stations. Did she say which line, or which station?"

"She said 'Metro Center.' I believe that's a specific location in the system."

"Yes, it's one of the busiest stations. I think three of the Metro lines have interchanges there, so there are a lot of ways in and a lot of ways out. Several thousand people must pass through that station at rush hour."

Both men were quiet for a few moments. Then Ben spoke.

"So tell me, Julian, why would she confide in you? Why give you the details? For that matter, why did Joseph give you any details?"

"Captain, you and I could discuss that for several hours, but does it matter? No, what matters is preventing a potential disaster. Do you agree?"

Ben agreed, of course. Which was the problem. If the FBI got their hands on Julian, their chief concerns would be his relationship with the terrorists, who he reported to, and what his legal rights were, including his right to remain silent. They would follow all the proper procedures. At least until the actual attack occurred.

"I understand. Wish us luck, Julian. You, too."

A minute later Ben was on the phone to Donniger.

"You what? You just spoke to Julian? Why didn't we know about it?" was the assistant director's first response.

"Well, you know about it now. How should I know how he got my office number? Maybe he just called the main post switchboard," Ben answered. He didn't mention that it wasn't Julian's first call to his office.

Ben told the FBI team leader what Julian had told him.

"Great. The Metro system. And you believe him?" was Donniger's second response.

"Yes, I do. For reasons I've already given you. So what do we do?"

"First thing I'm going to do is give the information to my boss, who'll give it to Homeland Security. They'll want to consider evacuation, which I'll recommend against."

"Because...?"

"Because one, we don't know if the information is credible. Two, how do you evacuate the city of Washington, D.C. when the mass transit system itself is the target? But mostly, because three, all that would do is spook our suspect, who would look for another target at another time and place."

"That all makes sense to me. But I'm glad it's not my call."

"OK, I have to pass on the info and get mobilized. We have a lot to do. I'll be pretty busy, so I may not get back to you, but you can check on the website. Call me only if it's urgent—and that definitely includes if you hear from Julian again. You got it, Captain?"

Ben didn't respond to Donniger's challenging tone. "Is there anything else I can do?" he asked. He had been involved since the chemical weapon was stolen and he wanted to see it through to the end.

"Yes, try and stay in touch with Julian. He's the key to this whole thing. And keep me posted. We'll alert Metro Transit Police, plus we'll send in some of our own people. We've worked with them before. The trick is to increase security without alerting our suspect. And I want to get some additional eyes to monitor the video surveillance throughout the whole system."

Ben was relieved. He had gone out on a limb, and it seemed to have paid off. He was pretty sure the FBI and Homeland Security wouldn't have the information on the planned attack if he hadn't broken protocol. Now it was up to the FBI to stop it.

Still, it was one thing to lose an FBI tail in order to meet with a suspect, as he had done with McNair. It was a whole other ballgame to arrange secret contact with a possible foreign agent, and then give that agent sensitive information, such as a suspect's phone number. Yes, he had really gone out on a limb this time.

Well, what's done is done, he thought to himself. *Jeez, it was tough just waiting it out!* Then he called Sara to make sure she would not be in the Capitol.

Ben spent the next few hours checking the team website for news about the search for Elena Santana and reviewing the case against McNair. McNair's daughter had been questioned extensively by the FBI, and then released. She had been able to provide several photos of Elena and descriptions of the people who had held her captive in Seville, but that was about it.

Jennifer had visited her father several times in his holding cell at Ft. Belvoir, but the visitor log didn't show a visit in the past several days. McNair said something about her going back home to Tupelo. He would ask the sergeant about it.

Finally, he couldn't stand waiting around any longer. This was still his case. He unlocked his 9mm Sig Sauer sidearm, picked up a dozen photos of Elena Santana, and stuck his head in Corliss' office.

"Boss, I'm heading into town. FBI offices. See if there's anything I can do there."

Twenty minutes later he was on Route 395 approaching the Potomac River Bridge. He was almost across the bridge when his cell phone rang. Only this ring tone was different. It was the phone Julian had secretly delivered to him.

"Captain, this is Julian. I don't think your FBI has made any progress."

"None that I know of," Ben answered. "But what makes you say that?"

"I just received a call from the woman." *The Americans don't need to know her real name, or the story of her family and Flight 655,* he thought.

"She says there is increased security throughout the Metro system. She wanted to know if I leaked the information."

"What did you tell her?"

"I told her maybe Joseph talked. Maybe he's in custody right now. Or perhaps it is just a precaution because of Sunday's attack in Richmond. Maybe there is increased security in New York, too."

"And did she believe you?"

"She's doesn't think I gave information to the FBI, if that's what you mean. She was upset about the thought that Joseph might be in custody. *Of course, I can't tell you that I used his real name—Mahmoud. And that I called her by her real name, Saman.*

"You still have her confidence," Ben said, wondering what Elena's— and their—next steps would be. Yes, they had stopped a major chemical weapons attack, but Elena was someplace in the D.C. area with a pound of VX-212, still enough nerve agent to cause several thousand deaths. This attack would make the anthrax scare of a few years ago a minor annoyance in comparison.

"Yes, but she wouldn't tell me her exact plans. She's being very careful."

"But you knew one terrorist was targeting an oil refinery in Texas. And you knew she was targeting the Metro system."

This man is no fool, Kashani thought. He couldn't tell Ben that he had learned about the probable target from a phone call to Qazvin. The CID investigator had seen the contradiction.

"And now I believe she will go after Union Station. I'm sure of it."

"What makes you say that?" Ben asked, trying to put the pieces together. An unknown foreign agent helping them track down another foreign agent. A terrorist cell that operated out of Seville, Spain. Middle Eastern. Probably Iranian, the NSA woman had said. An American GI who stole a deadly nerve toxin and turned it over to terrorists. And an Army CID investigator who gave sensitive information to an unidentified voice on the phone who was probably working for a foreign government. Information that had just helped one foreign agent contact another one. And maybe one terrorist contact another terrorist. Great.

"What do you call it? A hunch? No, something more. She wanted to target a travel center in the heart of your capitol. If the Metro is too protected, that only leaves your central train station."

Kashani couldn't tell Hawkins that Saman, the woman the Americans knew as Elena, had practically pinpointed the target.

"It's too risky to wait any longer," she had said only a few minutes ago. "Don't worry," she told Kashani. "Mahmoud and I picked another good place to hurt the Americans." From what Major Heidari had divulged to Kashani in Qazvin, the primary target was one of the Metro stations. If that target was untenable, the secondary target was to be the central rail terminal—Union Station.

Ben knew about Julian's so-called hunches. He hadn't been wrong yet.

The target made sense. Union Station was the hub for all rail service into the capital, including all Amtrak and Acela trains. It also served as a Metro station, linking the terminal to the Metro transit system via the Red Line. With dozens of shops and restaurants in the shopping arcade, and just a few blocks from Washington landmarks such as the Capitol Building and Senate and Congressional office buildings, the station was a popular shopping and sightseeing spot for tourists and government workers even when they weren't using the subways or trains. More than 50,000 commuters, tourists and shoppers used the station every day.

Ironically, it was only eight blocks from Donniger's office at FBI headquarters in the J. Edgar Hoover Building on Pennsylvania Avenue.

Ben was almost across the Potomac River and he noticed dark rain clouds closing in on the city from the west. He could stay on Route 395 and be at Union Station in 10 or 15 minutes.

"Julian, I'm heading for the station. I can be there in 10 minutes. I hope you're right about this…I think."

Ben ended the call, thinking how close to the edge he was. *Donniger is gonna hang me out to dry,* was one thought. *And Sara is gonna kill me,* was another. But he knew he had to make the call. He stepped on the gas as he made the call.

"Tom, this is Ben Hawkins," he began.

"I assume this is important, Captain."

"Very important, Tom. Julian just called me."

Ben was doing close to 90 mph when he braked hard to take the Route 395 ramp into the city. The highway went underground beneath the National Mall, and two drivers leaned on their horns as he cut around and ahead of them to make the exit marked "US Capitol." He was still doing nearly 40 mph as he approached the end of the exit ramp. One car was stopped ahead of him at a red light. Ben pulled around it, looked quickly and raced onto C Street, and he heard another angry horn behind him.

Fortunately, he was familiar with this part of the Capital from the many visits Sara made to the Smithsonian. The tires squealed as he made a hard left turn, narrowly missing a taxi that was just entering the intersection, and raced down the two-way street, weaving around any slow-moving traffic. In just a few moments he was at Columbus Circle. He braked and made a hard right turn to the front entrance of the train station.

It was just under 10 minutes after the call from Julian when Ben pulled over, braked hard to a screeching stop, and jumped out. He figured his Army uniform and CID identification would get plenty of attention with a security force that had already been alerted. Donniger and another dozen agents should be just minutes behind.

The call to Donniger could have been worse, Ben thought, as he ran into the station. True, Donniger had promised to prosecute him for interfering with a federal investigation and providing classified information to a foreign agent, and whatever else he could think of.

"You what?" he had asked Ben incredulously. "You've been having private phone conversations on a secret phone a foreign agent supplied you with? Are you nuts?" By then Donniger was screaming.

Ben hadn't even tried to calm him down. Or to explain.

"Union Station. Elena saw security all over the Metro lines. Julian said he's sure she's switched her target to Union Station. I'll be there in 10 minutes."

The two men hung up at the same time. Donniger immediately began assembling a team of agents to descend on the station, including several members of the FBI police force stationed at the J. Edgar Hoover Building. His office would alert the agents who were on the Metro security detail and Metro Transit Police that Union Station was a likely target. How long would it be before the terminal was swarming with agents and police? And would that stop Elena—or force her hand?

The rain was just starting to come down as Ben hurried into the terminal and looked for a Metro Transit Police officer. He spotted a uniformed Metro policeman by one of the ticketing areas. The officer carried a sidearm and handheld radio. He approached the officer, holding out both his ID and a photo of Elena Santana.

"Officer, I'm with Army CID. You know about the alert. You're about to get another one from the FBI, an imminent threat alert on Union Station. Come with me and try to stop this woman. And while we look for her, contact your HQ and get some help out here."

The transit policeman looked at Ben's uniform. "Hold on, Captain Hawkins. Let me call this in first."

"Look, this woman is carrying some very lethal nerve gas, and she's about to disperse it in *your* terminal. So either keep up with me or hand these out to your security people." Ben gave the guard several more photos of Elena Santana and began to move into the terminal's grand lobby. The guard remained behind, talking into the microphone pinned to his uniform.

It wasn't unusual to see uniformed military personnel in Washington. Ben tried to look like any other Army officer coming into D.C. from the Pentagon or one of the surrounding posts, perhaps to meet with a Congressional staffer or to attend a hearing.

He walked around the terminal's main lobby, keeping to the outer areas and scanning in something as close to a grid search as a single person could do. Nothing unusual. Hundreds of train and Metro riders went by him, government employees, shoppers, and tourists who had just come to see Union Station, some hurrying to their destination and others just strolling around the lobby enjoying the sights.

Ben was familiar with the impressive grand lobby. It soared almost a hundred feet high, with stairways leading to the upper levels where more shops and restaurants were located. The marble floors and decorative white granite walls and archways gave it a solid, substantial look.

He looked up at the granite statues on the upper level. There were several dozen of them, stone Roman legionnaires holding their shields. They seemed to be standing guard over the terminal, but Ben didn't think they would be much help against a chemical weapon designed to attack the human nervous system. He wondered what the legionnaires would make of a weapon that didn't train, didn't fight, didn't march. It just killed.

He noticed a little girl looking at the statues and overheard her ask her mother if those were angels looking down from above. Maybe that's what they needed—guardian angels, not guardian legionnaires.

"No, honey, those aren't really angels, they're statues of soldiers. You know, soldiers are like policemen or police ladies, who help protect us."

"Is he a soldier, mommy?" the little girl asked, pointing over at Ben, standing a few feet away in his Army uniform.

"Yes, I guess he is, Jessie. But it's not polite to point." The young mother smiled at Ben, and he smiled back and gave a little wave to the girl. As he began to move away, Ben overheard the girl ask her mother yet another question.

"Is *he* here to protect us?"

Ben moved further into the lobby before the mother could reply and he wondered what she said to her daughter. *Is he here to protect us?* He knew what this case was about. It wasn't about stolen Army property. It wasn't about solving a case. It wasn't even about saving the U.S. Army and the United States government from the disgrace and embarrassment of having its own weapons turned on American citizens.

I am here to protect them, he thought. *I couldn't stop the attack in Richmond, an attack that killed 28 people. And this one would be a lot worse, with thousands of people moving through the train station. I've got to stop this one!*

Where would Elena go? Where was the best place to launch a chemical attack? Out in the open? In the waiting areas by the platforms? On an upper level?

Ben thought he heard sirens in the distance. He hoped Donniger's team wasn't going to show up with sirens blaring and agents running around Union Station.

He looked up at the second level again. The upper level arcade overlooked the main terminal area. Ben saw a man casually looking around the main terminal below him. Had the man just been watching him?

That's when he noticed the two young women heading toward the train platforms. They looked like college students, in jeans and sneakers, and wearing baseball caps. Each was carrying a small backpack. What had caught his eye? They seemed intent, even more intent than the people hurrying to catch a train or a subway.

That was it. They looked intent, purposeful, but they weren't hurrying. Both women seemed to look around the terminal, but they weren't heading for a particular location or platform. They weren't scanning video displays or looking over the shops and restaurants. *They were looking around to see if anyone was looking at them!*

Now several security officers were entering the lobby area from side hallways. The two women seemed to pay attention to them. Ben still couldn't see their faces. Keeping his eye on them,, he stepped inside a Gotham news shop and picked up the first magazine he saw. He gave the clerk a $10 bill.

"Can I have a bag for this, please?" he asked. He put the magazine into the shopping bag and carried the bag so it could be seen easily. Just a guy passing through and picking up something from one of the shops. Not an armed CID investigator trying to prevent a terrorist attack.

He exited the newsstand and began strolling across the lobby on a path approaching the two women. He carried a train schedule that he pretended to study. *Two women?* he thought. *Probably not Elena. Unless she's got help, of course. But Julian didn't say anything about two operatives. Still, I should rule them out.*

A few moments later Ben was about 10 feet from the two women, his closest point of approach unless he changed course. He was about to turn directly toward them when there was a flurry of activity at the main entrance and a half dozen agents appeared. Both women reacted, first staring at the team of agents for a second or two, and then at each other. Ben got his first good look at their faces.

What's going on? he thought, in one of those moments of confusion when there's a disconnect, when what you see contradicts what you know or believe. He recognized the woman closer to him. It was the woman in the photos he had just handed to the security officer. It was Elena.

Holy shit! The woman standing next to her was Jennifer McNair. It didn't make sense!

Ben was shocked, and without thinking, he blurted out, "Jennifer, is that you?"

Both women turned quickly to Hawkins. The one Ben thought looked like Jennifer called out first.

"It's the Army guy who arrested my father!" she called out. "Run, Elena," she said in a firm voice, and grabbed her arm.

Both girls bolted for the train departures area. They moved quickly and Ben could see them exchanging words. He ran after them, yelling over his shoulder at the agents entering the terminal behind him, "Over here! Over here!" No one seemed to have focused on the trio moving quickly through the station.

That's Jennifer, Ben thought. *I saw her just a few days ago. She told her father she was on her way back to Alabama. It didn't make sense to me, not with her father in custody at Belvoir.* Ben couldn't quite grasp it, and his mind was working overtime trying to make sense of Jennifer's appearance as he tried to catch up to the pair of women.

One of the girls' backpacks bumped a man standing in their way and then both of them elbowed several people as they hurried through the terminal. Ben heard a stream of complaints called after them. Suddenly, Elena headed left toward the train platforms and Jennifer turned right. It looked as if Jennifer was heading for the stairway to the upper level.

Where was the FBI team? Where was Metro Police? Ben had been frozen for a few moments, physically and mentally, but now he realized—he *accepted*—that Elena and Jennifer were working together and that their attack was imminent.

"Move, Move!" he yelled, as he tried to make his way through groups of travelers and sightseers. He couldn't follow both of them. *Which one to follow? Where were Donniger and his team?* He decided to stay with Jennifer, but too many people were getting in the way. *There she was, still heading for the stairway to the restaurant and shopping arcade on the second level.*

He needed help and he needed to get the team's attention, but nobody seemed to be aware of what was going on and the FBI agents were moving into the terminal very slowly and carefully. Ben drew his service weapon, a Sig Sauer automatic pistol, standard issue, aimed at one of the beautifully detailed Beaux-Arts granite pieces in a nearby archway and fired.

The boom of the 9mm reverberated throughout the terminal and then there was the sound of chips of granite raining down on the marble floor. The crowd of people moving through and around the terminal froze and went quiet. Then someone saw Ben standing there holding a gun in the air, there was a scream, and people began dropping to the floor.

Well, that got some attention, Ben thought. Now the agents who were working their way through the terminal saw Ben, and Ben thought he saw Donniger with a knot of three or four agents just entering the terminal.

"There's two of them!" he shouted in the direction of the group of agents. Then he heard another yell.

"Drop it. Metro Police, drop it NOW!"

He saw a transit police officer by the newsstand he had just left. The officer had his weapon drawn and leveled at the CID officer.

"I'm Army CID!" Ben yelled in response and started to turn for the stairway. Jennifer was halfway up the stairs, taking them quickly. *Where had Elena gone?*

"Drop it. Now!" the Metro police officer yelled again. Several FBI agents were converging on the center of the lobby where Ben was.

You idiot, Ben thought. *She's getting away! They're both getting away!*

"I said put your weapon down!" the Metro security man yelled, his own weapon drawn.

Ben turned back just in time to see a man quietly approaching the security officer from behind. The man suddenly turned and side-kicked the officer behind the knee hard and the man went down.

That gave Ben the few seconds he needed. He took off for the stairway, heading after Jennifer. The man who had just decked the security guard was running in the direction Elena had taken.

Ben took the stairs two at a time and was on the upper level in just a few seconds. Jennifer had turned left, toward the western end of the arcade. There she was, on one side of the arcade, where it overlooked the grand lobby below, with her backpack on the floor.

He realized now what made him notice the two women moments before. It was a sunny, warm day in Washington, and bright sunlight was streaming into the terminal through the tall side windows. Both women were wearing long pants and long sleeve shirts. That wasn't unusual, but now he could clearly see Jennifer was also wearing gloves. Tan-colored gloves. That must be what had caught his attention. Who wears gloves in the spring?

Ben heard running steps, but he didn't have time to look behind him. Jennifer had her backpack open and was grabbing at something inside. He could see that she had just put on a full field respirator, basically a very sophisticated gas mask. He still had his automatic weapon out and he kept it pointed at the strange-looking girl in front of him, her skin fully covered and her head covered by the ominous looking gas mask. She was about 35 feet from him, but he was closing fast. He kept his pistol trained on her and he could see a fierce, determined look in her eyes through the mask.

"Hands in the air! Federal agent, hands in the air!" he yelled, even as he heard a voice behind him. The woman ignored him and was digging into the backpack again.

"Drop the weapon! Drop it!" someone was yelling at him from behind.

Now Jennifer had something in her hands and she was fumbling with the cap. It was a small container, like a thermos. She was struggling to open it. Ben was only 20 feet away, but he wasn't going to make it to her. If the police or security guard or FBI agent, whoever was behind him, interfered, she would have time open it.

"Drop your weapon," he heard someone yell again from behind him in a voice that sounded far away, although he knew it wasn't, and the girl was about to activate the canister. She hadn't hesitated or slowed down yet. Ben's mind had finally added the pieces together.

For a brief instant he remembered the words of the little girl downstairs. *Is he here to protect us?* Then he fired his 9mm weapon twice, just before he was tackled and knocked to the ground.

A few minutes later

Ben was in the Union Station security office. Even with handcuffs on, he felt pretty good about stopping at least part of the terrorist attack on the station. Two men in suits escorted him down the stairs and into the terminal security office. Then their very angry boss showed up.

"What the hell are you doing?" Donniger exploded. "You think you can just run around a train station shooting people? We had a team on site! You're lucky Metro Police didn't shoot you! Or that one of my own people didn't shoot you upstairs!"

"Shooting people? Shooting people?" Ben shot back. "A chemical weapon attack was about to take place. I stopped it. What about the other girl?"

"What are you talking about? What other girl?" Donniger countered.

Ben had had enough.

"You idiot! Instead of threatening me, why don't you look for the other terrorist? I told you there were two of them. I got Jennifer, McNair's daughter. The other one is Elena Santana. Are you looking for her?"

"Two of them? What are you talking about?"

"Listen to me, Tom." Ben looked at the other two agents in the room. "And I want you two to listen up in case you get questioned about this later. The girl I shot was Jennifer McNair. She was with our other suspect, Elena Santana. They split up. I followed Jennifer and stopped her from activating some kind of canister. I think we can assume it's the missing VX-212. Now, what are you doing to capture the second terrorist, who, for all we know, is about to, or already has, launched her own attack?"

Donniger looked over at the two agents. Then he looked back to Hawkins. "The girl you shot—that wasn't Santana?"

"That's right, Tom. It was *not* Elena Santana. It was Jennifer McNair. And the two of them were working together—McNair and Santana. Now do you get it? "

Just then, Donniger's handheld radio chirped. He picked it up and said, "Donniger," then listened for a few moments. "OK, thanks."

"Well, Captain Hawkins, you're right about two things so far. That *was* Jennifer McNair. And the stuff she had? We just confirmed it's VX-212. About half a pound of it."

"Alright, we got some of it. That means there's still another half pound of it out there. The other woman—Santana—was heading for the Amtrak waiting area. I couldn't follow both of them," Ben answered, realizing that the threat wasn't over yet.

"We locked down the whole terminal. None of the trains or subways are moving and we're evacuating people from the station. Now tell me how you heard about this. And a Metro transit officer tells me he was attacked by a second man. Just who exactly are you working with?"

"Jesus, Tom, will you get your priorities straight? Let's work on getting the other terrorist. We can do the debriefing later."

"I need to know about this call from Julian. I assume it was Julian. And how come...?" Donniger's radio chirped again.

"Donniger." Ben saw the agent relax as he listened, then his eyes narrowed.

"And the ID is confirmed?"

A moment later, the assistant director said, "Thanks. Good work. I'm in the Metro security office. I'll be up there in a few minutes."

He disconnected and looked at Ben.

"There's been another shooting. One dead, a female. Our agents confirmed that the victim, if that's the right word, is our suspect, Elena Santana."

"Then maybe it's over," Ben said, with relief. He really didn't care what happened to him next. "Maybe we were lucky today."

"Maybe not so lucky, because it's certainly not over," Donniger answered in a terse voice. "It wasn't us who got her. Witnesses say some guy, white male, medium complexion, about 5'10", never said anything, just approached her from behind, got up close, then shot her. Twice, in the head, once up very close. Everyone screamed, ran for cover. He disappeared."

"OK, someone else shot her. At least she didn't release the last of the nerve agent."

"No, she didn't. Problem is, there's no canister. Several witnesses saw the guy take her backpack. The security video tapes show him leaving the station with it. Now you want to tell me who it is?"

A few minutes earlier

Kashani had been on his way to Union Station when he placed his last call to Hawkins. He was already inside the terminal when Hawkins arrived and he saw Donniger's FBI agents arrive a few moments later. Then he saw Hawkins approach the two women.

That must be Elena! And someone with her! He watched as the Metro policeman tried to stop Hawkins, just as the two women split up.

Kashani had a split second to make a decision. *Could the Army investigator handle this? Would the FBI agents reach them?* He was so close... dangerously close.

But he hadn't come this far to leave anything to chance. He took several steps forward, then he sidekicked the policeman's knee, and the cop went down. Kashani kicked his gun away as he sprinted after the girl, who was moving away quickly.

He caught up to her just as she reached the train platforms. There was no time to waste, not with FBI agents and Metro police swarming through the terminal, and he didn't have to think twice about what he had to do. His first shot, from about three feet away, was to stop her. The second one, the one he took when she went down, when he could put the gun right up to her temple, was to make sure she wouldn't talk. And he was not about to leave a half pound of nerve agent behind.

He left the station through an exit on the western side of the terminal and headed up G Street, a backpack slung over his shoulder. He was in the middle of Washington, D.C. with a half pound of deadly nerve agent in his possession and he had another decision to make.

That evening

Ben was sitting out on his deck, overlooking the loblolly pines that came up to the edge of the lawn. He was working on his first beer while he waited for Sara to show up. Normally he would have waited for her to join him, but not tonight.

It was a warm spring evening, not quite moving to dusk yet. It had been quite a day, and he didn't think it was over yet. He had never shot his personal weapon in the line of duty before, much less kill anyone, and this was a young woman he had met and talked with. The image of him talking to Jennifer about Seville and about her father kept re-appearing, even when he tried not to think about it.

Assistant Director Tom Donniger, with the help of several of his FBI agents and the director of Metro Transit Police, had beaten him up pretty good just a few hours ago. Not physically, of course, but that might have been easier to take.

No, it was Donniger's threats of federal criminal charges, local criminal charges, aiding and abetting, withholding information, and making false statements, that had gotten to him. Somehow the threat of federal prison took all the joy out of stopping Jennifer McNair's attempted terrorist attack on Union Station. Finally, when Donniger threatened to put in a call to the Justice Department, Captain Benjamin Hawkins had had enough.

"Tom, I'd like to call my commanding officer, Major Corliss, now, thank you." He was still a commissioned officer in the United States Army and he wasn't going to put up with Donniger's crap any more. "Arrest me, or put the call through."

Donniger had already been in touch with Corliss. He made the call and gave the phone to Ben. Ben invited Donniger to listen in as he briefed his commanding officer. Somebody else was probably listening in already.

"I understand both Elena Santana and Jennifer McNair were stopped," Major Corliss opened.

"Yes, sir, that's right," Ben answered. I shot Jennifer McNair and an unknown person—I'm pretty sure it was Julian—shot Santana."

"So what the hell was Jennifer McNair doing there? She was supposed to be a kidnap victim."

"We haven't sorted that out yet. I'm not sure we ever will. Was she a part of it from the beginning? Or was this a 'Stockholm Syndrome' kind of thing, where the kidnap victim ends up identifying with the kidnappers?"

"You mean, like Patty Hearst, where she ended up participating in her kidnappers' bank holdup."

"Right. I guess that's something for the FBI to sort out."

"Captain, I understand they're still trying to sort several things out," Major Corliss responded, and Ben noted the formal tone. "I understand not all the VX-212 was recovered at Union Station."

"No, sir, there's still a half pound of it missing. Whoever killed Santana took the other half pound of it with him."

"Yeah, well, your friend Assistant Director Donniger called me a little while ago and gave me a quick rundown." Major Corliss knew that Donniger was listening in on the call. "Apparently he has some questions about your involvement with Julian."

"Yes, sir, I've explained to him that everything Julian gave me, I gave him, including the information on the Union Station attack, which we wouldn't have prevented without Julian's call."

"But you had some secret contact with him, Captain, contact that neither I nor the FBI knew about."

Ben realized that he was being questioned closely by his boss, someone experienced in interrogation. Someone who knew when to ask questions and when to just listen. On the other hand, Ben hadn't heard any threats or demands yet, and he had nothing to hide. He hoped their conversation was being recorded. Or maybe his boss was just heading for cover.

"I wouldn't call it 'secret', sir. Julian said he was concerned the FBI was more interested in capturing him than in stopping the attack. He delivered a phone to me so he could give me information without looking over his shoulder. I think he knew the FBI almost picked him up previously. I didn't ask him to do that, I just found the phone on my doorstep."

"And did you report it?"

"No, sir, I did not." Ben had thought this one through and he knew the question of "secret contact" is what could land him in a court martial right next to Staff Sergeant Harry McNair. He also realized that his boss was walking him through a very careful explanation.

"First of all, sir, I only had this so-called "secret" phone for a few hours. Julian dropped it off late last night. But the real reason I didn't report the contact was that he was giving me good intelligence, intel that I passed on to Assistant Director Donniger as soon as I got it. I wasn't prepared to have that information source go quiet. It was too important and too good. And today's events proved that."

"Alright, Captain, that makes sense to me. But there's still a half pound of dangerous stuff out there, so I'll let you finish up with the Assistant Director. I'll be here at Belvoir if you need me."

"Sir, one more thing...." Ben talked to Major Corliss about McNair and his daughter for a few moments and then hung up.

Donniger and several agents continued the debriefing with Ben for another hour before releasing him. No formal charges had been filed, at least not yet. Now he was sitting out on his deck on a lovely spring evening, and he was pretty sure there would be another phone call. At least he hoped so. If not—well, Assistant Director Donniger had been pretty clear about the repercussions, Army officer or not.

He was thinking about opening another bottle of beer, which was unusual for him. But it had already been an unusual day. In nearly 10 years as a CID investigator and Army officer, he'd never actually fired his weapon except in training, much less killed someone. His brain told him he had no choice but to kill. His brain also told him he had prevented that person from killing hundreds, perhaps thousands, of innocent people. And the person he killed wasn't innocent herself. But still, he had taken a life, the life of the daughter of someone he knew. He didn't understand it, but he was feeling almost sick. He also knew he would do the same thing again, without hesitation.

And how was Sergeant McNair handling the death of his daughter? Fortunately, Major Corliss had volunteered to break the news of Jennifer's death to McNair when it became clear that Ben wasn't ready to face him. Ben wondered which would torment McNair more: the death of his daughter, or the knowledge that she had become the accomplice of someone intent on committing mass murder, a terrorist who attacked the country McNair had chosen to defend. And that in a convoluted way, McNair had been a part of his own daughter's death. *Terrorist attack. Nerve gas. Mass murder.* Ben shuddered, knowing how close it had been.

There were still many unanswered questions. How long had Jennifer been involved? Had Elena Santana recruited her, or had Jennifer come to identify with her captors—a victim of the Stockholm Syndrome effect? It could take weeks and months to answer those questions, and many would remain unanswered forever.

Ben was deep in thought when one of his phones rang. He was still carrying the phone Julian had given him, but the FBI knew all about it now. Donniger and his team were monitoring it in the hopes that Julian would call. Donniger thought there was another demand coming. Ben didn't.

In fact, he was thinking about Julian when the phone call interrupted his thoughts. *Who was he? Where was he from?* NSA suspected Iran.

The phone rang again. It was Julian.

"Captain Hawkins, my congratulations again. I saw the news reports. You were successful stopping the attack at Union Station."

"And my thanks to you, Julian. I wouldn't have been there without your tip." Ben was glad the FBI was listening in.

"So we are both satisfied with the results. No more innocent lives lost."

"Not exactly, Julian. Two innocent men died in Texas. Along with two guilty ones."

"Yes, of course, Captain, you're correct. My apologies, and I wish I could express my condolences to the families of those two men."

"I get the feeling you will be unable to do that personally. But as you know, Julian, I only stopped one of the attackers in Union Station, and I only reached her with your help. I should be thanking you, as well, for stopping the second terrorist. And perhaps my government should be thanking your government." Ben had decided not to bother asking questions. He had learned from dozens of interrogations that making clear, assertive statements often made the person assume you knew more than you actually did.

But Julian was clever too. "Oh, no governments are involved, Captain. But yes, I did stop the second attacker when I saw there were two of them and only one of you. It didn't look as if your FBI was going to catch her or prevent the attack." Julian smiled to himself, since he was pretty sure that several FBI agents were listening in on the call.

Ben smiled also, knowing that Donniger himself was probably listening, the microwave transmissions being pulled out of the air by a nearby FBI listening station. He was pretty sure Julian knew that also.

"And we recovered *almost* all of the nerve agent," Ben answered. "Witnesses saw a man running out of the station with the attacker's backpack, probably with the rest of the nerve agent. About a half-pound of it."

"Perhaps the material was too dangerous to leave around in a public setting, Captain. Who knows? And perhaps you plan on going sailing soon." It wasn't a question.

Ben smiled again. He had been wondering how Julian would deliver the remaining VX-212. But he was confident he would.

"Again, Captain, my congratulations to you, and everyone in your group. I believe this unfortunate business is finished, and it is unlikely we will speak to each other again."

"Thank you, Julian, or whatever your name is." Then he used a phrase he had learned a few days before. *"Travel safely, my friend,"* he said, using the only words in Farsi he knew.

Ben couldn't see that Colonel Kashani was smiling. He hung up, took a deep breath and exhaled. *Well, it was only one drink, and I'll have plenty of drivers around who can take over at any time,* he thought, knowing there was an FBI team nearby. Then he placed a call to Tom Donniger on the team phone. He assumed Donniger himself had been listening in, but he wanted a record of his initiating a direct contact to the FBI.

If he had learned anything, it was that when the going gets tough, cover your ass.

After informing Donniger about the call from Julian, Ben went outside to his car. The rain had let up and seemed to be moving out to sea. There was still plenty of evening light in the western sky, although it was getting dark toward the east.

Ten minutes later he was at the boatyard. The parking lot was almost empty, so there was plenty of room for the three other vehicles that pulled in right after him.

"OK, Captain, just show us which one of these boats is yours."

Ben was still standing on the ground with Tom Donniger a few minutes later as two FBI agents in yellow hazmat suits went through the lockers on board *Blue Lady*.

"Got a backpack here," an agent called down, his voice muffled by the helmet of the hazmat suit. A moment later, they heard, "Container inside. Matches the one we took from Union Station. No leaks. Safe to transport."

So it *was* over. Ben was anxious to get back to his place. Sara should be there by now. They could actually relax and enjoy their evening for the first time in nearly two weeks. *Had it really only been two weeks?*

He looked up, where faint stars were beginning to light up the evening sky. Then he looked north, toward Washington, toward where he thought Julian might be.

"Travel safely my friend," he said again, this time in English, and this time to himself. Then he drove himself home.

A few minutes later, Ben was just pulling in front of his condo when his mobile phone rang. He looked at the screen and saw it was Major Corliss. He pressed "Talk."

"Yes sir? You heard the news?"

"Yes, I did, Ben. I just got a call from the Assistant Director. All the VX-212 is accounted for. Thank God, it really *is* over. Outstanding work, Ben."

"Thank you, sir. I don't suppose he said anything about those federal obstruction charges he was threatening me with."

"Actually, Ben, he did."

"And?"

"There won't be any charges, Ben. Not after Donniger got a call from the President himself, asking him to pass on his personal appreciation to the Army investigator who opened this investigation in the first place."

"The President? Of the United States?"

"The one and only. He asked for your name. Tom Donniger must have choked when he gave it to him. Hell, you might get a call from the President yourself."

Ben laughed, and looked at the lights in his condo. Sara was there, waiting for him.

"That would be great, Boss, but do me a favor."

"Sure, Ben. Anything."

"Ask him to wait until tomorrow."

Epilogue

USA Today, Washington, D.C.—The U.S. Army announced today that Staff Sergeant Harry McNair has been found guilty of theft of government property following a court-martial in Ft. Belvoir, Virginia. Colonel Barbara Hase of the Judge Advocate General's Corps sentenced McNair to 8 to 15 years in federal prison. McNair served two tours in Iraq and had more than 22 years of service in the Army.

Tehran, April 19, IRNA—The *Islamic Republic News Agency* reported today that the bodies of two Republican Guard officers were recovered following a serious auto accident. According to the report, Major Ali Heidari and Capt. Alireza Ashkani of the 19th Armored Division were traveling in a military vehicle when the vehicle went off the road several miles east of Qazvin. The cause of the accident is believed to be poor weather conditions. There were no other victims.

Associated Press—The CIA announced today that it has revised its estimate of when the Republic of Iran will be capable of producing a nuclear weapon. According to the agency, Iran is now producing enough enriched uranium to produce a nuclear weapon within 12 to 18 months. Previous estimates predicted it would be 3 to 5 years before Iran had such capabilities.